June

Forever Faithful

Shandal Publishing,
Saint-Petersburg, Russia

FOREVER FAITHFUL

Copyright © 2003, by Dr. June M. Temple

Published by Shandal Publishing,
P.O. Box 614, St. Petersburg, 197198, Russia
e-mail: julia@shandal.ru

Designed by Litvinova Maria

June M. Temple (nee Speake)

U.S. address
P.O. Box 237
Sumas, WA. 98297
USA

Canadian address:
C325 – 1909 Salton Rd.
Abbotsford, B.C.
Canada V2S 5B6
 e-mail: june.temple@interactministries.org

ISBN: 5-93925-001-7

Printed in Russia

Contents

Forward

*E*nglish history books record a part of the story of the Speke family from the years of the early ten hundreds through following centuries. This novel weaves some of the history book stories into the telling of the lives of William Speke and his descendents. All of the Speke men in the story actually lived in the time span recorded, but many of the every day experiences of these characters are pure fiction.

Some of the stories were told to the author by her parents, grandparents and great grandmother.

Chapter 1

Spring 1065

The message to William Speke Sr. simply said "Father, I've found it, come immediately," signed Walter. William ran up the stairs of his castle calling, "My dear wife I must leave Old Warden immediately for Normandy."

The castle became a buzz with activity. There were messengers preparing to go to the captain and his crew at the coast to make ready the ship Madeline (named for William's wife). William's traveling companions began their preparations. Maids started packing food for the trip and others packed raiment. Within a few hours William would ride toward the coast with his sons Edward and Richard, plus their four guards. But before leaving home, William and his sons took time for prayer in the Chapel.

William Jr. was already kneeling in the worship area. He rose as he heard the footsteps behind him. In filed his brothers Edward and Richard. Behind them walked William Sr. who spoke, "Son, ask God's blessing and safety as we must travel to France."

William Jr. was the Castle vicar, and he prayed, "Oh, Almighty God you have said in the Holy Scripture

'Know therefore that the Lord your God; He is the faithful God.

Who keeps His covenant of love to a thousand generations of those who love Him and keep His commands,' we praise you for you faithfulness from generation to generation. We thank you for your gracious love and pray for your love to surround my father and brothers as they travel. Keep them safe on land and sea. With your powerful arms encircle them; let no bandits fall on them, no wild animal attack them and no wave come to swamp the boat in the water. Because of who you are we completely depend upon you. In Jesus, the Son of God's name we pray. Amen."

On leaving the Chapel William put his arm around his eldest child and said, "Son, I want you to watch over your mother and care for her. Look out for the management of this home and the other manors. Maybe it would be a good idea to ride over to my Northhill manor and see what you could do to help the Johnson's. They have been having a terrible time since the plague went through the area.

We will probably be gone six weeks and if you need to contact me send a messenger. Please tell your wife and my grandson good bye for me and tell them I love them."

With all of these details taken care of the men walked toward the stable area where they found William senior's two young daughters and his wife Madeline waiting. There were hugs and kisses, then the father, Richard and Edward, plus the four guards mounted their horses. Two of the guards, Joseph and Nathaniel took the lead. The three Speke men followed and in the rear sat the other two guards, Samuel and John. With a unanimous "get-up" the horses broke into a trot.

Tears filled Madeline's eyes as she thought of the coming days without husband or sons. But she blinked them away for the sake of her two young girls standing beside her.

The road to the coast was very familiar because the men made at least one trek a year across the country while conducting business, or else to sail to visit family members in Europe. For most of the way the dirt road was wide enough for a cart, but some of the short cuts were as narrow as a footpath. Then once in a while the men would ride on the wider, hard surfaced roads, built during the Roman occupation. These were constructed to accommodate the passing of two chariots. The terrain inclines were modest and there were many flat areas. All of the men expected to make good time.

Edward asked, "Father, will we be staying at our manor in Eyeworth tonight?" The response was, "Our departure was so late it will be a hard ride to arrive before dusk. But then the Eyeworth manor is our objective."

The seven men rode in silence while pushing their horses as much as they dared because they did not want to be riding on the road after dark as they knew it would be dangerous then. While each man kept their daggers and swords in an easily accessible place they did not want to be accosted in pitch-blackness. Six hours later the men found themselves in a-darkness only a cloudy night could produce. Fortunately the turnoff to the manor was soon seen, because in the distance hung a torch light by the building to show the way.

As soon as William formed the plan to travel word was sent by a fast riding messenger on ahead to Eyeworth, and the seven men found cheery flickering lights greeting them down the lane from the main house. Three servants were ready to put a hearty meal on the table for the hungry men.

After all of the men became content with good food and were relaxed by the glowing fireplace, Philip, the manor keeper, came in to chat with them. The first thing he said was, "The town-crier announced this afternoon, "Harold's leading more skirmishes into Northumbria." But the crier also talked about a possible soon negotiation with the North-umbrians."

Then the men began to talk among themselves and soon the whole upsetting story about King Edward's life came out. They commiserated with the fact about Edward, who, as a boy of age ten, was required to flee to Normandy in France because of the Viking attacks upon this homeland. During those days he was only away from home for a year.

But again Edward needed to flee as a young teenager. This time he was gone from England for twenty-five years. During the years in exile he lived in the home of his cousin, William, the Duke of Normandy. For twenty-five years Edward built firm friendships among the Norman's.

At this point in the conversation Richard angrily spit-out, "Edward never should have married that woman Emma. She was his downfall. And that brother-in-law Harold is always causing trouble.

"William responded, "Richard, I believe you are correct. My dear patient cousin, who shows so many of the attributes of the Saviour he loves, should not have married into the controlling, angry, argumentative family of Emma's. But he did and now he needs to deal with the consequences."

Joseph broke into the conversation with, "You know the King brought on himself most of his troubles by transporting so many Norman's to our country. The very idea of putting them into places of authority!"

By now the tension in the room was thick, and Edward said, "Who else could my father's cousin trust? Those Norman's were the people our king Edward knew for a good part of his growing up years, and then even on into manhood. They were people he could depend upon."

A silence descended as the men mulled over the last few thoughts. In the quietness William said. "Men, I think we better retire. We must get an early start in order to make it all the way to St. Neots by tomorrow's nightfall."

Before dawn the next morning all seven men were at breakfast. Shortly after eating they approached their mounts and were on the road east as the first rays of the sun shone.

With the beauty of the rising morning mist and the sparkling drops of water on leaves and wildflowers William burst out in songs of praise. He sang one line of a Psalm. Then antiphonally the two brothers sang the same words, followed by the four riders singing in harmony. The rolling terrain reverberated with the Psalm

> *I will praise You O Lord, with my whole heart*
> *I will tell of all Your marvelous works.*
> *I will be glad and rejoice in You;*
> *I will sing praise to Your name, O Most High."*

The sights they saw and the sounds in their ears were thrilling. They couldn't help praising God.

In an hour's time their pace slowed because there was the traffic of farmers pushing carts full of produce, and there were other travelers starting to fill the roads. From time to time they would greet a familiar face. Every person they met was on their way to the town markets to either sell or buy. However by nine thirty most of the traffic began to thin out and the men could again pick up the pace of their horses.

About midday a bubbling stream came into view. They stopped, and the Speke party opened their knapsacks filled with food. Early in the morning Philip's wife prepared fresh baked soda bread, and into the knapsacks put large servings of it, along with chunks of cheese and beef. The hungry men set about devouring the ample portions. In a short time they were just about ready to be on their way again, so they collected the grazing horses. Then both men and horses quenched their thirst at the clear stream before beginning the afternoon ride.

By late afternoon the party of seven cantered into the town of St. Neots, where, when they saw the town market ahead, they slowed their horses. The men were planning on staying in the house church by the square where the Speke travelers usually stopped.

The vicar was already standing in the doorway, because the town lookout sent a message to him as soon as the men were sighted on their approach to town. The host and visitors greeted each other warmly.

Delicious odors wafted in the air as the stew bubbled over the flames in the living quarters of the church. Anna, the vicar's wife and the wives of the four monks in residence were busy preparing dinner. A multitude of children played on the kitchen floor and others ran in and out of the back door.

While the men were chatting in the sitting room the town crier passed bye calling out, "Battle in Northumbria over. The peace treaty should be signed any day." William exhaled a deep breath and exclaimed, "Praise the Lord! That's good to hear."

Once again the two sons started railing against Harold, the king's brother-in-law, and all the problems he brought to the monarchy. The vicar responded, "There is a rumor Harold might force the king to claim him as heir, with the king having no son."

In unison both Edward and Richard cried out, "Oh, no, how can that be? A few years ago King Edward appointed his cousin William, the Duke of Normandy, as his heir." Before anything more could be said the vicar's wife Anna, who was standing in the doorway, called the men to dinner.

The guests, vicar, monks and teenage boys gathered around the table for the first serving. The women and small children would eat after all the men finished.

Each plate was heavy with potatoes, carrots, onions, celery, meat and gravy. Then huge platters of fresh baked bread generously spread with sweet cream butter were placed on the table. After the saying of grace the men attacked the delicious food.

All the time they were eating the men discussed the Northumbrian situation, the actions of Harold, and what could possibly ensue if Harold ever managed to get on the throne.

When the well-satisfied men stood to retire to the sitting room they each carried a tankard of steaming tea in one hand. In the other hand a cup of egg custard with aroma- tic cinnamon and nutmeg gleaming on top.

Chapter 1

As they walked out of the room the vicar said to William, "Can you imagine how your cousin William in Normandy will react when he hears the latest news?"

Once that topic of conversation was exhausted Anna joined the men while the younger wives of the monks attended to cleaning up the kitchen and putting the children to bed.

Now the Speke men wanted to know how things were going within the church and the town. Anna said, "God is blessing! One new family joined the church just this week. Now we have thirty adults and their children coming to worship on Sundays. It is so wonderful to see some of the superstition lifted."

Richard responded, "Good, good. I see you have a beautiful new communion service on the alter." Immediately the vicar said, "Well, you know we needed one to compliment the exquisite alter cloth Walter found for us on the continent. The weave is exceptional and the faces of the figures are the clearest we've ever seen. Our members are constantly talking about it."

William expressed his thankfulness for the pleasure the cloth was bringing. Then he said, "We are on our way to the continent now. Walter has sent for us to come and I wonder what treasure he has recently uncovered. Which reminds me, we better get to bed as we want to make the coast in forty-eight hours."

The next two days became a blur of travel. Despite the hurry there were times when the men would round a corner to be awed with a meadow of beautiful wild flowers. Dotted here and there were yellow poppies, or roses and violets. Then there would be clusters of light pink lady smocks, rose red campions and purple chicory. Off and on daisies nodded their heads and in wet areas the beautiful water lily laid placidly.

Many times when the beauty would be outstanding one man or the other would break out into song and the other men responded. This was their only enjoyable diversion during the long hours in the saddle.

Then there were two less pleasurable events. Early in the morning after leaving St. Neots, even before sunrise, the men heard much yipping, barking and howling. As the sounds grew closer they realized a pack of wild dogs were pursuing them.

The first decision was to try to out-run the dogs. The horses were fresh and should have no trouble staying well ahead of the pack.

However, after a half hour of riding hard and still not hearing the sounds become any fainter Edward said, "If the horses tire and the dog's hunger drives them on, we will be in real trouble." Stephen responded, "If the dogs surround one of the horses, they'll shred his legs and the animal will collapse. Not saying what will happen to the rider."

With these words John untied the strings to his knapsack and began to throw the chucks of meat onto the ground. The other men followed John's example. Shortly the sounds of snarling began to fill the air as the dogs pounced upon the meat and fought among themselves for the meat's possession. The Speke party was sure now their escape could be completed.

This night was spent in the Inn at Haverhill. It was well after dark when the men stopped riding. The Innkeeper was just ready to extinguish the last wick when the knock came. He rushed to the door and said, "I expected you before dark, and I'm glad you have finally arrived."

No one could be exactly sure what would detain travelers. Usually bad news traveled quickly. The Innkeeper heard none and he was not upset. However dinner was cold and it would take a while to build a fire to warm it. The men opted to eat a cold meal of lamb with vegetables, drink tepid tea, and then fall into bed.

On the next day the three Spekes and four guards followed the same schedule as the day before. The men began riding long before sunrise. They kept the horses at a medium fast trot, and at times traveled the back roads to avoid the merchant traffic traveling to or from the towns.

Mile after mile passed. By nightfall they knew they would make their destination, the town of Manningtree, by nine p.m.

Chapter 1

Daylight turned to gray late in the afternoon. The closer the men approached the coast the more mist and fog rolled in.

Right after sundown an eerie darkness surrounded the riders, but their pace did not slacken, because they knew the road well. In a short while the thrumming of other horses hooves could be heard in a distance. William said, "Slow your pace men, we don't want the noise of our hooves to attract attention."

The sound was definitely coming toward the Speke party. Who ever it was appeared to be traveling at a fast pace and the group sounded like it consisted of a good number of people. They could be bandits, or another party of noblemen, or a band of the occasional Viking marauders.

Samuel said, "We should take to the woods instead of having a confrontation. In the darkness we cannot tell who the other people are. Rather than to meet an adversary and fight twice the number of people we have in our group it would be better to take the longer path." William responded, "With the vision in this type of weather, who could tell who the other person would be until we were upon them. Then they and we could be attacking unnecessarily just because we didn't know who the other person was."

Once into the woods the Speke party could see a glow from the road caused by men carrying torches. The light rolled through the fog and twenty forms were seen in the eerie glow as they passed on into the night.

Now William's group began looking forward to only traveling one more hour in the saddle before they would settle into the home of Jerome, the ship's Captain.

Jerome was a widower with seven children, five of whom were still living at home in Manningtree. Their grandmother (Jeremy's mother-in-law) and her sister all lived in the three-room cottage located very close to the river's edge. The two women were excellent cooks who also enjoyed looking after the Captain's brood of youngsters.

As soon as the Speke party of seven men entered the cottage the two women smeared grease in huge frying pans to cook bubble and squeak (potatoes and green cabbage fried together), plus bengers (sausage).

When the men did not arrive by five o'clock the women fixed dinner in order for the women and children to eat. It would only be Jerome and his guests who would be eating at nine o'clock at night. The eight famished men were ready to consume volumes of the food.

Three wicks in oil slightly broke the kitchen darkness, but that didn't hinder the men once they were called to the table. They just followed the succulent odors their noses picked up, and once seated the food was quickly blessed and consumed.

The out going tide was not until nine-twenty-nine the following morning, this meant the men were able to talk for a short while before going to sleep. The topic of conversation Jerome brought up was the wonderful qualities of the new boat they would be sailing on. His pride in the craft could easily be detected in the way he pointed out the roominess of the eighty-foot long craft and the wonderfully swift travel brought about by the combination of both sail and oars.

Edward said, "I hear there is covering for some of the people. That will be a help when the storms come." Jeremy's reply was, "Yes, eight people, sometimes ten, can easily fit under the tent." William kept interjecting into the conversation his thankfulness for the fact his Viking Uncle and their cousins were into building boats unusually long and looking like a ship for royalty. Of course William felt compelled to also share the fact about the economy of having relatives in the boat building business.

Suddenly Jerome began to snore and the men knew it was time to sleep. There was a pile of blankets in a corner of the sitting room. Each man grabbed one, then he laid down on the floor and rolled the blanket around himself.

At daybreak all of those sleeping in the sitting room woke to the sound of banging pans in the kitchen. Hours before the two women began quietly creeping around, over, and between the sleeping forms. In almost complete silence the food was prepared and now it was almost time to put the biscuits, slabs of ham, coddled eggs and mugs of tea on the table. The best way to wake men was with noise.

By eight-thirty the men walked up the gangplank onto the ship. Richard, Edward, Joseph, Nathaniel, Samuel and John sat on the first three benches under the tent. Twenty-six other oarsmen sat behind them on the remaining thirteen benches. This put one man on each side of the boat beside one oar lock, making a total of sixteen oars on each side of the boat. The tent covered the first eight rows.

Jerome and William walked to the bow of the boat and turned to face the men.

Jerome shouted, "Bow your heads." Then he continued in just as loud a voice, "God, the All powerful God, look at us. We pray for your miracle as we cross this sea. Go beside us and keep the water calm. Keep the wind calm, but give us enough of a breeze to make the passage swift. Amen."

In the same breath and at the same volume Jerome bellowed, "Release the ropes, set the sails, insert the oars." The craft pulled away from the shore and began it's way east on the river Stour until they entered the chop of the English Channel. Once free of the river Jerome yelled, "Hard on the oars." As the craft eased toward the southeast the captain yelled, "Oars together, pull hard."

The sky looked gray and overcast. Wisps of fog wafted by, but every once in a while the sun would break through the clouds. There was a mild breeze and from all indications there would be no threatening storms.

When the boat finally nudged into the shore of Le Havre, France the men saw Walter waiting on the bank with six men and their mounts, plus seven extra horses. The Speke party, along with Jerome, strode up to the waiting group. Much good-natured hugging and backslapping followed. Walter, his father and brothers all acted like the time being away from each other was much too long.

The ride to Falaise would take a good twelve hours and the men knew it would be wise to begin the journey the following morning. William turned to Jerome and said,

"My good friend, you should have the boat back here a month from today. I will be waiting on the shore for you."

As the party of fourteen rode toward an Inn they could hear Jerome bellowing, "Right oars up, left oars pull."

Late the next day, when traveling the last mile of their journey, a hill came into view upon which sat the home of William, Duke of Normandy. Slowly the horses plodded up the hillside and around the large stone structure where William lived. Fourteen men alighted from their horses. The four Speke men walked toward the luxurious home while the other ten took their horses to the stable.

The clomp of William, Walter, Richard and Edward's feet on the wooden planks leading to the castle steps sounded like thunder. These men were big people! William stood around five feet, ten inches, and his sons ranged around six feet. They were of heavy build and muscular, weighing-in between 190 and 225 pounds. Walter was the largest. His hands looked like baseball mitts.

Duke William and his wife Matilda were sitting with coffee by the fireplace when the men strode in. The Duke rose to greet his cousins from across the channel. All of the men were glad to see each other and the host asked, "Have you eaten yet?" When the answer was "No" the Duke notified his servants to prepare food.

It was midnight before the men finished conversing. Each one spent some sharing time about what was going on in their lives. Then too, much was said concerning the politics going on in both counties, plus the world activities. Naturally some talk dwelt on Harold and his sister's influence over King Edward and the problems this caused.

The Duke's castle spread over much land. There was a section his family lived. Then there were many wings where relatives and visiting dignitaries stayed. A chapel occupied another section. The servant's quarters were in one more area. Even the prisoner's quarters and stables for the horses were all confined into the monstrous sprawling building. Walter's quarters were on the top floor in the northwest wing.

Servants brought breakfast to Walter's suite the next morning. As the men ate they enjoyed the vast panoramic view from the third floor on the hilltop.

Walter said, "Tomorrow we will be riding to Le Bec-Helouin." Naturally questions followed about why they were going, what is there, etc., and Walter responded, "Forty years ago a knight by the name of Helouin faithfully served the former Duke of Normandy. He was a very brave man who fought in many skirmishes. The knight was well known for his skills in battle. However, this man exchanged his charger for a donkey in 1034, with the goal to live a simple life and to be of service to God.

Other people saw his cause and decided to follow Helouin. They began to be a part of an Abbey in a place they named Le Bec-Helouin and their work is becoming renown."

Richard said, "Tell us, what exactly it is we are going to see?" Walter responded, "It is best for you to wait to view what I have discovered in order to determine its value for yourselves."

On riding with Walter toward the renown town William, Edward and Richard could not help but notice the closer they came to it the more they saw men in simple robes working the fields and vineyards.

When the horses were slowed to a canter Walter began to explain the magnificent house of Worship now under construction in the center of Le Bec-Helouin. He told about the foundation being almost finished and about the huge collection of stones piled around it to be used in the building project. Walter said, "The plans are for a structure the size of which has never been seen before in the world. Their reason being — God deserves such a house."

Once they were inside the town's gates everything Walter talked about came into view. The enormity of the project lay before their eyes. Mountains of stones almost encircled a foundation two city blocks long and one city block wide. The project would take a lifetime to complete. Everyone working on this project also wore the simple garb of the people working in the fields.

Around the Abbey grounds were several long, low buildings. Some were cottages for families. One was a men's dormitory, another a women's dormitory. The dining hall occupied one more spot and there were four buildings for the production of artwork. It was into one of the latter Walter led the way.

Inside the building the men saw people working everywhere. The Spekes were in the tapestry-making workshop. Several women were sitting at low tapestry frames. Some were attaching the natural ecru colored threads from the top of a frame to the bottom. These threads were called the warp.

Other women were in the process of weaving the weft (multicolored threads) through the warp. The frames were of varying sizes. Some were laptop size, and from there they graduated on up to the size of an eight-foot by ten-foot wall piece. The smaller frames were called low warp and the larger ones high warp.

At the four feet by six feet and five feet by seven feet frames the men and women were bending over their work. This tapestry was sitting in a horizontal position on top of posts. Artisans worked on the smaller frames while they sat on stools. Then, where the extra large frames were located some women were bending over the frames while men were lying on their backs on the floor underneath the frame. This way the people bending over passed the weft through several threads of the warp until it was beyond their reach. Then the person on the floor took the weft and passed it on through the warp while the person on top moved into a lying position on top of the canvas. Again, the one on the canvas top took the thread in order for the one on the floor to move. So it continued until the whole width was covered.

Each craftsperson kept a comb-like instrument by their side. This they used to tamp the weft together. The comb passed through the warp threads and pushed the top thread tight to the one below it.

All four Speke men walked through the smaller pieces of work to examine the excellent craftsmanship. Many of the scenes depicted were of every day experiences or of historical events. Then there were the religious portrayals.

William stopped at each altar cloth to closely look at the workmanship and the authenticity of the scene depicted. In time they reached the largest canvas in the room. When they approached, the workers lifted the frame against the wall for William and his sons to receive a better view. The men stood there with their mouths open and a look of awe on their faces.

The tapestry scene portrayed Jesus walking on the water. In the distance could be seen a fishing boat with the occupants looking toward Jesus. Their faces showed surprise and unbelief. Around the boat the water looked angrily choppy with white caps. Where Jesus walked the water was smooth and calm. A glory appeared around His figure and His rugged features were full of peace.

The contrasting colors were what was most striking. The weft threads must have been impregnated with silver and gold ones. It almost looked like sunlight shimmered on the calm water while gray storm-like water lapped around the boat. In the distance a sense of mist seemed to be approaching the boat as if it would engulf the craft.

Walter said, "What a perfect picture of life! When Jesus walks with us there is calm, no matter how fearful our everyday storms." His father responded, "Yes, you are right. You are also correct in assuming I would be interested in coming to see this magnificent tapestry. I do want to purchase it. Perhaps King Edward will want to hang it in the new Abbey he is having built in London. From what I understand the Westminster Abbey is about in the same stage of progress as the one being built here."

William also purchased several tapestry Altar cloths to supply a few of the Abbeys, Cathedrals and Monasteries in England.

From all appearances the time it would take to finish the work on the wall hanging of Jesus walking on the water would be about two weeks. William told Friar Herlouin to notify Walter when the purchases would be ready to pick up.

During the following two weeks Walter took his father and brothers to other Abbeys and craft workshops to inspect their wares. The men also looked at exceptional pieces of metalwork. They were intrigued with the gilt bronze on the gold chalices, also on the crosses, and on the high altars. In some of these were imbedded gems; rubies, emeralds, sapphire and diamonds.

A few days were spent in Paris at the school for metalwork. Not only did they see more of the beautiful religious artifacts, but also pieces for other uses. For over two centuries students came from all over Europe to attend this school in order to learn the craft taught after the style of Eloi who lived during the eighth century.

As the men became ready to leave Edward stopped by a chair and remarked, "Father, look at this piece, see how extraordinary the legs are!" William, Richard and Walter all came to kneel by the guilt bronze lion-headed legs on a curule-type of folding chair.

One of the students came to the kneeling men and said, "Sirs Le Espek, (French for Speke) this is a reproduction of the chair Eloi himself crafted for a throne for the eighth century king Dagobert."

William, Walter, Edward and Richard all expressed their admiration with different comments. Then Richard said, "Father, do you think King Edward would be interested in sitting on a throne like this one? Do you think we should purchase it to take home?" William replied "It is a handsome chair. However, it is far too ornate for Edward's concept of a Godly ruler. No, it would not be a good idea to buy the chair for Edward's use."

Walter decided he would purchase one of the swords for his collection. He chose one with rubies and diamonds imbedded in the hilt.

By the time the notice came from Le Bec-Helouin concerning the completion of the tapestry, William and his son's purchases were almost a wagonload full of artifacts to take to the churches in England. There would be just enough room left for the half dozen alter cloths ordered. Then the large wall tapestry would sit on top.

The weeks quickly passed from the time when William, his sons and men met on the shore of Normandy until they left the Duke's home. Of course many words of thanks passed first from William, Edward and Richard to their host and hostess. Then when William extended the gift of a spectacular gem laden shield (from the school in Paris) to his cousin and gracious wife the thanks flowed in the other direction.

As the wagon approached the channel bank at La Havre they heard the bellowing voice of Jerome say, "Greetings men! The ship is over in this direction." The seamen and William's sons pitched in to unload the wagon; which took about forty-five minutes to complete. Then a tent-like covering was assembled around the cargo before the ship disembarked.

Three hours after leaving the safety of the harbor one of the famous channel storms struck. Very quickly thunderclouds assembled, ferocious winds descended and the water was whipped into monstrous waves.

Jerome and the oarsmen battled with the heaving, jostling boat for two hours. William knew his men were the best on the seas, but there were anxious moments and concern, not only for the men, but also for the expensive cargo. The boat sat low in the water because of the weight of the metal pieces they bought in Paris and the men were beginning to consider throwing overboard some of the pieces before the wind and waves started to abate.

From time to time through the storm Jerome's voice could be heard over the moaning of the wind, "Oh God, way back in Lamentations you said "It is of the Lord"s mercies and loving-kindness that we are not consumed, because His tender compassions fail not. They are new every morning; great and abundant are Your stability and faithfulness.' Now we rely on your faithful compassion to protect us."

Many men in the boat lifted other silent or quiet prayers. William kept picturing in his mind the tapestry he just purchased and he continually prayed for the Lord to give them peace through the storm as they sensed His presence. Now it seemed the mental picture was coming into reality, just as if Jesus was walking on the water and causing the churning channel to begin to calm.

Because of the storm the ship was much later in docking. Jerome's mother-in-law, her sister, and a few of the children were anxiously looking across the water. They knew the storm would affect those who were sailing and they were concerned. Finally, when the well-known sail came into view relief flooded their faces.

As the boat was docking Jerome called out, "Please go get the wagon." One of the children ran to his oldest brother's home to tell him to bring the wagon down to the water.

The young man put aside the shoe he was working on and told his wife, "The shop is closed for a short while. I'm taking the wagon down to Sir William at the dock." Then off he went to help load the wagon and bid the Speke party a "good day."

When, on the following morning, the party began to travel toward home they knew they would move at a much slower pace than when they traveled on horseback. The time would almost be double from Manningtree to Old Warden.

Williams's two young daughters, Grace and Hannah, were playing on the turret when they looked across the field and saw the wagon approaching. They went skipping down the stairs calling out, "Father's coming, Father's coming." Madeline and the girls ran out of their home to greet their loved ones. What a joyous hugging and kissing followed.

Madeline looked at the wagon and said, "It looks like you have had a successful trip." All three men began talking about all of the art pieces and of the wonderful things they saw in Normandy. Then William replied to his wife's statement, "Walter did let us know about a most wonderful tapestry. Let us unload the wagon and then we will show you many marvels."

All seven men set to work. Once they were finished Nathaniel, Joseph, Steven and John went to join their families. William, Edward and Richard began unwrapping the parcels and spreading them across the floor for Madeline and the girls to gaze upon and touch. Last of all William called two servants to help them hang the tapestry on the wall. Madeline gasped at the beauty and remarked about the picture's significance. Edward said, "Mother, we lived this sight when we crossed the channel. There was a terrible storm, yet God brought us safely through it." William stood looking at the tapestry then told his family, "We will keep this tapestry for ourselves. It will hang beautifully in the chapel. At first I thought we would offer it to Edward to be put in Westminster Abby, but because of our experience on the channel it seems to me the appropriate place for this scene is our own home."

In a short while William began to wonder where his eldest son and family were. It was unusual to not have them greet him. So when he asked Madeline why William wasn't around she said, "William is well, and I'll let you know about his absence at dinner."

Sitting at the table Madeline began telling how William did go to Eyeworth to help the Johnson family. However, the plague caused life to be extremely difficult there. For two weeks William helped with the sick. Ben Johnson lost his wife, his two daughters and two of his three sons. Many of the other families experienced similar grief. William dug graves, buried the dead and tried to put life back together for the village.

Then William himself came down with chills, fever and all indications of the sickness. He lay near death's door while Ben and his son Robin nursed him. It took almost ten days for him to strengthen enough to return home.

Shortly after he arrived back to be with us word came to William's wife Arlene concerning sickness over at Speke's woods, out by Liverpool, where Arlene's folks live. Now the two of them have gone there, but young William remained here. This evening he is visiting his fiancee, Elizabeth.

The next morning the two Williams, grandfather and grandson, met in young William's quarters. The talk centered on William's coming wedding to Elizabeth. Then young William told his grandfather about his plan to build a Hall close to Speke's woods because his mother's brother, Uncle Octred, offered him property in the area.

As young William placed the plans before his grandfather it appeared to both of them that Speke Hall would be a magnificent home. There were many wings designed as a place for royalty to stay when they came to hunt in the woods around the Hall. Young William was excited about the prospect of his overseeing the building and the management of the estate. He felt truly blessed to have such an opportunity offered him. A bride, plus a home would soon be his and the exciting future appeared to be secure.

Chapter 2

January 1066

Across all of England two voices could be heard. One voice, "The king is dead, long live the king." The other voice, "The scoundrel Harold has usurped the throne."

On the very day of Edward, the Confessor's funeral, the Archbishop of Canterbury crowned Harold as king. The Coronation took place in a wing of the partially constructed Westminster Abbey.

All of those living on and working the land of William Speke (fifteen towns in all) were angrily giving their opinions. In one form or another the words indicated that upon Edward's death the brother-in-law committed perjury by claiming the throne as his own.

No one was more vociferous concerning the matter than those in the Speke household. William kept saying, "Everyone knows Harold was sent by King Edward to Normandy two years ago to reconfirm William as being the heir to the English throne."

Edward followed these words with, "The records even show Harold in the church with one hand on a shrine and the other on the altar swearing his allegiance to our cousin William."

As soon as these words were finished Richard would speak his opinion about Harold's interpretation of King Edward's deathbed charge. "The dying king said he 'commended his wife, the queen, and the kingdom of England to Harold's protection.' How dare Harold claim this request as a bequest meaning he was to ascend England's throne. Surely Harold knew King Edward wanted him to protect his possessions until Duke William arrived from Normandy."

Madeline, son William, and grandson William all kept saying, "It is impossible for Harold to be king, because he is not a blood relation to the reigning line." Even Grace and Hannah repeated over and over what they heard their elders saying.

All over England dissent could be heard. The pubs became a cacophony of arguing. There were those who emphasized all the points the Speke family were adamant about, versus those who criticized the fact the Duke was Norman. The latter people would keep pointing out an idea about William bringing many different systems of government, religion and culture, from the continent. They believed any change was not wanted, nor would it be tolerated. They said a Norman king would not be good for England, even if he appeared to be the rightful heir.

Harold was informed of all the dissent but he ignored it all because he felt he could over throw any rebellion in the island, or any attack from Normandy. The man did not realize what he had gotten himself into.

Meanwhile, across the channel, the Duke was holding a banquet for his noblemen and knights when the news of Harold's action reached there. A messenger shouted three times over the large hall, "King Edward is dead and Harold has proclaimed himself as king of England!" A hush immediately descended over the crowd and everyone turned to see the Duke's reaction.

William stood in shock for a moment. Then while his words were few no one doubted his anger from the expression on his face. He shouted over the guests, "Harold is not the king of England. He has committed the crime of perjury. My next step will be to contact the church leaders in Rome."

The news of Harold usurping Britain's throne spread like wildfire across the other French Provinces and on to Germany,

Italy and Spain. Tongues were spitting out vengeance and rallying behind the Duke of Normandy.

Duke William himself traveled to Rome to the heart of the church fathers in order to learn their opinion, plus he wanted their blessing on retrieving what was rightfully his.

The church leaders constantly brought into their conversation the fact about Sligand, the present Archbishop of Canterbury, not ever being officially Canonized by the church. Because of this he possessed no church approved authority to crown anyone as king. Other leaders emphasized the oath Harold took before God to bind himself to William as his vassal and feudal man. In the church's sight Harold committed one crime after another when he usurped the throne. All of the church leaders, including the pope, encouraged William to forcefully regain his rightful throne. They prayed God's blessing upon the capture of the English throne.

It seemed a good part of Europe rallied behind William and men were ready to take up arms for his cause.

One more contender angrily claimed the English crown. This person was another man named Harold, also called, the Ruthless, who was the king of Norway and Denmark. He announced across his land, "My forefather, as King of Norway and claimant to Denmark, made a pact with the King of England stating 'If either ruler died without a son the other ruler was to inherit the kingdom.'"

The Viking Harold rallied men from Norway and Denmark to follow him. In September hundreds of men (enough to fill 300 ships) met at the docks to sail to England. Men armored with battle-axes, spears and swords. The archers were the last to assemble at the Viking fleet's boarding area.

To compound Harold, the King of England's impending problem, his own brother Tostig, allied himself with Harold the Ruthless. Vengeance was the motive for this union because Tostig was the former recently deposed Earl of Northumbria. When Harold's army conquered Northumbria (the year before) he sent his own brother into exile. The victory seemed to have backfired when Tostig allied himself with the king of Norway.

In the meantime, on the Norman coast, William's men and ships were gathered while waiting for favorable weather to sail.

All summer long the King of England anticipated the Norman invasion. Troops were stationed along the southeast coast of England. Then when September came the men ran out of provisions and were dismissed to return back to civilian work.

In mid September Harold the Ruthless issued the order, "Board Ships." The same Viking ships which struck fear for several hundred years into Northern English hearts. Stealthily they sailed across the open water and up the rivers toward the town of York. Quickly the whole area was captured and the populace turned their allegiance to the Norse leader and his ally Tostig. When Harold the Ruthless entered the city of York these citizens vowed to follow him into conquering the south.

As soon as Harold, the King of England, heard about a Norseman conquering the northern portion of his country he assembled a large sized army. With the English king in the lead, a forced march was ordered, and they covered the 200 miles north in exceptionally quick time. Above York at Stamford Bridge the army from London made an early morning surprise attack on the Norse troops. The army from Norway was so unprepared for the unexpected attack they were quickly defeated.

In the fierce hand fighting a great company of the Norse army were killed. Of the few remaining men there were only enough to fill twenty of the 300 ships waiting off shore.

Harold Hardrada, the Ruler of Norway and Denmark, was killed, along with Tostig, the English ruler's brother. Harold of England felt no more fear of his being attacked after this overwhelming victory at Stamford Bridge.

However, even as the Stamford battle was occurring, the weather cleared over the English Channel and William's fleet set sail for the southern coast of England. They landed unopposed.

Harold unaware of what was occurring in the south, marched his men back to York and haughtily entered the city as a victor. The army shouted and leaped as they went through the streets and into homes. The British ruler announced to the city officials, "My men and I will stay until a Victory feast is celebrated."

Several days later, when all the preparations were finished, a banquet was held with hundreds of townspeople, plus all of the town officials, plus Harold with his army in attendance. Much revelry and drinking took place. As the evening was winding down a messenger came running in and up to whisper in King Harold's ear, "The Duke of Normandy is camped near Hastings." Harold turned to his highest officer and said, "Announce to the men there will be a march south at sunrise."

A few days before king Harold's northern victory Water Le Espec was standing in the bow of the flagship of the Norman fleet in order to oversee all of the loading processes. Along side of him stood Duke William. The armada of ships proved to be extremely large and they were filled with thousands of foot soldiers as well as the men of the cavalry. Some of the ships contained only the knight's coats of mail. These were knee length with three quarter sleeves completely made of interlocked metal rings. The noblemen's helmets, swords and lances were also part of the cargo. Other ships contained only horses (never before was the feat of transporting horses across water ever attempted).

The Norman armada sailed from St-Valery-sur-Somme two evenings before the Stamford Bridge battle took place and the town of Pervency, on the English coast, became the arrival point where the army settled into an old Roman fort. This did not seem the ideal spot. In a few days they moved to Hastings to raise a base camp and the foundation of a castle.

Outside of town Walter rode across Telham Hill watching for the expected English army. In the distance two lone riders were spotted and he thought he recognized them. The closer they came the more sure Walter was as to who they were. He rode out to meet his eighteen and sixteen year old brothers Edward and Richard.

The older brother was glad to see them, but also apprehensive because of the situation he knew soon to be coming upon the area. He didn't want his brothers wounded or killed. They were so much younger than either their eldest brother William or himself, and actually they were half brothers.

William and Walter's mother died when they were young. Then their father waited ten years before marrying again.

Edward and Richard jumped off their horses and ran toward Walter. Both grabbed him so hard they almost knocked him off his feet. Because of Walter's huge size the boys always tried to tackle him and get him to the ground in good-natured brotherly competition.

Walter asked, "What are you two doing here?" The answers alternately came tumbling out of the young men. "Father heard you were here." "William is home to help father." "He said we could come." "Father thought we might be helpful to you." "Mother wants you to know father is not well."

Then the young men gave a tidbit of information helpful for the Norman army. "We skirted London and on the city's perimeter we heard about Harold collecting a vast army. He is already marching south to Hastings."

Later in the afternoon the first contingent of the English army could be seen from Telham Hill. The English scouts also saw the Norman army on the far hill and then they notified their commanders about a ridge in the area that looked like it would be a good place for them to camp. The ridge later became known as the area of Battle.

Harold's goal was to initiate another surprise attack, as he had at Stamford Bridge. In his haste to accomplish this he arrived on the ridge with only a portion of his army and the hope of the remaining soldiers coming before morning.

Because the Norman's who were standing on watch saw the English presence any hope Harold held of a surprise attack was extinguished. All night long the men on Telham Hill kept watch for fear of an attack. The men in their quarters incessantly prayed. Believers and unbelievers all were petitioning God for victory and safety. It was like a blanket of murmuring covered the area.

Walter went to his brothers and put his arm around each as they went before God in supplication. The elder brother prayed, "Lord, we join with the Psalmist who said 'I will praise and give thanks to You, O Lord, among the peoples; I will sing praises to You among the nation. For your mercy and loving-kindness are great, reaching to the heavens, and Your truth and faithfulness to the clouds.' Heavenly Father we believe this is a just cause. We believe it is your will to put William on England's throne and we are only your instruments in implementing the plan. Oh, mighty God put your protecting hands around your servants. Give us your safety and victory. This we pray in the name of your son, our Saviour." Both Edward and Richard entered in with a soft "Amen."

The three men felt more relaxed after praying and were able to get a short nap in before the call to arms.

Early, before dawn the next morning, the entire Norman army of approximately 7000 men went down into the Valley and approached the ridge where the English army of numerous men sat. In reality the surprise attack came from the Normans.

King William, the Duke of Normandy's army, advanced in three divisions. He, along with Walter Espec sat mounted in the central position. The French scribe, William of Poiters, was also in the center division and that night wrote in his journal, "The battle began with a terrible sound. Horns were blaring. The French were screaming, 'God help us' and the English were yelling, 'Holy Cross.'"

At the front of each Norman division the archers and cross-bowmen advanced. Next followed the men with spear, sword and battleaxe. In the rear came the mounted knights in heavy armor.

Walter made sure both Edward and Richard were at the very rear of the foot soldiers. Most of the youngest men were put in this position.

The English divisions were lined in a shield wall across the ridge. Men stood ten ranks in depth and held their shields in front of themselves. They surrounded Harold and his two brothers who stood with him and the shield wall extended about 400 yards on each side of the monarch. The men in the shield wall stood so close together (after the old Germanic and Viking style of warfare) it would be impossible for a man to fall when he was hit.

As the French army marched up the hill the going was slow. Therefore the knights, on horseback in the rear, passed through the foot soldiers and on up to the front. The Englishmen who were standing in the army shield division eventually could not stand against the mounted knights. When they collapsed the hand to hand fighting began. It was terrible and went on for hour after hour.

In the early afternoon William's left division began to give way. A rumor concerning William being killed was started and passed from mouth to mouth. As it spread one French soldier after another turned around and began to run away from battle.

William spurred his horse through the men until he reached the very rear of the division and then he pulled off his helmet shouting, "See, I'm alive!" A loud roar, "William's alive!" rose from the men as they about-faced and fought even more fiercely.

One English soldier who lay on the ground feigning death, stood up in back of William and started to swing a battleaxe toward the Duke's back. The action was caught out of the corner of Walter's eye. With an instantaneous reaction he threw a lance at the bold man. This pierced the man's shoulder before the thrust of the axe could be completed. William turned to see the man fall and moved over to finish the job with his sword. The Duke then turned toward Walter and put his fingers to his helmet in salute.

For several more hours the battle raged until there came a point when the French began to feign a retreat. This lured the English off the ridge in order for them to pursue the apparently fleeing men. However the French turned back into them. More bodies of young English and French men continued to be strewn in the area. Still the battle continued. The Frenchman, William of Poitiers, wrote in his journal, "As daylight faded the clashing of weapons still rang in our ears."

King Harold and his two brothers finally were killed at the foot of the monarch's standard. At this point the English turned and retreated while the Norman knights followed them in pursuit.

With complete darkness surrounding them the fight finally ended. William was the Conqueror and the French Duke rode back into camp with a broken lance still held in his hand.

Walter stepped into the barracks area and heard a great deal of moaning. The wounded were laying everywhere and then he saw the abject face of Richard, who was standing over a body and fear gripped his heart. When Walter saw Edward lying on the floor in a pool of blood he knew his fears were grounded.

There were two things the older brother needed to do after he cried, "Oh God, help us!" First he sent Richard to the mess hall to bring back a pouch full of salt. Then he examined the deep leg wound caused by a lance passing all the way through Edward's left thigh.

Around the wound there seemed to be some clotting, but there was also quite a bit of blood still leaking. Walter contemplated the amount of blood on the floor, plus what must have been lost during the time Edward was carried back to camp. The older brother cringed and thought came - any more blood loss could be fatal. The wound needed to be cauterized immediately to stop the bleeding.

Walter built a fire. Then he took Edward's spear, which was lying on the floor, and thrust it into the flames. There it was held until it glowed red. With tears in his eyes Walter thrust the red-hot spear into Edward's wound. The groaning young man screamed and fainted, but the flow of blood ceased.

In the meantime, Richard stood in a long line of men who were waiting to obtain salt for the wounded men. When he almost reached the barrel the men found it was empty and they started yelling for the cook to bring more. Finally another keg was rolled in, and Richard was able to fill his pouch.

He quickly ran back to his tent and was shocked to find Walter sitting on the floor by unconscious Edward. He thought his brother was dead until Walter explained the situation. Then Walter carefully packed salt in and around the wound to prevent any infection. In the meantime Richard tore one of his nightshirts into strips to bandage the wound. The next day Edward woke and smiled, but he was very weak and in much pain.

Duke William announced, "Today we will bury the no longer reigning king of England. He will be given the proper honor of a former monarch." First a small party of French soldiers were sent to dig a grave a few miles from Hastings; set at the very spot where Harold's standard still stood on the battlefield. Then the complete number of men from each French division marched to the site and stood at attention as the priest (who accompanied William's force) conducted the ceremony. During this time the soldiers who remained from the defeated English army stood around the perimeter of the gravesite.

Following the ceremony the French divisions, with William on his steed in the forefront, marched into Hastings singing victory songs. To the very waterfront they marched. Then across the extremely pebbled beach to circle the town and from there back to headquarters.

For the next couple of weeks much strategy planning took place. The Norman leaders knew the conquest would still be opposed because many people in the English populace did not want a Frenchman as their ruler. The opposition would be tough, with many skirmishes, until William could become the legally crowned king in the city of London.

Finally the plan formulated was for the army to march toward Winchester while squelching any opposition, and in key areas build a castle in order to house the new town official who would be a man with Norman leanings. Before beginning the march west a messenger arrived for William from the pope. The message began with a hearty congratulations on the victory at Hastings. Then it went on to say, "The battle fought was a right and honorable one in order to gain the throne God chose for you. However the Almighty says, "Thou shalt not kill." Men were killed in this war. Your penance for disobeying scripture is to build a house of worship." The message concluded with the thought there would probably be a need for more battles before the monarchy would become William's. Therefore an Abbey, or a Cathedral, or a Monastery must be built for every skirmish where men are killed.

William was pleased with this directive. He felt all of England was in need of a religious revival. As the Norman nobleman thought about the prospects of building places of worship he believed a beautiful house of God could draw people to it. If the reason they came was out of curiosity, or just to study the artwork, they would still hear about the Lord Jesus Christ while they were visiting and could possibly come to believe in the Saviour.

The march west was postponed for another week as William made plans and gave directives for the first church to be named Battle Abbey. The structure would be built in the area where Harold fell and the high altar placed over the very spot where the grave lay.

During the week William talked with Walter about Edward's wound and what the future could hold for the two younger brothers. Each day Edward appeared to be healing and gaining strength and he constantly thanked the Lord for not allowing any infection to develop. However, everyone knew it would be a while before he could travel again; either on horse or on foot. There was a question in both Walter and William's mind as to whether Edward would ever walk once more without assistance.

William suggested for both Edward and Richard to remain in the battle area to help where possible, and to observe the construction of the Abbey. He was sure they would learn much which could be of assistance in the future construction of houses of worship. Walter thought the idea was a good one and when he presented it to his younger brothers they listened with interest. In a few days Edward and Richard both determined they would stay in the south to learn what they could about massive construction.

Camp was broken. The French army moved northwest. Along the way they met various receptions. There were people who raised their arms and gave a victory sign. There were people who simply stayed on their farms, or in their houses while shunning the moving mass of soldiers. By word of mouth these people already heard of the power of this army and preferred to stay neutral until the final consent came from the English government as to whether William, Duke of Normandy, would be accepted as their monarch.

Then there were those who were definitely opposed enough to take a sword in hand. Minor skirmishes ensued with these men. The next major opposition was at Winchester. Here the people retreated within the walls of the city and barred the gates. For three days William waited outside the walls hoping the city officials would come to their senses and order the gates to be opened. When this did not happen the walls were breached, the gates were forcefully opened and hand-to-hand street fighting followed.

William and the army once more stayed put for two weeks while the conqueror organized the new city government. The work on a castle and another house of worship was begun before the Normans were ready for their trek on to London. But before actually marching away William made sure the city residents understood the castle belonged to him. His, to return to if he wished, as well as for the use of any official he placed in it.

The Norman force zigzagged across all of southern England until all of the communities were conquered and under their control. They met the same types of reception previously encountered from Hastings to Winchester. Early in December the army approached London and filtered in through the city gates. There was not much opposition, although from time to time skirmishes broke out in the streets.

On Christmas day in Westminster Abbey a second coronation took place in the year of 1066. This time the man crowned was William, Duke of Normandy.

Two days later, again in Westminster Abbey, William called a ceremony to knight several men of exceptional valor who fought with him. One of these men was Walter Espec. After the ceremony was finished Walter was again called to the altar where William presented him with a magnificent gold ring (set with two diamonds) for saving his life at the battle of Hastings.

The ring was made monstrous in size due to of Walter's unusually large hands, with the gold being quite thick and intricately molded with a crown and a cross.

William and his men continued to remain in London. Days were filled with the business of constructing a kingly castle on a site by the bank of the Thames to be William's future palace when he was in London.

News kept filtering into London from the north concerning unrest and also unacceptance of the new king. William decided to take his army north to squelch any and all rebellion.

The lovely town of Norwich appealed to William as a place for him to make his domain. Once the townspeople's discontent was settled, the English-Norman ruler ordered the construction of another castle for his use to be located on a rise overlooking the town center. From there he could watch the business of the town market, the movement of patrons in and out of the small shops and in and out of the pub (located in an old Roman ruin), plus he was able to see all of the commerce moving along the roads into and out of the town. Right away William realized the community needed two landmarks: a Cathedral and a Monastery. These were the next projects for him to keep an eye on. Once they were underway William determined to proceed further north and continue settling the rebellious people.

This king would sometimes travel north with his army. Other times he would travel to London to conduct government business there. Always there was a need to take a good-sized force where he traveled because of the uncertainty of just what they would encounter. Walter always accompanied William in the traveling party.

Then too, officials would come from all over England and Europe to Norwich to confer with William concerning matters of politics. The meetings would be held in the magnificent Norman style castle with its great rooms and many suites.

As William considered the continuing need for revival and reform within the English church he felt led to request for church leaders to be sent from Europe. In his estimation the church needed new bishops and pastors to bring forth any revival. The move by the new monarch brought even more dissent, disapproval and rebellion from his subjects.

The king of England now realized he must completely focus on matters of state to make all of the necessary transitions go more smoothly. No longer would William be able to travel with his forces and he knew someone competent must be put in charge. As the ruler thought about the need the name of his cousin, Walter Espec, kept coming to mind. Finally he decided to ask Walter if he would oversee the movements of the army. Walter responded, "If you think having me in charge will be best, I will take the position and do it with my utmost ability. But before we go any further we should ask God's blessing on this charge." The two men walked down into the castle's chapel and up to the altar. There they dropped on their knees, and Walter prayed, "Lord, I feel like David looking unto the hills while seeking help from you. I feel inadequate for the job before me and claim your help. Oh, Almighty God in a Psalm you said, 'How blessed is he whose help is the God of Jacob, Whose hope is in the Lord his God. Who made heaven and earth, The sea and all that is in them. Who keeps faith forever.' Now Saviour, please give me the blessing of help as you promised your servant David." William added a hearty "Amen!" to the prayer.

As the king and Walter rose, and turned, they saw their Pastor standing at the back of the chapel. When the Pastor walked toward the men William informed him of the new posting for Walter. The man of God took the time to give congratulations then said, "Walter there is a messenger waiting for you outside." Walter quickly walked up the aisle.

The message was from his brother William stating, "Father is failing greatly. You better come now." Walter was stunned for a moment, and then he approached William who was talking with the Pastor.

Walter's face displayed his concern and his cousin blurted out, "What is the matter?" When Walter explained what the message contained, William replied, "No! It doesn't seen possible for my strong uncle to be dying. Just last year he strode into the castle at Falaise. You must go. The army's move north can wait."

Distraught Walter quickly contacted half a dozen soldiers to ride with him on the six-day journey southwest to Old Warden. He instructed them to gather supplies as quickly as possible while he would go pack for the trip. The seven men were on horseback and leaving the castle grounds within the hour.

They rode hard. From time to time it was necessary to stop long enough for the horses to get rested. The seven arrived at William Speke's castle just past midday and Walter found his father in bed, extremely pale with labored breathing, but their hug was warm and it was satisfying. The two men talked of every-day matters for twenty minutes. Then Walter said, "Father, I want you to know I love you and I'm thankful for all the love and care you gave me during my growing up years." There were tears in both men's eyes because they knew before long there would be no more earthly contact between this father and son. Then Walter realized his father was tiring and excused himself to join other family members.

Gathered around the table in the dining hall were Walter's mother, his brother William and wife Arlene, nephew William and wife Elizabeth, and his two young sisters, Grace and Hannah. Walter sat to join his family. The serving bowl of soup on the table was now cold because the others ate at noon. Madeline ordered the servant to heat it when she realized her son had not taken time to eat.

The homemade vegetable beef soup tasted very good. Walter ate two big bowls full with huge chunks of freshly baked bread while the family told him all about his father's illness.

The information he was hearing spilled out from one member after another. It seemed shortly after returning from Normandy his dear father started with a dry cough. Many different herbs were given, but no matter what herb was administered it didn't help. In a few months strings of blood began to appear in the coughed-up mucous and then they knew he had the coughing sickness. Now there is a daily choking with massive amounts of blood loss during the coughing spasms. With tears and a tight throat Madeline choked out, "Everyone knows your father cannot last long."

When Walter asked if Edward and Richard were notified William assured him a messenger was sent to them at the same time as the one who traveled to get him. The older brother thought Edward and Richard should be arriving any time soon.

William Sr. wanted to be with his family at dinner, therefore his two sons carried him to the table. Walter saw his father's face was flushed and he felt extremely hot to the touch. All food neither appealed to the patriarch, nor did it taste good. The man who once enjoyed an extremely good appetite now ate little. But he was content to just sit at the table and listen to the conversation. It reminded him of happy past times when all of his children lived at home.

Later in the evening Edward and Richard rode in. They too went straight to their father's bedroom. He was asleep and the two young men decided it would be best to wait until morning to greet him. They returned to the sitting room where the rest of the family sat conversing.

Immediately questions started flying. Edward and Richard wanted to know all about their father's illness. Once their curiosity was quenched the two young men began answering questions about themselves.

Edward said he was getting along well and he talked about having no use of his leg. Then he went on to say how thankful he was for the wound to be completely healed and also for the fact he was able to get around on a crutch.

This was the first time his mother, sisters and oldest brother's family were able to see him since the time he was wounded in battle. They kept interjecting their sorrow and sympathy between almost every sentence Edward uttered. Then finally this young man said, "Yes, the wound was terrible and the pain was awful, but my soul is right with God, and He gives me daily strength to function as a whole man. I am thankful this happened to me, because due to my incapacity I stayed at Hastings and have spent hours with the architects for the Cathedral at the battle site. I've learned much about design and construction and I am fascinated with the process enough to make it my lifetime occupation. Your need to realize such an interest would have never happened if I hadn't been wounded. God had a purpose in the injury."

Next Richard joined in telling about his experiences while fighting for a cause he thought just, and how before going, he believed being in a battle would be an exciting thing to do. However he felt he learned that even though sometimes war is a necessary action, to actually witness combat and see death is a terrible thing.

Then Richard said, "Edward's wound and suffering broke my heart. Many a night I approached the Lord with tears in my eyes for Edward's healing and for his return to strength. God answered! Now I too can see the good coming from the injury. My interest was caught in watching the stonemasons at work in the Cathedral construction. I want to become as efficient in that craft as those working on the Battle Abbey. There are a couple techniques apparent to me where I could make the laying of the stones more precise. God willing I hope to perfect them."

For the next two days the senior William coughed more and more. He silently died in his sleep on the third night. A quiet weeping filled the home. The father figure, the family leader, the gallant servant of God and a greatly loved man now gone from their presence and with the Lord.

In the morning the eldest son dispatched riders to neighbors and to all of his father's tenants and workers. The purpose was to notify everyone about William Speke's death. Also to inform them the body would be in state in the evening. The family wanted their father to be buried the following day.

Men servants were dispatched to build the coffin and prepare the ground. The women quickly began the extremely large job of preparing foods for the hundreds of people who would be coming and going for the next twenty-four hours.

Son William went to the Chapel to pray and to prepare his heart and mind for the duty of conducting the funeral. That evening the relatives, friends and neighbors of the family began to arrive. This continued all night long with wagons full of people and men on horseback filing into the Speke estate. Tenants and serfs from Eyeworth, Southhill and Northhill settled within walking distance of the castle. Each brought food to share with the several hundred people who would be gathering.

Among the guests who came for the funeral were members of Elizabeth's family. Walter noticed the attractiveness of the older sister of his niece by marriage. His mind went back to about eight years earlier when he left for Normandy and this beautiful young woman was only twelve years of age. He thought, what a transformation has taken place in those years! The skinny little girl was now a lovely young woman. Walter couldn't keep his eyes off of her. Naturally he kept drifting over in the direction of the blue-eyed blonde named Joanne who diverted his thoughts from some of the solemnity of the moment.

Joanne herself was quite surprised in the muscular handsomeness of the young man whose Norman fame reached her ears from time to time from Elizabeth's lips. She thought back how, even before Walter left for Europe, she would notice the big young man who often would ride to her home with messages from Sir William to her father. Now it almost seemed like electricity crackled between them. She thought, "Hmm, I wouldn't mind if he came riding to see my father every day now."

Before the afternoon funeral began, everyone from all of William's holdings within a forty-mile radius began arriving. The new comers were from Beeston, Biddenham, Roxton, Steppingley and Streatley. All of the manor lords, landholders, tenants, farmers, plowmen, mill workers, slaves and many of the villagers crowded around the grounds.

During the funeral service eulogy, given by Walter, the faithful leading of God in William Speke's life was stressed. This included choices the man made, which were honoring to his Lord and Saviour and how blessing after blessing followed. Walter ended with, "And now my father is experiencing the final blessing, which is life everlasting in heaven for all eternity with the God he loved." William closed the service with a sermon and prayer. Then the coffin was carried to the cemetery by the side of the castle.

Following the funeral, as the guests mingled around the many food-laden tables in the courtyard, Walter kept gravitating toward Joanne. He thought she was the most enchanting young woman he ever met. Being one of the hosts, he often offered her choice food items for her plate. Her father, Solomon Edwards watched, with a twinkle in his eye, as he saw apparently more than friendship was going to develop.

By the next morning all the guests were gone and the family gathered in the sitting room. As was the custom, the son William became the heir to all of the Speke holdings. He went to sit in the chair his father usually sat in.

Conversation was slow at first, as each person remained deep in thought concerning the events of the last few days. Then the chatter started about who was seen and what was said. Finally the talk worked around to the future plans of each individual.

William said, "Hopefully the transition in leadership will present no problems. Of course, this will always be home to you my dear mother, and the girls. Home also to you Walter, Edward and George, that is as long as you want it to be. But I know you will want to set up your own estates sometime in the future and I'll help you in any way possible. Your valued advice will be welcomed on any concerns for the home and family. Please always feel free to offer it. I won't say I'll always take it."

Then William asked his brothers if it would be possible for them to ride with him to all of the Speke owned areas that were so far away the people could not come to the funeral. He wanted to make sure all of the tenants were aware of the change in authority.

All of the tenants who attended the funeral, were given the paperwork to cover the change in property ownership before they left the grounds.

Because of Edward's leg injury he declined from traveling with William. He said there was still pain in his leg whenever it was jarred by the movement of the horse's hooves striking the ground in any faster pace than a walk. Also, with no strength in his leg Edward needed to be careful of his balance on the horses back in order to not fall. The young man felt just traveling back to Hastings would be the most he could endure.

Richard thought it would be wisest to travel south with Edward. There was no question as to Richard knowing his brother's endurance and he wanted to be available for any need.

Then too, the youngest brother was anxious to get back to positioning the stones on the now twenty foot high Abbey walls.

Walter said he would be willing to make the trip with his brother. "Good" replied William. Then the eldest brother turned to the two youngest and asked them if they would mind stopping at Chawton and Stanford on their way to Hastings. This would save the two eldest a trip south and it would not be more than a few miles out of George and Edward's way. The two young men said they would be happy to take care of the business and William responded, "So glad you will be able to do this, I will leave the matter in your hands.

Now Walter, you and I will travel north in a few days and make the people in Hinwick, Holcot and Wymington aware of who now is the owner." "That sounds good to me," answered Walter; mean while he was thinking, this method will give me time to see Joanne some of the days before traveling with William. Then I will also be able to see her for a few days after the trip and before I return to my post.

There was just one more matter William was concerned about. Before everyone filed out of the room he went to his son and asked, "William, will you and your wife stay with your grandmother until Walter and I return from our trip?" Young William replied he would be pleased to help in any way.

Chapter 3

Summer 1067

*W*alter bid Joanne good-bye with a kiss, plus a ring to seal their betrothal. With all of the business at Wardon being completed it was time to return to Norwich and take up his duties there. He rode off with the same seven men who accompanied him months earlier to attend the death of the beloved patriarch; men who were kept busy assisting Walter while they were staying in Wardon. Then when Walter and William traveled north the men traveled with them to help combat any dangers on the road.

Shortly after Walter arrived back in Norwich, King William called him for a consultation concerning northern problems. All the time Walter was down in Old Wardon there were reports of rebellion constantly filtering back to the king. Small battalions were sent to put down each minor conflict. There was no question about a need for a major offensive to settle the matter more completely. The king knew Walter would be able to plan a sensible march to put all rebellion down. He waited restlessly day by day for his cousin's return to take care of the problem. Now William would be able to relax concerning the matter.

Walter announced a meeting of the knights involved with the strategy planning. For hours, then for several days the men debated. The conclusion to all of the discussion was to make "an all out" offensive on the major cities to the north. Even the order of the march was determined. The army planned on going toward Nottingham first, then on to Sheffield, York, Thirsk, Newcastle-Upon-Thyne, Edinburgh and ending at Aberdeen. As the previous year's offensive in the south progressed, so it would be in the north. Once each area was subdued the building of a castle and a place of worship would be started. Then one who is a noble or a leader from the marching army would be left to govern the region.

Many of the king's men became restless during the period of time Walter was away. They were anxious to complete the job of subduing the rebellion, because after it was finished they could return home to civilian life. The men were "at the ready" which made possible a swift departure from Norwich.

For the next two years Walter led the offensives until all of the rebellious areas settled down. When the land between York and Edinburgh became subdued Walter chose this area to be under his domain. He began to think about the building of a castle at Helmsley, close to York, and another one at Wark close to Newcastle upon Thyne. He would reside at Helmsley and assign someone reliable for the position of governor at Wark.

Now with his military assignment completed Walter rode toward Wardon on June first 1069 to claim his beloved Joannne. The date decided for the wedding was to be the seventeenth. Already preparations were underway for the lavish festivities of the nuptials and the reception. New gowns were being assembled for all of the women who would be attending the bride. Diagrams of the large gardens of Joanne's father's estate were drawn in order to arrange for the location of the ceremony, plus how to place the decorations, and where to set the reception tables.

Joanne asked her older sister Elizabeth, and her younger sister Isobel to stand for her. Walter's two younger sisters were also prepared to be a part of the bridal party.

One day, during the preparations Joanne's father asked, "Walter, are you going to have "Speke or Le Espek" on the legal marriage paper?" Walter replied, "With all of my art dealings in France and Europe it would be better to keep the French nomenclature of Espec. God willing, I hope to resume my trade now that I have a wife, a home, and our country's peace is secure. People across the water would not understand, nor know me under the name of Speke."

Just a few days before the wedding Walter's brother Richard drove a horse and wagon north. In the wagon sat Edward and his fiancee Kathleen, plus a chaperone by the name of Naomi. The trip was not as difficult for the cripple as when he tried to travel astride a horse.

As soon as Richard finished greeting everyone he went to build the arbor in the rose garden under which the ceremony would be performed. Once it was finished the gardener began stringing garlands through the latticework. The wedding was scheduled to take place the next afternoon.

Joanne asked William to perform the ceremony and her brother Alexander to give the blessing at the reception.

Alexander recently returned from a Pilgrimage to the Holy land. He was gone from home for five years and during part of the time away took some studies in Jerusalem. Everyone kept asking him questions about his trip; what he saw and what he did. Many family members were concerned about the problem some of the Pilgrims experienced while on their way to the Holy Land. Foremost in their minds was the atrocity of being attacked by Muslim radicals.

At two p.m. on June seventeenth Joanne appeared exquisite in a very simply designed white silk gown with a garland of tiny pastel blossoms circling her head. Joanne's hand rested on Sir. Edward's arm while she proudly walked the path between the multicolored roses. Both Walter and Joanne's sisters were adorned in gowns the same pastel colors as the flowers in the bride's garland. The attendant's gowns were of the same material and design of the soon to be Mrs. Le Espek.

All the brothers and sisters were gathered under the sweet-smelling arbor when William began the age-old words, "We are gathered here." As this family's Pastor led the couple through the well-known vows a joy was on his face and also in his voice. Walter's oldest brother felt very privileged to be the one joining in wedlock two people he loved and on whom he knew the Lord's blessing would rest.

Alexander presided as Master of Ceremonies throughout the entire reception. After everyone gathered around the tables his deep resonant voice reached across the expansive grounds saying, "Family, friends, before the toast, before the food, before the dancing let us take the time to praise God for the joining together of Walter and Joanne in marriage." Everyone bowed their heads and he continued with, "Oh mighty God, You have said You are the Rock, Your work is perfect, Your ways are just, You are a faithful God who does no wrong. You are upright and just. We claim these truths You gave in the book of Deuteronomy, and depend upon You to be the protecting rock through all the married life of Walter and Joanne. Now we pray for Your blessing upon this food."

With the last words still echoing across the tables everyone began to sit in their seats. Alexander continued with, "Let us toast the bride and groom in order for the festivities to begin."

The tables were laden with goose, duck and lamb, all kinds of cheeses, dark breads, plus bite-size fresh vegetables carved into the shapes of various flower blossoms.

Off to the side of the garden stood a large platform where different drama troupes put on skits during the time the guests were eating. The other side of the garden held the area where minstrels and troubadours performed. The people chose their seats in one area or another in order for them to listen to the type of entertainment they preferred.

After every appetite was satiated and as twilight began to descend the orchestra musicians began gathering. Many torches were lit as the bride and groom ascended the steps to the platform to begin the evening's dancing. The bride and groom danced two pieces of music by themselves. Then the guests joined the newlyweds. After a half dozen dances Walter and Joanne were free to either mingle with the guests sitting at the tables or they could continue dancing.

Walter wanted a little time to speak with Edward and Richard before he and his bride left for Europe. The appropriate time seemed to be now and the couple meandered around tables while greeting people until their family's table was reached. All of the Speke clan was there. Of course it was necessary to carry on a general conversation for a while.

Finally, the time came when Walter could talk with Edward and Richard individually. To both brothers he began the conversation with "You have learned much about the construction of massive buildings and have been involved with just such a building program in the south. Now your skills are needed in the north as well. Would you consider going there?"

Walter proposed to Edward a permanent residency on his property at Wark. To Richard the proposition was the same but for him to reside at Helmsley. One stipulation in the contract would be for the men to finish building the castle. In each castle's design was to be located a wing for Walter and Joanne to live in.

Edward agreed right away. He said he would go north as soon as possible to oversee the craftsmen already working on the building. Once the castle was completed he would marry Kathleen and they would be glad to live at Wark while he supervised future construction.

Richard said, "Let me think about this a little while. I'll let you know my answer before the evening in over."

Just before the last of the guests retired for the night George walked over to Walter and Joanne to explain why he needed time to consider the offer made to him.

To bring the topic up Richard began with, "Walter, when William's army marched into the town of Bath do you remember what kind of town it was?" "Well yes," Walter replied, "the place was quaint and relatively quiet with an interesting old Roman bath. People came there, even from a distance, to soak in the hot pools for their medicinal purposes. Many of us in the army went into the waters to relax while we were there.

When I came out from the pool I went into the Saxon church, along side of the bath house, to pray for Edward and you back at the Battle campsite."

Richard was pleased with the answer because within the last six months he was invited to visit Bath's little square-steeple Saxon church several times. There he learned the church stood at the Roman poolside site for almost three hundred years. Now the congregation desired to build one of the expansive Norman Abbeys. They wanted Richard to be in charge of the stonework.

When Richard told Walter the reason he was reluctant about going to Helmsley the older brother completely understood, but he was disappointed. Then the younger brother said he would go to Helmsley and oversee the building of the home. However once the bride and bridegroom returned home from Europe he would travel south to Bath.

On the next day every one of the guests began departing for their homes. Walter and Joanne left for France and they took the usual route the Speke family traveled when they went across the water to Europe.

This was the first trip across the channel for Joanne and every aspect of the coming travel appeared exciting to her. Through most of her growing up years she heard many things about France through her family's closeness with the Speke family and their ties with the foreign country. The history of the city of Paris intrigued her. She knew Julius Caesar himself captured the city and then named it Lutetia. She knew about the early local rulers in various regions and about Hugh Capet, Count of Paris becoming king of France in 987. Now she would meet the present ruler, King Philip the first, and she would actually walk around this city now known for its commerce, its courtliness and it's being the location of the King's residence.

King William of England, as part of his wedding gift to Walter and Joanne, contacted Philip, the king of France (long before the ceremony) to make the ruler aware of the honeymoon plans of Walter and Joanne. He knew the French king would feel obligated to invite the couple to reside in one of the palace's apartments while they were in Paris. When the invitation was confirmed the English king quietly told Walter the news.

Joanne's eyes were wide in wonder to see the king's coach waiting for them at the Channel's edge. Walter chuckled when he saw her expression and he was quite content at being able to keep the palace apartment opportunity a secret from her. Down to Paris they rode in style with people by the wayside straining to see who was riding in the King's coach.

Through the bustling city of Paris they traveled and on into its very heart. For a while they drove along the river street in front of the venders and shops. Joanne's ears picked up the bickering conversations among the merchants and she mentioned it to Walter. His reply was "Do you realize Caesar said the very same thing about the people when he came here. It's recorded he said the French are, 'clever, inventive and quarrelsome.'" Joanne laughed when she heard this, and thought, how unusual to be so progressive, yet bickering all the time.

After the coach left the river bank it turned through a set of gates into the king's palace and servants met the vehicle to assist the newlyweds to their quarters. Once all the luggage, plus Walter and Joanne were comfortably situated a servant told them the king would stop to see them in about two hours time.

Joanne immediately told the servant to bring them warm water in order to wash. She felt dusty and grimy from the long trip.

In half an hour a large basin was filled in their bedroom's annex where the toilet facilities stood. After the couple washed themselves the servant poured the water into the latrine, which exited down the outside of the castle wall.

Walter and his wife were refreshed and relaxed by the time the sixteen-year old king made his appearance. This king Philip the first of France had ascended the throne two years earlier. He looked very polished and hospitable, while underneath the French ruler seethed with uncertainty and distrust. Philip did not like the apparent power of a Frenchman, the Duke of Normandy, on the English throne. The French king feared William's possible influence on his own monarchy. Walter and Joanne were viewed as possible spies in the eyes of Philip. However the newlyweds did not realize this. The only thing they were aware of was the thrill of being man and wife while staying in the palace of the king of France.

Walter's plans were two-fold. One was to show his bride the sights of major cities on the continent. The other reason for their being away from England was in order for Walter to search out various art works to purchase and send home. William commissioned his brother, at the time of their father's death, to continue in the family trade when Walter was free of his military service.

For two days the young couple rested from their journey. They marveled at the beauty of the palace grounds and the floral gardens. They relaxed on the banks of the Seine and ambled through the shops while looking at the various wares. Then Walter took his bride to the metalwork school.

Joanne was almost speechless, as she looked at all the beautiful pieces of work. Then she said, "My dearest, lets purchase one of the communion goblets for use in our chapel at Helmsley." Walter agreed. Her idea was a good one and they bought the one of Joanne's choice, plus several others to take back for some of the new Abbeys being built in England.

On Sunday the newlyweds went to worship in the five hundred year old monastery and abbey of St. Germain-des-Pres. Both felt a thrill as they stepped into the ancient wooden structure and thought of the faithfulness of God through generation after generation of worshippers. The Le Espek's knew the Almighty established this place of worship in 542 and now they were looking over how laymen continued to preserve the buildings year after year.

Walter said, "What a privilege it is to be a part of God's family." The two of them knelt and Walter whispered from a Psalm, "I will declare that your love stands firm forever, that you established your faithfulness in heaven itself. O Lord God Almighty, who is like you? You are mighty, O Lord, and your faithfulness surrounds you."

In a few minutes the silence was broken when a plain song began echoing from the rear of the church. It grew louder as the Pastor, monks and choir strolled down the isle. From that moment on the holiness and majesty of God impressed itself in the minds of those in attendance. Two hours later the building was quietly vacated with the people concentrating on the awesomeness of God.

About halfway through the next week the time came for Walter and Joanne to travel. One of king Philip's coaches was offered for their use and their itinerary took them north to Cologne. But on the way the bride and bridegroom stopped first at Le Bec-Helouin. Walter wanted his wife to see the tapestry work. He himself was anxious to see the progression of the Cathedral's construction. Then too, there was the possibility of purchasing more tapestry. Joanne planned on looking for objects for their own chapel and Walter hoped to locate pieces to be shipped back to England. Neither of them were disappointed in what they saw or purchased.

In preparation for this trip Walter made the arrangement for transportation of all the goods he would buy. Now he need not be concerned about the carting home of the many objects to be attained.

Cologne proved to be a fascinating city. Together the couple explored shop after shop. Because this city was located on a major trade route they found many items they never saw before. Goods from as far away as the Far east and the Orient. Joanne especially appreciated the fine embroidery from China and

Walter kept his eye out for the fine linens from Egypt. The main reason for the trip to Cologne was for Walter to purchase meter upon meter of the linen for embroidery to be worked by the women in England's churches.

Because of the ancientness, the largeness and the richness of this city, the honeymooners spent a full week just going places, looking at things and walking along the banks of the Rhine River. There was a special aura about Cologne, with it being an important member of the Holy Roman Empire and the home of Germany's Archbishop. The floral gardens took on a new life. The artwork breathed a beauty and the uniqueness of a very apparent ancient Roman civilization caught their awe. Love and contentment walked with Walter and Joanne.

From Cologne, the king's coach carried the couple toward east central France. Along the way they would often mention how much they appreciated the use of the comfortable transportation. Their destination was Lyon; another ancient city. This one was located on the strategic waterways of the Rhone and Saone Rivers.

Walter and Joanne only stayed a few days exploring the city founded forty years before Christ was born. The purpose for their stopping was in order for Walter to purchase wine for the English church's communion tables. This did not take long to accomplish.

Now they were off to Bologna. A city even older than any of the previous ones they visited on the trip so far. Bologna began as a Roman colony in 190 B.C. Once again the reason for the city's stability was due to being located on a major trade route; one traveling through north central Italy. Walter chose to visit the city because he heard artists living there were considering the establishment of an art school. He wanted to see their work and possibly attain some.

The honeymooners enjoyed a week of sightseeing. The University of Bologna was well known for its law school whose classes began during Roman times. The school did not own a building of their own, but presently held the lectures in the great halls of the convents and the attendance was open to the visiting public. Out of curiosity Walter went to two of the afternoon law classes while Joanne attended a class on incense making.

At this point in history one of Bologna's main attractions was the construction process of four Cathedrals being built all at one time. They were of special interest to Christians because they were being laid over the foundations of four pagan temples. The Christians believed this was a sign of the power of the Lord Jesus Christ over heathen beliefs. The area for the four Cathedrals was called Santo Sefano.

Hand in hand the couple climbed the steps into the churches while admiring the beauty of the workmanship around them. They strolled the tiny lanes and on into the shops. Two afternoons they walked around the town center where the artists gathered. Some artists were making pottery, some were drawing pictures and some were carving figurines. Walter and Joanne were fascinated as they watched the pieces of art being developed.

Joanne purchased some of the pottery for use in her home. One of the water pitchers especially caught her attention and she bought several various pieces from the artist who made it. Walter commissioned one of the artists to draw a picture of Christ on the cross. The artist already displayed several religious art pictures along one side of the square and Walter appreciated the facial features on them. He felt the workmanship would be excellent and wanted such a picture to be placed over the Alter at Helmsley.

As the two were walking back from the riverbank toward their accommodations Joanne told her husband she suspected he would become a father in late spring. Walter was ecstatic over the news and immediately became concerned about Joanne's health. He wondered whether it would be wise to continue their stay on the continent. She assured him she would be fine and told him she was not as yet even experiencing the often talked about morning sickness.

Joanne believed the next and last stop of their trip was, for her, a culmination of all their travel. They were going to Rome and the thought of not being able to go there, because of pregnancy, would be a terrible disappointment.

When the coach approached the seven hills on the central west coast of Italy's peninsula the couple saw several lights beginning to twinkle while dusk settled in. Walter and Joanne were anticipating a hot meal, a good nights rest, and then the exploration around Rome would begin on the following day.

While they were growing up the couple heard many stories about the early history of the city they saw sitting before them. Now they would be able to go into the buildings and imagine what life was like during the well-known days of the Roman Empire.

Joanne wanted to visit the Christian sites before viewing any of the Roman ones. Because the plan was to allow two weeks for sightseeing in this place there was no rush. They could sleep-in until after sunrise. Then go to one or two places each day. In the other daylight hours there would be shops and gardens to visit, plus stops at places where different types of craftwork or artwork were being created.

On their agenda the first place they wanted see was St. Peter's Basilica, whose construction was begun in the year 325 by Constantine the great, and was completed around fifteen-fifty. What Walter and Joanne walked into, was a church built on the style of a Roman meeting hall, something the Romans called a Basilica. There were four rows of columns dividing the isles and a nave within the building. The couple chatted about the many things they knew concerning the history of the Basilica. Joanne's focus was on the people involved in the church. Her voice took on a tone of awe as she talked about the apostle Peter's tomb below the structure, and about the Emperor Constantine's desire to build an edifice to God's glory. Then on she went about all of the popes being crowned within the building's walls.

The masonry, the carpentry, the architecture, the artwork were what Walter concentrated his conversation around. After their tour of the Basilica Walter wanted a good look at the wall encircling the church. Because, when Pope Leo IV saw the result of pagan plundering within the church he ordered the wall to be built to prevent any such future action.

After seeing the wall the couple went down into the catacombs. Walter experienced difficulty maneuvering thorough the Christian place of hiding because of his great bulk. The thought of escaping from an Emperor's death decree to live in such a closed-in dark space sent chills up Joanne's spine. She could not picture herself living there for weeks, months, perhaps longer. Yet she knew it was a welcome place of refuge for many first century Christians. Babies were born there. People died there. Hundreds lived part of their lives there. What a cruel part of Christian history to think on.

Lazy days of enjoyment followed. There was no rush to cover a great deal of ground, or to look at all there was to see. But there was the desire to not miss anything of importance. Walter and Joanne decided to next start viewing Roman relics. The first choice of these was the Roman forum, where, under all of the Caesars, the political and religious life was centered. This area included a market place, plus many important buildings and monuments. The couple walked where the Roman senate formerly met, then meandered over toward the triumphal arch. On they strolled toward the temple of Saturn and the Basilica of Julia.

As the late afternoon sun reached well toward the west, Walter was concerned Joanne could be overly tiring herself. He watched her all of the day and she seemed fine. Still he wondered if there was some discomfort he could not see. Once Joanne took a good look at her husband's face she realized he was concerned about her and assured him she was fine.

Chapter 3

On the following days all of the sights on Rome's seven hills were visited. The Coliseum, which once held fifty thousand spectators absorbed one morning's time. It was empty, except for some athletes on the field going through their morning run. Joanne and Walter watched them for a while. Then swordsmen came in and went through their routines. The Le Espec's minds and conversation became centered around the Christians who were martyred by wild beasts on the field before them. They talked about the gladiators who also fought wild beasts and of the beasts winning. Then too, there were also the gladiators who fought other gladiators to the death, while the crowds roared. Both agreed once more to the terribleness of that period of time.

On several mornings Walter and Joanne made trips to the public baths to enjoy the cleansing care of the people working there. They received from the employees the skin scraping, the massaging and sponging after coming out from the steam rooms. A few of the morning's when the water was especially hot Joanne felt light-headed after leaving the pool. She wondered why. One morning while being scraped alongside of other women Joanne did faint. No one was concerned as they thought she was experiencing a common symptom of being pregnant. Many pregnant women fainted after coming out of the hot baths.

The public baths were luxurious and well attended. Most of the homes of the wealthy contained their own private hot baths. Therefore the ones for the public were not overly crowded.

On other mornings the couple's time was spent inspecting the Palatine, or the ruins of Nero's house, or the mausoleum of Augustus, or the second century emperor Hadrians' family's mausoleum.

When the second Sunday morning in Rome came Joanne and Walter worshipped at the Roman Pantheon (built in 28 BC), which became a Christian church in the year 609 AD. Memories of the catacombs and the Coliseum and early Christian martyrs filled the couple's mind as they sat in awesome silence in the reverent setting before the actual worship time began.

Before Walter and Joanne now stretched the last week of their trip on the continent. There were still ancient archeological treasures to visit, - palaces, temples, royal homes, and gardens. Then too, Walter wanted to make some art purchases. He was interested in the marble stonework (Marble mined close to the city and brought into Rome to be carved by local men). Some of the artists designed elegant tables, chairs and lattices of marble, while others carved figures. Walter wanted to establish the work of this trade into England.

Joanne didn't know about it, but her husband arraigned for one big event to take place at the end of their Rome visit. They were to meet pope Alexander II. When Walter told his wife they would spend several hours with this compassionate man of God she was thrilled. For two days Joanne constantly expressed her excitement. Then the actual afternoon of the meeting arrived and the LeEspec couple were dressed in their finest clothes when they walked into St. Peter's Basilica.

One of the monks met Walter and Joanne at the door to escort them to the pope's apartment. There were a few comfortable chairs, but most of the furniture reflected the humble childhood home of this man born near Milan, who, as an infant was given the name of Anselm.

Immediately Alexander II came forward and greeted the couple warmly. He invited them to sit and they talked for quite a while. Naturally the church leader asked about Walter's family first. Then he followed with many questions about king William; the man he blessed and counseled about claiming his title to England.

The Le Espek's answered the pope's questions and then began questioning the church leader about the present church reforms and the papal authority issue. The next topic centered on the Jewish people's fears and problems with the influx of Muslims into France and Spain. Walter expressed his concern for the race of people God called out to be His own, but Alexander assured him he was doing everything possible to protect the Jews from danger.

Joanne asked "Father Alexander, are the German people more ready to accept you as their church leader"? Both Le Espec's expressed their sympathy over the angry church rebellion and how embarrassing it must have been to Alexander to have a German pope (named Honorius II) elected while he was leading the church. Everyone spoke about their relief concerning the situation calming and the stepping down of Honorius from office. Alexander said, "I am thankful the Norman people stood-bye to protect me through all of this."

The visit concluded with Pope Alexander praying for God's blessing upon Walter, Joanne and their future life together. Then he asked Walter to deliver a message to king William.

Throughout the trip the luggage kept getting heavier and heavier. Joanne kept buying wool shawls, wool blankets and wool lap robes. She knew the weather for traveling this late into the fall would be quite cold. Now during the final leg of their trip back to the coast and then on home every wool piece would be tucked around their bodies.

The weather was cold, gray and dank in England. Early on a December evening Richard lit the fire in the fireplace at Helmsley and he was standing by the blazing logs when the Le Espec's walked in.

A great deal of hugging and backslapping followed, especially when Walter told his brother, "In six months time you will become an uncle." Then Richard broke the news he was waiting to tell, "Edward and Kathleen are going to be married during Christmas week while we are all with Mother down at Wardon."

Three days later Edward rode into the Le Espek yard in his horse drawn wagon. He came to help Joanne, Walter and Richard with their unpacking and to get the furniture set up in the living quarters. The castle was far from finished, but the wing for the Espec's was livable. All of the objects sent from the continent, all of the objects brought by Walter and Joanne, plus the pieces of furniture Richard personally made for the newlyweds were unpacked and placed. By the middle of December the four, (plus the four riders who came with Edward) would travel south. Joanne rode in the wagon with Edward.

The Speke family and members of Kathleen's family all gathered at Wardon three days before Christmas. The few next day's plans all centered around the ceremony soon to take place on the evening before Christmas day. William would officiate.

Much preparation, with not much time, made the castle halls alive with business. Everyone became involved with the activity of decorating for a wedding with a Christmas theme. One hour before the ceremony was to take place everything was completed.

The back doors and the side doors of the small castle chapel were open with available seating outside in the hall as well as inside. No matter where anyone sat they could see the ceremony in plain view in the beautifully decorated, candle lit worship center. The service was lovely and the reception in the huge castle hall was grand.

Whenever William asked a blessing on people he always reminded them about the faithfulness of God. This wedding was no different. At the reception William began his prayer, "O God, "Thy kingdom is an everlasting kingdom, and Thy dominion endures throughout all generations. The Lord is faithful in all His words, and gracious in all His deeds." Because the Holy Spirit constantly reminded William about how faithfully God led the Speke family through generation after generation he couldn't help but use the thought in his ministry.

There was one difference between this reception and the one of the previous June. Edward could not lead the dancing, but he could stand on the dance platform after his brothers lifted him there. There he held his bride and swayed from side to side while the orchestra played the music for the first dance. Everyone applauded and then the guests began dancing

Early Christmas morning the family and all those visiting once more crowded into the Chapel area to sing Christmas carols and read the scriptures concerning the birth of Christ. Everyone felt this was a blessed way to begin Christmas day. Usually the Christmas Eve worship service was conducted the evening before, but with the wedding being held at that time William chose to prepare this year's Holy Child celebration before the Christmas day's activity began.

Later on Christmas day, Elizabeth came to hug her sister Joanne and congratulate her on the pregnancy. She said, "I couldn't come to you earlier. While the news makes me happy and excited for you, it hurt me. William and I have been attempting to conceive for several years and I am barren." Immediately Joanne encircled her sister in her arms and cried with her while whispering, "I'm so sorry." When Elizabeth's emotions calmed she said, "I know it's ridiculous, but a thought keeps coming to me about beautiful Speke Hall not being filled with Speke descendants. If William and I bore a son he would inherit the property from Uncle Uctred. Now, unless a miracle occurs, the Hall will pass on to another niece or nephew of my Uncle."

The day after Christmas Edward and Kathleen left for a honeymoon (north of their home in Wark) to the city of Glasgow. Up until now neither of the two traveled farther north than Wark. Preceding the wedding both of them spent some time reading all about the ancient fortified Celtic city. They wanted to see the prehistoric area for themselves. Then too, the city was known for the religious community established in 550 by St. Kentigern. They heard about the Christian music being sung and played there was exceptional and they read some about material concerning the renowned Music Fests. Edward and Kathleen hoped to see and enjoy all of these events while in the north.

A few days after Christmas Richard rode south toward Bath, while Walter and Joanne began their journey northeast to Helmsley. William the third, and his wife Elizabeth, remained at Wardon for a few weeks to stay with Madeline and the girls because his father Sir William, and his brother–in–law, Alexander soon planned on riding down to London.

In this century numerous knights were concerned about the dangers many Pilgrims experienced while traveling to the Holy Lands. The Christian travelers were meeting all kinds of opposition, from being prevented in completing their journey to being raped and killed. As the pilgrims returned to their homeland they told of what they experienced or saw happen. A great resentment and anger was fermenting toward Islam. The English church leaders called a meeting for men in London to discuss measures to resolve the problem. This is the reason William and Alexander were traveling south.

In May of the year 1070 Walter Espec Jr. was born at Helmsley. The labor was not especially long, nor difficult and the ten pound, six ounce, twenty-one inch long boy became the pride and joy of Walter and Joanne.

At Helmsley in 1082, twelve year old Walter Le Espek Jr. started playing hide and seek with his three younger sisters; Hawisa, age eleven, Albreda, age nine, and Adelina, age seven. The girls were well hidden and Walter was having a difficult time finding them. The boy looked everywhere he could think of and then sat on a stump by the front of the castle when he noticed a single forlorn figure riding up the road toward the castle. The knight was dressed all in black and slumped on his horse. It appeared he was crying something out periodically, but the man was too great a distance away for the words to be understood.

Walter shouted to his sisters, "Come out, come out wherever you are. We must go inside immediately." By the tone of his voice the girls knew something was urgent and they quickly ran out of their hiding places. The four youngsters ran up the stone steps into the castle entryway, then on up to their mother's sitting room.

The servants who were cleaning downstairs and the ones who were setting the table for the noon dinner wore a surprised look on their faces to see the children coming in so early. Then they heard the girls shouting, "Mother, someone is coming."

As the knight approached the entrance to the castle he could be heard calling out, "Sad news, sad news." For many days this man traveled and shouted before coming to the Espec home. When he approached a town he would call out while riding through the streets. People would follow him to the market square where he stopped and with the crowd assembled around him told a terrible story.

Often on the road other travelers would stop the dejected man and ask, "What happened?"

Joanne met the knight at the door and invited him to the noon dinner. The man offered his thanks and responded, "A good location to tell my story would be around the dining room table."

After everyone finished eating the knight suggested perhaps it would be wise to invite the servants into the room because they too needed to hear his story.

Once everyone gathered the knight began to explain how several years before there were four families in a London church who felt the desire to make a pilgrimage to Jerusalem. They wanted to honor the Lord by taking this time in their lives to go to the place where Jesus walked, prayed and worshipped. It took months of planning and preparation, plus the job of obtaining a dozen knights as protection for the journey.

The man in black turned to Joanne at this point, and said, "As you know your brother Alexander has been going along with the pilgrimages for the last twelve years. He was one of the knights who volunteered to accompany these people. I also volunteered to travel on this trip."

Then the knight continued the tale about the group leaving London and singing praises as they walked. Everyone from the youngest to the eldest was filled with a sense of joy. They even danced as they walked to the channel. There they rented three boats to sail to Normandy.

The group marched cross France and then on down toward the boot of Italy. Around the area of Bari three more boats were rented to carry them across the Adriatic Sea to the east Roman Empire. On and on through one empire after another the march went. At a southern port in Lycia arrangements were made to procure ship passage to Joppa.

Now sweat poured from the man's brow and tears ran down his face while he said, "A few miles from Joppa a group of over one hundred sons of Ishmael surrounded us. We could not move. We did not have chance! They immediately subdued us. As so often practiced they separated one of the Christian men from the group and forced him to watch the massacre. I was that man.

I saw our women and girls being raped. Then their throats slit. I saw the men mutilated, followed by a swift sword blow, severing their heads. Your brother, my dear Lady Le Espek, died shouting, 'Christ Only!'

After the terrible ordeal was finished I was told, 'You have been kept alive to return home and tell what you saw.'

I cannot get the terrible scene out of my mind. For months now my mission has been to go to every family member of those within the pilgrim party to tell them of the ferocious slaughter my eyes witnessed."

Now trembling the man loudly exclaimed, "Oh, that I had been born blind!"

Chapter 4

Helmsley, year 1092

Young Walter walked out of the Chapel hand in hand with his sweetheart Adelina. They stopped to talk with the Pastor concerning the morning announcement.

For all of Walter's life he was kept constantly aware of the agitation among England's Christians concerning the Islam problems in the Holy Lands. There seemed to be a constant ongoing warfare. Islam fanatics would capture Christian sites, and then destroy the places considered sacred. Christians would recapture and rebuild. It seemed a never-ending cycle of war and violence. However, the announcement the Pastor made today seemed the most terrible. Everyone in the chapel gasped when he said, "The city of Jerusalem is now under the control of Mohammedan forces. Who knows what holy places will soon be rubble?"

The memory of the black knight coming to his home, and the terrible news he bore, often haunted Walter. The trips of Uncle Alexander to Jerusalem were something his family honored and often talked about. The Uncle was even Walter's childhood hero and role model. Then suddenly the admired man's life was no longer.

At sixteen years of age Walter joined with the other young noblemen to practice the art of protection and war. He often thought, perhaps some day down in the Holy Land there will be a need to use what I have learned. One very effective maneuver (for which he constantly trained) took a squad of men on horseback (leg to leg), and taught them to charge forward at a high rate of speed with heavy lances.

The exceptionally long lances were couched under each knight's arm and held parallel to the horse's body with the tips several feet in front of the horse's heads. For any enemy the effect produced was a frightening wall of approaching death.

During the three years following the announcement concerning the capture of Jerusalem there were validated atrocities and many rumors constantly being talked about. Then the news came about the Muslims destroying the sepulcher of Jesus and accompanying the news came a call issued from Pope Urban II for Christians to volunteer to "take the cross" and serve in a crusade.

The church leader's desire was for noblemen, well trained in combat, to come forward. However the outrage over the destruction was so great in all of Christendom that people from every walk of life came forward; noblemen, commoners, serfs; all good people. There were also criminals who joined forces, with the gain of plunder their only objective.

A huge mass of people spread east and much destruction, killing and raping followed in their wake. Not only were Muslim people attacked. The Jewish people were attacked as well, especially those living in southern Spain. The forces of the Islam people flew into an uproar and brought about an overwhelmingly large army of Turks to attack the army of the first crusade. They destroyed a major portion of the Christian forces while those who survived fled west to regroup.

When this news reached Helmsley Walter Jr. told his wife, "No longer can I just stand by. I must join the forces to combat this evil. It breaks my heart to think of leaving you and my infant son, but what has happened is too terrible for me to stay home."

Adelina responded, "To have you away will be hard to bare, but I know you cannot stay here while Christian men are being killed, and the places we hold sacred are being destroyed. I will be all right. Your mother and father will take good care of baby Walter and me. Do not fear."

Walter rode to where the squadron practiced their maneuvers to inform the lieutenant of his plans to join the crusade. There he heard a roar of noise. All the agitated men in his squad were milling around while spitting out anger about the turn of events in the east. The whole squad was determined to avenge the death of men serving in a Holy cause.

That evening all of the men met with one of the church legates. Individually they vowed their allegiance and were sworn in as a soldier of the church. Each man was given a cross of red material to wear on his shoulder. Then the Chaplain preached on the cause of freeing the Holy relics from heathen people.

The sermon was based on Isaiah 25, verses 1 and 2, "O Lord, You are my God. I will exalt You, I will praise your name, For You have done wonderful things; Your counsels of old are faithfulness and truth." The Pastor went on to speak of how God worked in the life of the Old Testament character Joshua. The sermon concluded with, "God enabled Joshua to take the walled city of Jericho and the Almighty will give you the power to capture the Holy city of Jerusalem."

In forty-eight hours several British squads gathered together in London and they were ready to advance toward the Holy Land. There was no hesitation, no lagging as the knight's horses hooves thundered across the land at a fast gallop.

Once over the channel, the English knights rode for many days to reach the perimeter of the city of Constantinople and there they set up camp. The plans were for the knights from all of the western countries to assemble in this city until everyone arrived.

Now the church leaders praised God for the members of this wave of the crusade's army being men well trained in the art of warfare. These were not people from different walks of life, as were many of those who enlisted in the first crusade. These were people who knew about precision combat.

The days spent at Constantinople seemed to go on forever for Walter and most of the crusader men. But one good aspect of the "standstill" was the fact that most of the knights who escaped the first slaughter came among the waiting men to talk of battles and about what went wrong in them. Then the battle weary men talked about an unusual agitation prevalent among the Islamic people.

Much of what Walter heard was an old story; the mutilation, the slaughter, the being forced to watch and then being released (this he heard many years before). But the new information seemed a very strange tale. Men were saying the Mohammedan people believed the end of the world was coming at this point in history. All of Islam was talking about the hordes of Gog and Magog who will appear, then disappear after drinking Lake Tiberias dry. They talked about the one-eyed anti-Christ with a following of 70,000 Jews. They talked about the anti-Christ performing miracles like Jesus did.

This was all new information for most of the Christian knights. As they talked among themselves they couldn't help but note the comparisons of the Muslim stories to those in Scripture. However this wasn't the most shocking part of the story. What seemed almost beyond comprehension was the fact the Muslims believed Jesus was going to descend from heaven, slay the anti-Christ and claim the world for Islam. They believed the dead would rise and be judged. They believed Islam would triumph over Jerusalem, Constantinople and Rome. How perfectly the massacre of the people in the first wave of the crusade fit into the Muslim time frame.

There were more facts, which to Walter seemed so very sad. One was the Muslim's prophet Mohammed at one time traveled to Jerusalem in his search for God. The man studied Jewish and Christian precepts. He accepted the facts about Jesus living a life without sin and that He now is sitting at the right hand of the Father. But Mohammed did not believe Jesus was the Son of God because he thought God would not allow His son to die. Mohammed believed Jesus was buried like any other man and He was only a prophet.

Walter kept thinking, "The leader of Islam came so close to the truth, but he missed the main point. Now we are going into warfare because of this. How wily is the deceit of Satan!"

Alexius, the ruler of Constantinople, became more and more uncomfortable with the growing number of soldiers and contingent after contingent arriving from the west.

The army practiced maneuvers during the daylight hours, but at night some of the men became unruly. Finally nervous Alexius offered to transport each army into Asia Minor. But first he extracted a promise from the officers to return to Greek ownership all the land they captured from the Turks; land once owned by Greece before the religious conflict began.

Year 1097

What a relief to Walter and his companions to finally be on the move. However unthinkable discomfort began to descend upon the army. Swarms of biting insects and extreme heat made the body miserable underneath leather and mail suits. It seemed unbearable. Through terrible itching and at times fainting from dehydration the men fought on: skirmish after skirmish, battle after battle. There were victories and cities were captured as the men moved eastward.

In October, the fortified city of Antioch in Syria came into view. Four hundred fifty towers flanked the formidable walls around the city. The army set up camp and thought the capture of such a fortified place seemed impossible.

The Lord arranged for a ship from Genoa to come into a local port. When the boat's officers heard of the plight of the Crusaders, they sent their carpenters, as well as their engineers to the Antioch site. Immediately these men began building battering machines and thus the battle was able to begin.

Because of the immense quantity of provisions stored in the city of Antioch the people could have withstood any siege for a long period of time. However with the breaching of the walls the city surrendered in June. During the fierce fighting many crusaders were killed. Then a plague followed and many more men died. The lieutenant of Walter's squadron was one who succumbed to the plague. Walter was next in line to take his place.

Months passed before the army was ready to move again. Finally, when health and strength returned and more Crusaders joined from the west they were ready to begin traveling south. Their next objective was the town of Safed. After months of travel the Crusade leaders knew there would be a need to have some place for future Christian armies to claim as a base. They already began plans to use Safed as this base.

Once the town came under the Crusaders control, the army bivouacked in an old Jewish fort; a fort used during the Hebrew revolt against the Romans. The Christian men traveled in groups around the city because located in the numerous ancient synagogues there were pockets of fanatical Muslims hiding with the hope of making a surprise attack. Because of this it was necessary to always be armed and ready to fight.

Walter assigned his men to begin refortifying the old fort. His squadron started to gather the many rocks and stones around the countryside to rebuild the areas of the fort's walls needing repairs. Once the rock accumulation was taken care of, then the buildings inside the fort would be repaired.

Through much of the marching and conflicts, Bernard, one of the French commanders, seemed to often locate his men close to Walter's squadron. A friendship began to build. Then, as the army left Safed a troop of Christian Arabs joined the massive marching men. The Arab's commander Peter knew the terrain well.

Peter's job was to guide the Crusaders. But, he was much more than a guide. Peter was a historian who took it upon himself to tell the Biblical stories of each location as the men in the army moved southeast.

Toward one evening Peter said, "We will bivouac on this hill for the night." Walter looked out and the land terraced down to a lovely body of water. Many beautiful wild flowers grew on the hillside.

After supper Bernard, Peter and Walter sat together around a small campfire. Peter said, "You are sitting in the area where Jesus spoke the Beatitudes. The Bible tells us Jesus went up this hill. Then after being here a while, Jesus walked down to give His sermon to the multitude of people waiting below. The message was concerning God's view of what in life are blessings. Our Lord was looking out over the beautiful Sea of Galilee as He talked, just as we are doing this evening."

A sense of peace and contentment came over Walter as he contemplated the words the Lord spoke. For weeks now the terribleness of bloodshed, of seeing the life of both Christian and heathen being sniffed out and seeing people being maimed for life was weighing greatly on his conscience. As Walter's mind mulled over this portion of scripture (which his mother taught him as a child) the verses ten and eleven of the fifth chapter of Matthew kept coming to mind; "Blessed are those who are persecuted because of righteousness, for theirs is the kingdom of heaven. Blessed are you when people insult you, persecute you and falsely say all kinds of evil against you because of me." Walter thought, Yes, We Crusaders have felt the ostracism, the insults, and the hatred because we are following the living God with our just cause. On to verse nine his mind roamed, "Blessed are the peacemakers, for they will be called the sons of God." Walter said under his breath, "We will be peacemakers after Jerusalem is captured, after peace reigns in Palestine and Christian Pilgrims will be able to travel to the Holy Land without persecution."

Before retiring for the night Peter said to the other two men, "There will be pockets of angry Muslims at all the historic sites between here and Jerusalem. These are people who must be removed, or else they will band together and follow us south to attack us from the rear when we are outside of Jerusalem's walls."

The next morning the troops marched southeast toward Capernaum; a once prosperous, flourishing town during Roman rule and Jesus' lifetime. While on the road Peter explained to the men, "You will find in Capernaum a Roman customs house and the remains of all the industry buildings prevalent in the city many years ago." Then he said, "This is where Peter lived and a town where Jesus ministered for two and a half years."

Once the Christian men approached the city they found Muslim men armed with knives, swords and bats. These men poured out of the run down buildings. The fighting was fierce, but the Crusading army outnumbered the Muslims and slaughtered the majority of them.

Toward evening Peter, Walter and Bernard walked along Lake Tiberias. Peter said, "In this area is the spot where Jesus told the fishing disciples to cast their nets on the other side of the boat. What a fish haul they pulled in!" They walked a little further and Peter talked about the feeding of the five thousand with a few fish and a few loaves of bread taking place in Capernaum. Then he said, "Do you realize it was here Peter was asked three times "Do you love me," by Jesus."

While walking back from the shore the three men chatted about the depth of meaning of the events that enfolded in this town. Peter led them into a beautiful old Synagogue while saying, "A little over a thousand years ago our Lord worshipped here."

The troops marched around the north end of the lake, toward Cana. In the distance ruins could be seen. Walter was fearful they would find clumps of Muslims hiding there, and he questioned Peter about the area. All fears were allayed when the guide said, "What you see is Chorazin. Do you remember the story in the Gospels about Jesus going there and performing many miracles, but He was rejected? Jesus told them, "Woe to you, if the mighty works which were done in you had been done in Tyre and Sidon, they would have repented." Jesus also told the Chorazim residents they would go to hell. At the present time Christians, Jews and Muslims believe the place is cursed. They will not go there. There will be no Muslims hiding there.

As the army continued south they walked past the spot where Joseph was sold into slavery. Then by the place where Jezebel fell down dead, to have the dogs tear her flesh.

From now on skirmishes and battles occurred in every place the Crusaders passed until they reached Jerusalem. At each place, once the fighting was over, Peter would elucidate on the history of the area. In Cana he talked about the first miracle Jesus performed; the one where the Lord changed the water into wine. Peter then expounded on the quality of the naturally sweet juice coming from fruit grown in Israel. Is it any wonder the wine made from this juice is exceptional? Then he said, "However, the wine Jesus made must have been even more delicious than any from the fruit of the vine."

Bernard said, "When I think of Cana, I remember a story my mother once told me as a child. I was very sick and she said, "Jesus healed sick children." Do you remember the story of the man who came to Jesus to tell him his little boy was dying? The man asked Jesus to come to his house and the Lord told the man to go home because his little boy would live. That miracle happened right here in Cana."

Over hills and down into valleys the procession went. They passed beautiful wild flowers and lush vegetation. Then the men seemed to be walking down and down until they were below sea level. On entering the city of Tiberias they encountered stiff opposition. Fishing boats lay abandoned on the muddy shoreline, because the men quickly left them to fight once they realized the Crusaders were approaching.

With Tiberias under control the army was ready to contin-ue south when a scout rode up to Peter and said, "Muslim clans are gathering in the caves of Nazareth and around Mount Carmel." Peter thanked the man, then turned to his companions and said, "We shall go in that direction tomorrow."

Once inside the town of Nazareth the men found a Christian church erected during the fourth century. They were told it was located on the site where the angel appeared to Mary and gave the announcement concerning her conception of the Messiah.

Walter mentioned to Peter his surprise at the site not being destroyed by the Muslims. Peter told his friends, "The Koran also tells the story of the angel's announcement. Mohammed himself spoke of it and his followers would not destroy what they too consider sacred."

Such information surprised both Walter and Bernard, but what Peter said next seemed even more unusual. He claimed Mary and Joseph's families probably lived in the caves they presently rid of the Muslims. Historically Nazareth was a very transitory place. People lived in the caves until they moved on to employment in another city and there were no homes in the area until many years after Christ's birth

Before moving on the scout told the men about Mount Carmel being where Elijah challenged the prophets of Baal and Asherah to prove which God was more powerful. The test was for a sacrificial fire to be lit by the most powerful Supreme Being.

Peter said, "As you all know neither Baal or Asherah can light a fire. Elijah even taunted the false prophets when their gods did not send one spark. Then Elijah told them to pour water over his sacrifice. They poured water three times and the wood was soaking wet! Then Elijah prayed to the great "I Am" to show His power and fire fell from heaven lighting the water soaked wood."

The Crusaders all cheered while Peter went on to say, "Tomorrow, on our way to Mount Carmel, we will be marching across the Valley of Armageddon, the Valley of Death. Think of the effect this will play on those encamped in the caves. The men have heard the Christian story of the Battle of Armageddon.

They will come out to meet us and inwardly cheer, because they believe this is the end time. In their minds they cannot be defeated. We will not need to go up the mountain to clear out the caves as they will be coming to us."

The battle took place exactly as Peter predicted and the Crusaders overcame their enemies. There was no need to proceed further west. The army rested, then they turned southeast retracing their steps through the Valley of Death and down to Megiddo.

At this point Walter, and many of the Christians, felt even more the ancientness of the land. Especially when Peter continued with his history lessons. Megiddo, they were told, was a thriving, fortified city during Canaanite times, and a city used by Solomon. When the army left this ancient place they proceeded to Beth Shean.

As the Crusaders stood on a mound along the side of Beth Shean Peter said, "Men, it was here Saul sought the witch's counsel and here Saul fought the Philistines. He, and his sons, including Jonathan, were all slain right on this spot. Then their bodies were hung on the city walls. The city ruins you are looking at have been destroyed and rebuilt over and over and over.

Walter remarked, "This is almost overwhelming! All the time we were traveling to Palestine I kept thinking about the privilege of being where Jesus lived and walked. The realization never came to me I would be where my Lord's ancestors, where all of the prophets, where all of the Old Testament people lived. I am actually seeing places spoken of in many a sermon to which I listened. The ever-faithful leading hand of God is so evident here.

From time to time other ancient relics (not noted in the Bible) came before their eyes. Especially noticeable were those of the Roman rule. There were forts, stadiums, official buildings and theaters. The men even saw evidences of a cruelty forced upon an ancient people under subjection.

While on the road to Samaria, Peter said, "The coming town is where Christians claim John the Baptist is buried. The terrible beheading of the cousin of Jesus is a well known fact to all of us."

Once they were inside the town Peter talked about Jesus meeting the woman at the well. Bernard said, "She was a sinner!" Peter replied, "Yes she was, but she confessed her sins and repented of them. Our loving Lord forgave her." Walter chimed in. "The wonderful ending to the story is how she went around telling everyone Jesus was the Messiah and the Saviour."

The Crusaders went down past Mount Ebal where Joshua erected an altar. Then they traveled through Schechem, the first capitol of the Northern kingdom. The men knew they were getting close to Jerusalem when they camped at Rama.

Peter expounded a good part of the next evening concerning Rama being the birthplace of Samuel. He told stories of the child's birth and of his growing up years in the house of the Priest Eli. One story which fascinated the men was about how God called to Samuel in the middle of the night and Samuel thought it was the priest calling.

The next topic of conversation covered the life and the convictions of Joseph of Aramathea, whose home was also located in Rama.

Toward the end of the next day's march the army saw Jerusalem in the distance. After what seemed an eternity of marching the objective was now before them in the sixth month of 1099. Here God provided another group of engineers right at the ideal moment by bringing a ship into Joppa while the army was in Samaria. The ship's officers heard where the army was located, and they knew the skill of some of their men was needed. The qualified seamen were sent to meet with the crusaders.

As soon as the engineers arrived they started building catapults and battering rams. When this was completed, all of the Crusaders took off their shoes and started marching around Jerusalem barefoot, just as Joshua's army did years before when approaching Jericho. Everyone prayed and claimed the city for the King Eternal. Meanwhile, Muslim men stood on top of the fortified walls taunting those walking below; hurling insults, curses and incantations down on the marching forces.

On July 14th the actual attack on the city began. The battering rams built by the engineers proved very effective and the Crusaders poured into the city the next day. They slew men, women and children. Then claimed Jerusalem for Christ. The jubilant men danced in the streets.

Several squadrons bivouacked in the Dome of the Rock. Among them were Bernard's, Walter's and Peter's squadrons. The men marveled at the beautiful mosaic walls of tile. They talked about the designs in nature brought out in the white and brilliant blue tiles. Then the men made a pact to not destroy the building because of the artwork.

There were other underlying reasons as well. One discussed was the fact the army was in Jerusalem because the Muslims were destroying sites Christians thought sacred. They were not going to stoop that low. Another reason was the fact Muslims, Jews and Christians thought the spot sacred, therefore why destroy a beautiful covering over it?

Much work needed to be accomplished in Jerusalem before the men could rest easy. Before anything else, the walls must be refortified and secured. Then any building within the city walls in need of repair should be taken care of in order for every Crusader to be able to have comfortable quarters. The sacred sites must be repaired and a Crusader church's erection must begin. Then even places for future Crusaders use must be built.

On several evenings, men would gather around Peter to hear in-depth the facts concerning the area in which they slept. First Peter began by talking about the wall located outside of the Dome of the Rock being a part of the original Temple built by Solomon. While most of the first Temple was destroyed, one wall has stood through history. For centuries the Jewish people have come to the wall. Many place their hands on it and rock back and forth while talking to God. They wail over the destruction of the Temple. They wail over family problems, over problems in Jerusalem, problems in Israel and problems of the world. Some people leave little pieces of paper in the wall's cracks to remind God of their petitions.

Peter continued on about the history of this place being even more ancient than Solomon's time. He talked about the rock in the center of the building being the place God told Abraham to bring Isaac to be sacrificed. Here is where God provided a ram as the substitute sacrifice. The men were advised to think about the exceptional picture the story tells to illustrate the perfect Lamb of God as a sacrifice for out sins.

One more bit of information surprised the Christian men. This was the fact the Muslims believe because Ishmael was the firstborn, he was the son brought for sacrifice. Firstborns have the natural right of inheritance in their eyesight.

Walter was curious as to why the Muslims would not destroy the birthplace in Nazareth where the angel appeared to Mary, but they did destroy Jesus' sepulcher.

Peter explained, "The Sunni branch of Muslims believe Jesus was conceived of God. That He lived a holy life and He is presently at the right hand of the Father. How- ever they do not believe He is God, or the Son of God. They do not believe God would allow His Son to be killed, especially on a cross. They do not believe He rose from the dead. To their way of thinking, our claiming Jesus rose from a sepulcher is heresy and the place should be destroyed.

Then too, there is a second branch of the Muslim faith called Shiite; a smaller fanatical group and they believe everything Christian should be annihilated. They are the people who are the cause of many of the acts of violence we hear about.

Peter told about the Muslim takeover of the property on which the Dome of the Rock is situated. He concentrated on the Orthodox Church built on the same site just after the Roman era. Once the Mohammedan followers captured Jerusalem the Dome's construction was begun on the foundations of the Orthodox Church they destroyed. The building was placed purposely over the older church to show their defiance against what Christianity stood for.

The guide continued with, "Here was where the Synagogue was located when Jesus surprised the priests with his knowledge at only twelve years of age. This happened following the feast of Passover at a time when His whole family was in Jerusalem for the celebration. Later in our Lord's life he drove the money-changers out of the courtyards of this Temple. Here Jesus taught again as an adult and the scoffers tried to arrest Him. Up these outside steps men dragged the woman in sin. You all know Jesus wrote on the ground and her accusers left. Then Jesus said, "I don't condemn you, go and leave your life of sin." Truly this area has much meaning for those of the Christian faith."

The last evening Peter spent talking about the Dome he used the time to dispel a myth. From ear to ear among the Crusade men a rumor circled concerning a belief they thought the Muslims held. This belief was that Mohammed ascended to heaven from the Dome of the Rock. The guide - teacher emphatically said, "The Muslims do not, I said NOT believe Mohammed ascended to heaven from the Dome of the Rock. Remember I told you the Muslims believe Jesus was a man, a prophet, no more. He died, was buried and is in heaven. They believe Mohammed was also a prophet who died, was buried and is in heaven. They do not believe he literally, before peoples eyes, rose and ascended to heaven."

Toward the end of September news came about the gathering of a Muslim army in Caesarea on the Mediterranean coast. Five squadrons stationed in Jerusalem (out of the ten squadrons located there) were ordered to march to Caesarea and contain the problem.

Peter and Walter's squads were among those ordered to go. Bernard's squadron was to remain in Jerusalem to continue the protection of the city, plus to go on with the construction work.

Early, before dawn, the next morning the five squadrons began a brisk march Northwest to the coast. The goal before them was the once showplace city of Herod the Great. A city built by his specifications in the year 22 B.C.

Good spirits prevailed in the march and the men burst into song. They were slightly awestruck in seeing the hand of God in all the victories and accomplishments. However, after two days of marching, the Crusaders became very aware of a horrible stench hanging in the air. Then they came upon rotting dead bodies contorted on the roadside and in the towns. These were the bodies of Christian and Jewish men, women and children who heard about Jerusalem being no longer under Muslim control. These people were attempting to return to the land.

The sight was sickening, the smell overwhelming and anger began to brew against the marauding army from Caesarea filled with fanatical men pouncing upon defenseless people. Once the armies met, the hatred and dislike on both sides, escalated into frenzied fighting. The battle did not take long and the town quickly came under Crusade domination. However, many of the leaders of Islam, who were camped inside the city of Caesarea, escaped before the crusaders entered. Their plan was to move to another area of Palestine, to regroup, to attack and kill unsuspecting Christians and Jews.

Evidence could be seen where the Muslim forces bivouacked within the Roman Fortress located on one side of the city. Then too, from the design of the newer buildings it could be determined the army's latest reinforcements were Turkish.

Late one afternoon, toward sunset, Walter sat high in the amphitheater looking out over the sand and beautiful water. The gold, russet and red hues of the dropping sun were spectacular over the Mediterranean. Then he noticed a figure walking across the sand. It was Peter coming to join him.

The two men sat in silence for a while; just drinking-in the beauty before them. Then Walter said, "Exceptional harbor, isn't it? Peter responded, "Yes, it is. Did you know it was man made?" With the surprised look in Walter's face, Peter continued, "Hundreds of years ago Herod the Great ordered it to be dredged in the shape of a horse shoe. Then he ordered rock to be brought from the hills to line the harbor perimeter to prevent any collapse. The work was quite a feat of engineering for Herod's time and the harbor continued to be serviceable for many years."

As the days passed the revamping of the old Roman fort progressed in order for it to be used in the future by Crusaders. One area within the building was put aside as a Chapel. Some men began carving an altar plus a communion service out of the beautiful local Olivewood.

Even though the sacred location was not yet completed men came there to pray and Sunday services were held. Several of the short Sunday sermons dealt with the Biblical history of Caesarea. In the first sermon the Chaplain talked about Paul being sent to Rome from this port.

Another sermon concerned the devout centurion Cornelius who dwelled in Caesarea and about how God met this man to advised him to send for the apostle Peter who was residing in Joppa.

The third topic delved into the dream Peter experienced concerning the unclean animals the Lord told him to eat.

On the forth Sunday the Chaplain brought out a truth the apostle Peter found when he traveled with Cornelius' servants to Caesarea. He was on his way to a gentile home; a place into which he would never have stepped before he became a Christian.

In the centurion's home Peter preached to the whole household. Everyone came to the saving knowledge of Christ. It was at this point Peter realized the significance of his dream. The Lord was telling him the plan of Salvation was for all people. Not just the Jews, but for the gentiles as well.

Following one of the Sunday services Peter asked Walter to ride north with him along the coast. In a short while the two men approached a viaduct looking like it went on forever.

Peter said, "This is what I wanted you to see." Then he went on talking about the viaduct being another engineering wonder conceived by Herod the Great in the first century. As the two men cantered alongside the marvel for a few miles Peter elucidated on the problem Herod faced with no potable water in the area of Caesarea. There were springs in the distant mountains and the viaduct was constructed to bring water to the city from a mountain spring eight miles away.

In early November two more Crusader squadrons arrived in Caesarea. They were made up of men fresh from France, Germany and Italy; men who were to be permanently stationed in the Crusader fort area. By the end of the month the newcomers were well settled-in and the all of the squadrons from Jerusalem were ready to return back there.

Peter, Walter and the men strode into the Holy Land's main city while Christmas preparations were underway. The streets were jammed with many of the once fleeing Christians, plus the Jews who recently returned to their homes within the city walls. Groups of Pilgrims were also among the throngs walking in the city to celebrate the holiday.

For the month of December two squadrons were ordered to escort and protect the many European people traveling on the road from Joppa to Jerusalem. These people too were coming for the holiday. Peter was the commander of one of the squadrons assigned to this duty. Everyone knew a need for this protection was necessary, because no one knew when a party of attacking Muslims would strike unprotected travelers.

Bernard and Walter's squadrons were ordered to the same type of service on the road from Jerusalem to Bethlehem. Every hour from eight a.m. until two p.m. a party of fifty people were escorted to the town where Jesus was born. The walk would take from one and a half hours to two hours depending upon whether there were elderly or young children in the group.

Most of the Crusaders rode on the perimeter of the Pilgrim group. Ten of the men were given the assignment of walking and talking with the Pilgrims on the road to share with them the facts about the ancientness of the community they were going to see.

Naturally, the first thing the men talked about was the fact of Bethlehem being the birthplace of Jesus. Then it was mentioned about Bethlehem being the birthplace of the renowned King David (who lived a century before Jesus) and who was one of the Lord's ancestors.

Getting closer to the town, in a hilly area, the men pointed to possible spots where the Shepherds passed after the angels appeared to them. Even some shepherds leading their sheep were sighted during the walk.

When the group was only a half-mile from town they paused for a few minutes while the speakers talked about this being the field of Boaz and the story of Boaz redeeming Ruth was recounted. Also pointed out was the fact this couple was one more ancestral link of the Messiah.

On the very outskirts of Bethlehem the speakers spoke about a most ancient Biblical person by the name of Rachael, the wife of Jacob and the mother of Joseph. Her burial site is located in Bethlehem. A story found in the book of Genesis came to life for the trudging Pilgrims.

Like a swarm of bees honing in on their hive the group of people were led to the Church of the Nativity. Before entering everyone was informed about the church being constructed on the site during the fourth century. One fact impressed over and over was that all of Christendom acknowledged the place as the birthplace of Christ. The Catholic, Coptic, Greek and Ethiopian churches were all united on this fact.

As a postscript, before leaving Bethlehem, the crusaders wanted the Pilgrims to know Bethlehem was also the town where the saintly Jerome spent his days in the fourth century while translating the Greek and Hebrew scriptures into Latin. They went on to explain Latin was the official language during Jerome's lifetime, just as it in our Crusader's day. All official documents were in Latin then, as now.

Thankfully life returned to normal in Jerusalem following the Christmas Season.

Now the building process and reconstruction filled most of the daylight hours for the Crusaders.

Toward the end of January word began to filter into the Holy City concerning more fanatical killings. These reports were coming from the southern Dead Sea area. Scouts, led by Peter, were sent out to verify what was being heard. They returned to report human cadavers in Beer Sheba, Hebron, Tekoah, Bathabara, and even as far north as the outskirts of Jericho. The Muslim camp was bivouacked in the old Roman fort outside of Masada.

Once more five squadrons were sent out to stop the problem. Bernard, Peter and Walter were commanders of three of the squadrons. Their order to march was in a direct line to Masada, with one stopover at Qumran. The purpose there was to see how the people who fled into the caves from the Muslims were faring.

The men of Islam in the Roman fort thought they were well protected. The gates and walls were strong and they were well supplied with food and water. They knew they could stay inside for months, perhaps a year. Even though the men in the watchtowers reported the approaching army must have a thousand men in it, what did they have to fear?

As a child, Peter used to be a shepherd his father's goatherds. His family was one of Bedouin people who camped from Beer Sheba to the dead-sea on the east, then north to Tekoah and circle around again. He was well acquainted with the land and any mystery it held.

On one of these trips the family camped close to the old fort. One day in Peter's childish wanderings he discovered an underground tunnel into the fort. Another day, he found the source of the fort's underground water supply.

While the army was moving south Peter weighed the different options of attack. They could use the underground tunnel during night hours and infiltrate the fort. However the spot where the tunnel exited into the fort was narrow. If a sentry were on watch the Crusaders would not succeed and lives would be lost unnecessarily.

Another option was to pollute the water supply. Then just wait until everyone was sick in bed and attack. The second option was the one Peter chose.

There was no fighting. The Crusaders literally broke down the gates and walked into the fort with no opposition. The Muslims were extremely sick and just lay moaning on their mats.

Before the return trip to Jerusalem Bernard wanted to ascend Masada. His desire was to see the place where the courageous band of Jews withstood the Roman army for quite some length of time. In the end the Jewish group committed suicide rather than surrender. They decided death was better than slavery under the cruel Roman rule.

The famous Masada is located on a plateau high in the sky and the only way up was by climbing an old, steep, narrow path. Masada was a perfect place to defend. Anyone coming up the trail to attack those on top would be annihilated before they reached there.

Peter and Walter joined Bernard for the arduous climb. A few hours later the three red faced, sweating, puffing men rolled over the rim into the plateau area. After catching their breath they wandered through the crumbling buildings trying thinking about what the days were like for the families living in cramped quarters while knowing their days were doomed.

On the plateau everything necessary to survive was in view; tiny living quarters, huge storerooms and a deep well, even a Synagogue. The buildings were all made from rocks hauled up the trail. The small rooms held many rock arches to support the huge slab stone roofs. At one time in history Herod built a home for himself in this natural fortress. It too was in use by the band of dissenters who barricaded themselves at Masada..

The view in every direction was fantastic. To the east lay the Dead Sea and much sand. On the west the Roman fort came into view with the crumbling ramp the Romans built for themselves to reach Masada. To the north and south spread miles and miles of barren arid sand.

The army soon left for their march north, back to Jerusalem, with a stop over in Jericho. It was uphill all the way. The fort in the Dead Sea area lay 1300 feet below sea level. Jericho was 800 feet below sea level and Jerusalem 2500 feet above sea level.

On the way Peter pointed out the spring of Engedi and said, "This is the place where David (while he was fleeing from king Saul) came upon the sleeping king. David had opportunity then to kill the man who was attempting to kill him. But he refused to kill his king. Then further north the place where David hid from Saul was shown."

The town of Jericho itself appeared to be mostly rubble. They walked through the thousands of years old deserted streets and on to the banks of the Jordan River where Jesus was baptized by John. Then the army turned back toward Jerusalem. This led them through the New Testament Jericho built by Herod and the place where Herod died. Here Peter reminded the men about when Jesus visited this town and the story of the tax collector Zaccheus climbing the Sycamore tree and Jesus calling to him to come down in order to visit with him.

Awesome describes the 3300-foot climb of the old road on which the army traveled from Jericho to their home base in Jerusalem while knowing Jesus walked the very same road when he traveled from the one city to the other. The roadway was steep, narrow and extremely windy with many hairpin turns. So narrow the men could only march six abreast, with a harrowing drop off to the chasm below, at both road edges. The rugged beauty appeared breath taking at each turn.

Spring and the Easter Season in Jerusalem was something Walter always felt he would like to experience. Now he was living it and the deep spiritual significance gripped him.

For several days Walter went off by himself outside of the city walls, to sit and pray in the garden of Gethsemane. Serenity and peace filled him. He would look at the ancient olive trees around him and imagine the Lord coming to the very same spot and looking at the same trees as He prayed.

Then Walter walked away to the area where Jesus withdrew after telling His disciples, "Sit here while I go over there and pray." Walter would sit on a rock and cast his burdens on the Lord. First he would praise the Lord for the protection in all of the travels and warfare experienced. Then the tears would flow while he spoke of the distance between his family and himself and of the lack of communication from home. He would pour out his love for his wife and son, and his desire to be with them. Lastly Walter prayed he would be able to return home quickly.

Twice Walter went to the spot where Jesus looked over the Kidron valley toward Jerusalem and wept. The Crusader would contemplate all the trials Jerusalem has since experienced. Trials coming upon the city from its founding day and on to the ones the Lord foresaw as he looked across the valley. But aside from the trials, Walter's eyes would tear as he thought of the populace in the city and their rejection of the Lord and Saviour. Then too the terrible mockery of justice around the crucifixion of the Son of God filled his mind.

From here Walter walked down through the valley. He passed Absalom's tomb and then the place where Steven was stoned before going through the gate into the city.

On Palm Sunday many Crusaders, including Bernard, Peter and Walter, plus numerous visiting Pilgrims, walked the road where Jesus rode on a donkey with Palm branch homage around Him. Everyone in this huge throng of people carried and waved Palm branches in recognition of the honor paid their Lord centuries earlier.

All of Good Friday people were going to the place of the Upper Room. As the three friends, Bernard, Peter and Walter walked toward the building. The master historian said, "Do you remember in the book of Mark where the disciples asked Jesus where they would have the Passover and Jesus responded, "Go into the city, and a man carrying a jar of water will meet you. Follow him. Say to the owner of the house he enters, 'The Teacher asks: "Where is my guest room, where I may eat the Passover with my disciples?"' He will show you a large upper room, furnished and ready. Make preparations for us there." Peter asked, "Do you realize finding a man carrying a water jar is very unusual and a definite sign because only women transported the water in those days. The man probably stood out like a sore thumb."

Bernard and Walter in unison said, "I never thought about that!" and Bernard continued, "What an unusual sign our Lord prepared!"

As the men strolled into the building Peter continued with more information which touched the hearts of the other two men. He talked about the portions of the Passover supper described in the book of Exodus where unleavened bread was eaten for seven days. Some Hebrew people call Passover the Feast of Unleavened Bread. Then Peter asked, "Do you think the disciples understood Jesus being the Bread of life when the bread was taken and He said, "Take, eat, this is my body?"

Walter responded, "Probably not. Not until after the resurrection."

Now Peter elucidated to his two friends on a new concept concerning the wine. First he shifted their thinking to a Hebrew wedding ceremony and around the first portion of the service dealing with the fixing of a high price for the bride. Then Peter went on to the next step where the groom fills a cup with wine offering it to his bride and saying, "This cup is a new covenant in my blood which I offer you." If she accepts the cup she indicates — I love you and give my life to you.

Peter concluded with, "Can you picture the surprise on the disciples faces when Jesus quoted a part of the marriage ceremony in offering the wine. Maybe even some of them chuckled. In essence the Lord was saying, "I love you — I offer my life for you — will you be my bride as a part of the church?"

The men left the building in silence as Bernard and Walter contemplated all the new concepts they heard this day. Going from there they walked pass the old Roman Antonia fortress where Jesus was tried before Pontius Pilate. The men went into the basement of one of the buildings. Here Peter pointed out a thick low archway.

Through the top of the archway appeared a six-inch hole and at elbow height on each supporting side there was the same type of hole. Peter said, "The Romans passed a rope through the top hole and tied it under the armpits of a criminal. Then each arm was tied at the wrist to the holes located in the sidewalls. A soldier would take a whip imbedded with sharp stones and beat the criminal until his flesh hung in shreds. In all likelihood this was where our Lord was scourged." Bernard and Walter's faces were very solemn when they exited this building.

Around noon on Good Friday, Peter took his two friends to a large area where many of the Roman soldiers formerly played games. In the paving stones markings were imbedded from the various games played and the building was called the Lithostrotos. It was now used as the place for people to gather to walk through the Stations of the Cross.

Bernard, Peter and Walter joined the throng going through the narrow passageway toward Golgotha. The men stopped at each station of the cross to pray.

Faithful Peter continued giving insight into historical events pertinent to Palestine. He talked about the Roman method of execution for criminals. First, in order for the shame of the punishment to be before the public, and to help deter crime, the uprights of the crosses were permanently placed along the roadsides of main thorough- fares into town. Usually just the crossbeams of the cross were what the person dragged through the streets to their execution, and often the criminals hung in agony before the public for days.

When the men reached Golgotha, Peter described the actual method of placement upon the cross. First, with the person lying outstretched on the ground on top of the crossbeam, a spike would be hammered through the base of both hands where it enters the wrist. Then that section of the cross would be lifted up and placed through an opening in the crossbeam upon the upright. During this all of the body's weight hung upon the wrist spikes.

By now a large crowd encircled the three Crusaders to hear Peter's description of a crucifixion. He continued, "The knees of the criminal were forced to bend sideways as the feet were pushed upwards and turned horizontal to the upright. A spike was then hammered in just below the anklebone with one foot on top of the other.

Peter concluded talking about the actual death being by asphyxiation. The twisted sagging diaphragm could only expand for air when the person succeeded in pushing straight his legs. Some criminals would struggle for days until they had no strength left to push up and they were not able to breathe any longer. The death was terribly agonizing.

Tears rolled down the faces of many people standing around Peter. A murmur could be heard expressing the awfulness of the tortuous death the Son of God went through to bring them eternal life.

In early May fresh squadrons of Crusaders began to arrive from Europe. Once the newcomers were trained the squadrons who spent almost a year in Jerusalem began to be released to return home.

One of the first squadrons to leave was Bernard's. A few weeks later Walter's followed. All exit routes went through Joppa, and then by sea to the homeland.

Naturally Peter wanted the men to know the history of their departure point. The three men sat together for their final nights. Each was excited about going home. But there was also sadness over the separation and the knowledge they would probably never see each other again. These last nights Bernard and Walter heard the stories concerning Joppa.

Peter told one story each of the last three nights about this most ancient of Palestinian cities.

1. It was to this port (as told in the Old Testament) the Cedars from Lebanon were shipped for the building of the Temple during Solomon's time.

Later in history, after the port was dredged at Caesarea, the Cedars of Lebanon were shipped there for the use of Herod.

2. As has been told in the first chapter of Jonah, it was to Joppa the prophet fled in order to sail to Tarshish. This happened while fleeing from God's command for him to go to Nineveh. From this time forward Jonah experienced nothing but trials because of his disobedience.

3. Dorcas lived in Joppa. The ninth chapter of Acts recounts the story of this gracious, kind woman becoming violently ill. Those who loved her notified the apostle Peter who was ministering in the nearby town of Lydda. By the time Peter reached Joppa Dorcas was dead.

Peter prayed by the body. Then through the power of the Holy Spirit said, "Dorcas, stand up." She rose completely healed. Peter remained many days in Joppa at the house of Simon the Tanner.

With a twinkle in his eye Peter closed the last story with, "If you noticed — that apostle has a great name! It is such a great name most of the Christian churches around Joppa are called St. Peter."

Chapter 5

September 30, 1100

*W*alter rode up the path to Helmsley castle. He could hardly wait to hug his wife and the now five-year old son. The Crusader's mind kept dwelling on two thoughts, "mother and father should be in their wing of the castle, plus, five years is a long time to be away from my wife and son." Then he scrutinized the buildings and they all looked in good order.

One of the servants ran into the parlor where Adelina was playing with little Walter. The maid kept saying, "A knight is riding up the path on a beautiful horse." Instinctively Adelina knew who it was. She grabbed the young fellow's hand and whispered, "Daddy's coming, daddy's coming. "Hurriedly the two made their way down the long ramp.

Walter jumped off his steed and ran as fast as he could to envelope his wife and son in his big arms. Tears flowed down Adelina's face while Walter kissed her over and over.

Little Walter appeared a wee bit shy toward his father, but mostly wonderment was the expression on his face. Almost daily, from the time he was an infant his mother kept telling him, "One your father will ride up our path on a beautiful horse." That truth now was fulfilled and the boy could hardly believe it.

Holding his son's hand, with his other arm around Adelina, Walter walked up the stairs in the castle where he was born, raised, and which was now his present home. Adelina stated, "Come sit in the parlor. I want to bring you up to date on all of the family news that has taken place in the past five years. Then you can go greet the rest of the family."

The fact Adelina took him aside before going to see his parents made Walter wonder what all transpired in the years he was away. First Adelina chatted about the joy of watching their son grow, and she talked about important events in the boy's life. Then she revealed to Walter the news of his sister Albreda's marriage. Adelina told about the wedding, which took place in 1098, plus all the fine qualities of the new husband. To top this information Adalina said, "Now, you are an uncle to one year old Martha."

After several hours of telling Walter all the good news Adelina stated, "There is sad news which I must tell. Shortly after Adelina's wedding a plague hit England. Uncle Edward and Aunt Kathleen came down with it. The sickness was terribly swift; with an agonizing death. In a few days your aunt and uncle were dead and buried. Then your father went to settle matters concerning the managing of the Wark estate. He decided to notify your sister Albreda and her husband to come be the overseers. As soon as your father left Wark to come home he came down with the contagion and was dead in the saddle when the horse walked up our entry way.

Your mother has been in mourning for the last six months. No one can console her. I want you to be aware of what to expect when you go to her quarters."

As Walter approached his mother's apartment he was shocked to see a very old looking woman clad in black and slouching in a chair by the window. The whole suite was draped in black and the vital vibrant woman Walter once knew was absent. Sadness radiated from her whole being as he stood in her doorway.

In a few seconds Joanne sensed someone's presence and she looked up. A spark of surprise lit her face. She stood quickly and moved quickly to greet him saying, "Walter, my son, I thought you too were dead."

Much hugging and tears flowed. Walter's with grief, because his father was dead. But Joanne's, face was with joy, because her son was alive.

For the first time since her husband's funeral Joanne left her apartment arm in arm with Walter. Adelina was completely surprised to see her mother-in-law walking toward her with a smile on her face. Joanne said, "We must invite many to a welcoming home party and a Celebration service for Walter's safe return. Even now we can start to send invitations to neighbors, family and friends. A week should be enough time for all of the preparations."

During the second weekend in October people came from miles away. Because of the inclement weather the great dining hall tables were moved along the walls in order for dancing to be held in the center of the room. Still the guests could be served at the tables after they arrived. Cold platters of venison, lamb, chicken, pork, cheeses, chunks of home baked bread and dishes of hot potatoes with cabbage were brought and served by the maids.

Children moved toward the game room for puppet shows and other entertainment, while the older people congregated in the parlor to reminisce about old times.

Sunday morning at 10:30 the Chapel bells chimed and chimed. All of the guests entered the place of Worship for the Celebration Service. On the side wall of the Chapel hung the beautiful tapestry of Jesus calming the sea, (bought years before in France by Walter's grandfather).

Walter's aging Uncle William stood by the pulpit and said," On this glorious Sunday morning let us begin our worship with praises to the Lord."

All in attendance antiphonally sang Psalms of Praise and read Scripture glorifying God. William's message followed his constant theme on God's faithfulness. This day's sermon began with the reading of a Psalm "He will cover you with His pinions, and under His wings shall you trust and find refuge; His truth and His faithfulness are a shield and a buckler. Then you shall not be afraid of the terror by night, nor of the arrow that flies by day." William brought out how typically their creator calmed the sea of fear in Joanne's heart by bringing her son home safely. And how God covered Walter with his wings through all of the conflicts in the Holy Land to preserve his life. The elderly vicar closed his message expressing God's goodness in giving life (as in the case of baby Martha,) in preserving the life of Walter while he was far from home, and in giving everlasting new life to those taken to glory (Walter Sr., Edward and Kathleen.)

After everyone sang the closing hymn William stated, "Now I would like for Joanne and Walter to please come forward." With surprise on Walter's face, he and his mother walked to the front. Then William continued, "Over thirty years ago King William (my father's Norman cousin,) presented to my brother Walter a gold ring; for preserving the monarch's life during battle. One thing Walter always told Joanne was "the ring is to be presented to my son after I enter the heavenly realm." Today Joanne will make the presentation.

Joanne took Walter's right hand with her left and placed the bulky gold band on his huge ring finger. Everyone applauded.

A few days after the celebration Walter and Adelina decided they should take some time away together with little Walter. They wanted to relax away from home, by visiting with family down south. Both of them thought Walter should do this before he settled back into an occupation. The two adult Especs and young Walter traveled to Warden with their Uncle William. For a few days they visited with the now bedridden grandmother Madeline who was nearing eighty years of age. Then they continued south to visit with Uncle Richard, his wife and their two children.

Walter, Adelina and little Walter thoroughly enjoyed being with the much loved family members. The little cousins Walter,

William and Jennifer played all types of games in the gardens and yard of the lovely home Richard built outside of Bath. The Espec family spent a whole week at this location before traveling northwest to Liverpool to visit with cousins William and Elizabeth.

Speke woods seemed to go on for miles and miles before Speke Hall could be reached. While traveling through the woods the family constantly caught glimpses of different creatures bounding by. Such sightings brought about an awareness of the varied abundant wildlife contained in the beautiful forest. When a handsome stag stopped and stared at the moving party Walter remarked, "No wonder the kings of England claim these woods as one of their most favorite places to hunt."

Again, as at Wardon and Bath, the Espec family were welcomed with open arms and rejoicing. Every family member felt the blessing of God in bringing Walter safely home.

William took his cousin hunting and little Walter tagged along. Elizabeth took Adelina into her tapestry making room to show her the design she was weaving. Already many lovely tapestries hung upon the Hall's walls and before long the scene Elizabeth was presently working would find its place among the other handiworks. The new one showed a picturesque country home surrounded with colorful flowers.

After Adelina told of her delight in what she saw the two women sat to chat about the exciting events and the hurts in their daily lives. Elizabeth talked about how she ached through the years for a child of her own. Then she expressed the joy she felt working with the orphaned children in Liverpool.

This quiet woman also talked about designing the exquisite flower gardens already surrounding the hall. Elizabeth now showed Adelina her drawn diagrams for future expansion of the flowerbeds, plus where to place the walkways to be installed by the gardeners.

Adelina constantly carried a bit of cotton thread with her and she showed Elizabeth a small designed figure she was making with it. Each small figure would eventually be joined together to make a chair throw for the Helmley home. This was the type of project she could carry anywhere because of its smallness.

Walter's wife also expressed the anguish she carried for five years concerning the uncertainty of whether her husband was alive or not. Then Adelina spoke about the frightening fear she carried when father Walter rode up to the castle dead from the plague. She told about how every day, month after month, she thoroughly examined little Walter fearing she would find a sign of the disease on him. Now this beautiful woman's face was aglow with the relief over the hurt and fear being gone.

Early the following morning William, Walter and little Walter returned carrying a young buck over the saddle of a spare horse. Immediately the servants set to work preparing the animal, plus a spit in order to roast it. Mouths began to water as they thought of the succulent venison for dinner.

That evening both noblemen and servants feasted until well filled with the tender meat.

Shortly after Walter and his family arrived back at Helmsley an official sent from king Henry (the first) came for a visit. He was there on official business, but first, the custom of general conversation must fill several hours. The men talked about the recent coronation of king Henry. Then the official praised his ruler for settling a northern problem through his marriage to the Scottish princess Matilda. Along the same line of thinking Walter talked about the goodness of the new Charter of Liberties recently established by the king. One point mentioned was how the Charter canceled many abuses the previous king set earlier into motion. Both men excitedly chatted about the fact Henry brought back to England the scholarly St. Anselm, the archbishop of Canterbury, from his banishment.

The topic turned to the recent crusade and Walter said, "I remember my French crusader friend Bernard talking about our king, knowing Henry of Normandy, who was a leader of another one of the French squadrons in the Holy land. I believe Henry was stationed at Shiloh after his squadron was involved in our successful capture of Jerusalem.

The guest replied, "Yes, you are correct. Henry returned home to France a year before you came home. Our king was quite impressed with your record while serving with the Crusaders. That is why I am here. Henry would like to bestow upon you the office of Justice of Forests and Itinerant Justice of the Northern Counties. He would like for you to govern this area of his country.

Walter responded, "Please tell our ruler I will be very honored to accept the position."

The King's representative stayed through dinner and the night. Then he was off for London early the next morning.

Year after year Walter maintained peace in the forests. He rode the roads through them and saw to their upkeep. He settled hunter's disputes and kept guard against robbers using the woods as a hiding place for themselves, or for their stash of stolen goods. Then too, there were hunting accidents and murders in the forests about which Walter needed to oversee the details of, and to carry out the justice needed. He was excellent in his job.

Often young Walter rode with his father on the observation trips and there were days they hunted together in the northern woods.

In the succeeding years, Adelina bore Walter four more children. None of them lived into adulthood. The two girls died in infancy. One boy died at six years of age. After the fifth child was conceived both Adelina and the fetus died in the birthing process.

The entire castle went into deep mourning. Walter fell into extreme grief and following the service the only way he could cope with the awfulness was to go into the solitude of the forest and pray.

Teen aged Walter and his grandmother Joanne found solace in working around the castle gardens, chatting during the evening hours and on their knees in the Chapel before bedtime.

Nine months later the Le Espek family life became more normal, with much of the grief laid aside. At this time young Walter turned sixteen. His grandmother doted on him. His father considered him a co-worker in guarding the forests. There was no question about what a fine, stalwart young man Walter the third appeared to be and he followed in his father's steps in many ways. Young Walter desired to serve God, country and community. He even joined the squadron in which his father had been a member and trained for in the defense of England and the defense of Christianity.

In the spring of the year 1121 some of the squadron members were out on a hunting trip. The men riding the horses at their utmost speed over barriers of many types was one exercise the squadron practiced often. The hunters were riding this way when Walter's horse's hoof caught on the top of a stonewall. Both animal and man crashed to the ground and Walter's neck was broken. He died on the spot at only twenty-six years of age.

The death shocked all of the squadron members. Foremost in the commander's mind was the dread of telling Lord Espec his son was dead. Banding together all ninety-nine men circled the horse carrying Walter's body and rode as a group toward Helmsley while intoning the death dirge. Mournfully the sound carried across the land.

Walter Sr. was at his desk filling out a report when the dirge was heard. He rose to look out the window to see where the sound was coming from. But from where he was standing he could not see the location where the chanting men were and he went out into the garden to get a better look.

Chapter 5

When the procession turned toward the castle Walter fell on his knees crying out, "Oh, God - No, Oh, God - No."

By nightfall the castle was shrouded in black and the criers were sent out to notify all of the people in the area about the death of the much-loved young nobleman.

Walter the third was laid to rest on the next day in the castle grounds. He was buried next to his mother, brothers and sisters. Hundreds of people came to share in the sorrow.

Immediately following the service Walter strode deeply into the woods. For six months he cried and prayed, and subsisted on whatever her could find. Then the grieving man returned home and walked into the Chapel.

Walter fell on his knees and said, "Almighty God, I feel like Job. You have taken away everything I hold most dear. True, you have not removed my material wealth like you did the Old Testament character. But my material things mean nothing to me.

Dear Father my thanks goes up to You for the wonderful family You gave to me. Oh, Almighty, You are to be praised for the days on this earth my loved ones were in my presence. Thank you for the knowledge I will see them again.

Now, Lord, my desire is to build a Priory to Your glory in memory of my son Walter. It will be erected near where he was killed. Please instruct me as to the proper way of going about this project. I pray this in the precious name of your son, the Lord Jesus Christ."

Walter went to his Pastor to talk about the project. He went to his Bishop, then to his Uncle William. Finally Walter traveled to the Archbishop. Through these men Sir Espec learned about the church's trend toward more modestly designed places of worship; toward isolation and solitude. The trend was called Cistercian.

Next Walter rode toward Malton, in Yorkshire into the area where his son was killed. The man purchased a lovely, peaceful, tranquil track of land situated on a bend of the Derwent River. Before the end of the year construction on a Priory was started.

Walter's cousin William, son of Richard Speke of Bath, came north to oversee the building of the Priory. His design was not towering, like many of the Abbeys and it was built of squared stones, covered with shingles. Beautiful stained glass windows were installed. Then bells were placed in the tower to call the monks to Mass, to prayers and to meals. The most modern of clay water pipes were laid underground to bring fresh spring water into the grounds.

In the foundation charter of the priory King William II name was mentioned. This king William, also known as William Rufus, wanted his stamp of approval upon the project, especially since he was both a distant cousin and a friend to the three generations of Walters.

Aged Uncle William came to bless the place of worship. Shortly after the dedication the Priory became filled with Augustinian cannons, young and old, who desired to draw away from the world into a wilderness place and commune with God. They felt their mission on this earth was to work with their hands. Some were farmers and some became involved with various trades; carpentry, woodworking, weaving, leatherwork, and all kinds of arts. The community on the grounds became very self-sufficient.

Ten years later Walter designated a tract of land two and a half miles from Helmsley, and located on the Rye River for the site of a house of Worship. He felt it was time to build a local edifice to glorify his God, and he called the place Rievaux Abbey. Again cousin William was invited to be a part of the designing and construction of the place to worship God. The younger Speke man felt honored to be a part of the plan.

Once more Walter wanted the same design followed as of the lovely, austere concept of the Cistercians. To him, an Abbey's main purpose was to promote contemplation, plus the teaching of arts and culture. The grounds were designed to be large enough and comfortable enough to house 150 monks, 500 laymen, and the many pilgrims who would pass through Rievaulx.

William began construction with the digging of the foundations of the church building. Along side of this work the men also dug areas to lay pipes to bring fresh water into the compound. One other important aspect of the lead pipe laying was for the removal of waste material.

As the beautiful huge squared stone Abbey was being erected by some of the workmen, others were building the Abbot's quarters alongside of the church building. The house contained two storeys, with 18 rooms. Some were for the Abbot's personal use, while other rooms were used by all of the clergy and the guests. Next to this building lay the infirmary. Then came the Monks quarters and guest cottages. Many rooms contained fireplaces for heat. Every building contained a latrine with the most modern plumbing of the day. The vent for the waste was either emptied below the cellar line, or else piped out underground.

The last stone placed high on the Abby contained the imprint of the king's badge. The royal monarch constantly kept in touch with his aging subject. Along side of the

King's approval, the Archbishop Thurston of York constantly condoned and aided all of Walter's works within the church.

On the west side of the precinct sat lovely meadows, over which the River Rye could be viewed. Then between the Abbey and the outer wall, on the east side laid the stable, the swine enclosure, the sheep-shearing pen, the well house, and the guesthouse. Also inside the wall stood the corn mill, the kiln, the brew house, a tannery, the plumber's quarters and a fulling mill. An inner and outer gatehouse, plus a Chapel were located by the entryway. There was no question as to Rievaux having everything a small town would contain.

Monks attended the gardens of fresh fruit and vegetables, plus beehives, in order to feed those living within the compound, as well as feeding many guests who came and went.

Within four years William's work at Rievaulx was finished. Then Walter decided to build an Abbey in Warden. It was built in memory of his grandfather and his Uncle William.

During the dedication of the Warden Abbey a special presentation was made to young William. At this time he was given the Espec ring. Walter explained, as the ring was handed to his cousin, "Because I no longer have an heir, and because your father, along with my grandfather fought at the Battle of Hastings I proudly honor you with this ring."

Before William returned home to Bath a messenger arrived with the news of King Henry's death. Walter and William rode south to attend the king's funeral at Westminster Abbey. Then they stayed in London for a few more days in order to also attend the coronation ceremony of Stephen the first.

Immediately, upon the crowning of Stephen, a conflict began between England and Scotland. King Henry's daughter Matilda claimed the English throne, even though her father chose his Norman nephew to be his heir.

"Empress Maud" the daughter of Henry, was also the niece of Scotland's King David, as his sister was Henry's wife. King David did not want another Norman on the English throne. Many Scotsmen supported his opinion. For the first time in history Scotland became unified under one cause, which was to put Matilda on the throne of England.

One reason the English did not want a woman on the throne was because such a thing ever taking place in their land was unknown.

Following the coronation in 1135 some sporadic attacks were made from Scotland into England. In 1138 king David earnestly went into the state of war.

Walter's castle at Wark lay in the path of king David's army. In the month of January the northern army, led by Walter Fitzaland (Scotland's High Steward) attacked the castle. The garrison within repelled the attack and the Scots withdrew. In June a siege was formed outside of the castle.

Late in August king David led his army into a major battle at Northallerton. Aging Walter was one of the English leaders against the northern army. Sir Espec was considered the "dux et pater" (a father who shows the way, or leads) by the other English barons. With the Scottish army on a northern hill and the English army assembled on a southern hill the battle began in the valley between.

King David's foot soldiers were exceptionally well armored. However, the Gallgael section of the army thought it was an insult for the foot soldiers to be better equipped than they. Therefore, to prove they were the better fighters, the men from Galloway insisted they be in the forefront of the attack in place of the foot soldiers.

As the Galloway men (with only pikes) ran down the hill Walter ordered the English archers to begin shooting. Many Gallgael men fell in battle and then the English knights rode in to finish the slaughter.

Upon seeing this the Scottish knights, led by Earl Henry, crashed through to the center of the English army. Immediately, the English military closed ranks around their enemy. Fear entered the hearts of the Earl's men. They knew they could not escape without a great loss of life, so they ceased fighting.

High on the English hill stood a float bearing the banner of the Archbishop of York. Also placed next to the float were religious banners and Holy relics; even included were the communion cup and the bread.

The standard, plus the relics could be seen by all of the opposing men and there was a discomfort among the Scottish soldiers over fighting with such a presence within their eyesight. Many of the men were hesitant and did not want to go into battle. In reality the number of the northern army exceeded in numbers those of the

English one, but there was much confusion. Fueling even more the confusion was a rumor spreading which said King David was dead. Finally king David's army quietly withdrew from their post.

The Englishmen claimed victory even though the Scotsmen knew the battle was theirs. However the "Battle of the Standard", the most important and devastating fight so far, was finished.

Skirmishes continued, one of them being the siege of Walter's castle at Wark. For five months, from June to November, there was no way to bring food into the castle grounds. The family of Walter's nephew, the servants, and the garrison were reduced to eating the horses in the stable. They were down to one live horse and one preserved in salt.

Walter, at Yorkshire, called a meeting with other leaders to decide how to resolve the Wark problem. In sympathy the Abbot of Rievaulx offered to negotiate with king David concerning a settlement. Terms were peacefully brought to the conclusion where all of the people within the castle were allowed to leave without harm. However the property remained in Scottish hands.

Six months later, April 1139, the English and the Scottish officials met at Durham to sign a treaty. At this meeting it was decided to use the Tees River as the boundary between England and Scotland. This made it possible for Walter to regain his Wark castle.

Until 1152 Walter continued to live at Helmsley. His black hair was now white and his large build was slightly stooped. However Walter's booming voice (like his father's had been) still rang out. The old man was revered and honored.

At this stage of the distinguished man's life he decided to retire to Kirkham to meditate and pray. Walter Le Espek passed on to glory at the Kirkham Priory on March 7, 1153.

All of Yorkshire and Bedfordshire mourned the loss of the Godly Le Espek, their "dux et Pater". They thanked the Almighty for this man's many years of wise leadership and kind governing.

Chapter 6

October 1190

$\mathscr{W}$illiam, the son of deceased architect and builder William Le Espek, was sitting on the floor of a shed in the back yard of his home located on the edge of the town of Bath. His two sons John and James were sitting along side of him. All three men were cutting stones into two-inch squares to build a playhouse (a surprise birthday gift) for William's five-year-old daughter Sarah.

When the three men decided to build the house they first constructed the wooden shed to conceal what they were about to do. After the work was completed it would stay hidden until the time of the birthday party. Then the wooden shed walls would be removed and the little house would sit on a permanent spot.

On designing the miniature home the men decided to make three rooms large enough for Sarah to stand, with enough headroom to allow for a few years growth. Then off of these rooms were smaller rooms designed as a home for Sarah's dolls. From each of the larger rooms she and her friends could reach in and play house with a half-dozen dolls.

As William, John and James cracked, chipped and shaved the stones they discussed the world situation. It seemed to them there were constant battles and fighting on every continent they knew of.

The first topic of course, centered on their monarch, Richard the Lion hearted, who now ruled England. This whole year while the king sat on the throne people all over England heatedly talked about England's relationship to France. Two questions were battered back and forth in all of the pubs.

1. Is it right for an English king to still be so involved with personal holdings in the land of France?

2. Is it right for king Philip of France to break up English holdings there?

Although it was now past history some men still grew angry over how king Henry II, Richard's father, tried to force Richard to give some French holdings to his brother John.

Other men shouted, "Yeah, but Richard engaged king Philip's help and in the skirmish which followed actually caused his own father's death."

As the three Speke men spoke about all of this they came to the consensus the whole terrible ordeal did nothing but bring England close to war with France. They realized the only reason war did not occur was because both king Philip and king Richard took the "Oath of the Cross."

James said, "I can understand both Philip and Richard's desire to become crusaders. I can understand their aim to lead an army against Saladin who recently recaptured Jerusalem. I can understand the importance of freeing the Holy City again. But I can't understand our monarch depleting the treasury and selling sherrifdoms, plus other offices to fund his army. This has the possibility of ruining our country."

John posed the question, "Do you think the arguing, or the fighting will ever stop?" William responded, "You know the Holy Scripture tells us "wars and rumors of wars" will continue until Christ returns to set up His kingdom," William Sr. responded.

"Won't that be exciting!" remarked James. Quietly William Jr. murmured, "The turn of the century is only ten years away. Maybe our Lord will return then."

Once this topic ended William gave his sons some good news. He informed his sons about their business being commissioned to do an important work for the Bath Abbey. They were to do the carving on the new doors and also the portal for the church's entryway. The oak double doors stood ten feet high. Into the wood were to be carved the apostles faces. The order for the portal was a carving of the figure of Jesus from the waist up, with His arms extended.

Excitedly the men talked about the personality and the emotion needing to be portrayed in each face. William Sr. said, "James, I want you to work on the door with the faces of James, Andrew, Bartholomew, Thomas, Simon and Judas. John, you are to carve John, Matthew, Peter, Philip, James the less, and Jude on the other door. I will do the portal.

While the men were talking about the carving project a knock came on the shed door. It was one of the kitchen maids to say dinner was ready.

William spoke up, "We've been so busy enjoying ourselves here I hadn't even thought of food. "Not my problem," responded the two sons. William Jr. went on, "My belly's been complaining for the last hour." The three big men briskly walked toward the home where their wives and children waited.

The large house was one these men built ten years earlier. While young John and James were not yet married at that time their father planned a big enough building for three families to live-in. The floor plan consisted of a large common area including a sitting room, a library, a den, a huge dining space and a kitchen. Placed to the east, north and south were three wings connected by halls to the common area. Each wing was spacious enough to contain three bedrooms, a sitting room and a room for bathing.

All of the afternoon the cook industrially spent time making "Pasties", while at the same time she boiled cabbage and also cooked a rice pudding with currents. The making of the pasties was the most time consuming. First the bread dough was mixed and while it was rising the cook tended the lamb roasting on a spit. Then the raised dough was rolled out and cut into four-inch squares. Next the cook took the juicy cooked lamb, along with some mint leaves and began the fine chopping necessary to put this concoction on one side of the dough squares. As a last step the other half of the square was folded over, then firmly pinched until closed. These were baked until they were slightly brown.

While the pasties were baking, a pot of carrots was boiling and the already cooked cabbage was gently fried. Next to the oven the rice pudding sat cooling so it would not burn any mouths, yet still be pleasantly warm when the rich cream was poured over it.

Once the men stepped inside and smelled the aroma of all the cooked food they knew they were famished and their appetites matched their body size. They could eat volumes of food and the cook knew it. Fifty pasties were waiting for the six adults and three children who were to come into the dining room. Probably ten would be left for the five servants who would be eating in the kitchen.

Rachael, William Sr.'s wife, James' wife Gertrude and their two sons, George, eight years old and Walter, four years of age, plus John's wife Emma and daughter Sarah were waiting in the main sitting room for the men of their lives. After the hugs and kisses they proceeded into the dining area.

Following dinner the Le Espek family returned to the sitting room where the chairs were gathered into a semicircle close to the blazing fire. After the adults sat down the children gathered on the floor with a game board. Coins were used as the pieces to move on the board after each child found how far they were to move by throwing dice.

While the children played the adults chatted about their day's business. Rachael began by exclaiming over the beauty of the day and the pleasure of working at the stream with Gertrude and Emma. Emma nodded her head and then spoke of her thankfulness for a certain place in the stream where a basket full of wool fit perfectly. Rachael joined in with her joy over the gentle force of the stream's water being just perfect to remove most of the grime, mud and twigs from the newly shorn fleece.

All of this time Gertrude quietly, said, "yes, yes" in agreement with the other women. Then she spoke up, "Hopefully the wool will be dry enough by tomorrow to do the carding. We'll spread it all thinly on mats to dry in this afternoon's sunshine and when dusk approaches bring the mats indoors."

Even though the men were well aware of the carding process Emma wanted to remind them of all which would take place on the next day. She told how each woman would take paddles (called tow cards) with thin spikes imbedded in them and pull the tow cards through the wool. This would remove any remaining dirt and also straighten the fibers so the spinning process could follow.

During the time the women were talking their busy hands held bone knitting needles as they were making wool stockings from the wool they spent the evening before spinning.

Before retiring for the night William Sr. mentioned the commissioning of the Abbey doors and portal. All three women excitedly expressed how glad they were for the opportunity before their husbands.

The next evening Rachael, Gertrude and Emma sat spinning while listening to their husbands discussing their plans for the carving.

Sitting on the floor by the right side of each lady was a basket of wool. From the basket a strand of wool was pulled taunt across the right knee and held tight with the left hand. All the time they chatted the right hand kept rolling the fiber downward over the thigh twisting it into a thread. As the thread lengthened the left hand would wind it around a stick nailed to a flat board sitting on the floor on the left side to form a spool full of wool.

Gertrude mentioned it would probably take another day to finish spinning the wool and Emma said, "Yes, then we will be able to dye the wool. I want some of dark green and some of dark blue to make vests." Rachael wanted to color some maroon to make shawls and Gertrude thought lavender would make lovely lap robes.

As the conversation of the women died down Rachael asked the men what their plans were in regards to the latest carving assignment. William responded. "Our sons made an appointment with the abbot to learn all they could about the apostles. Depending upon what they hear they will then sketch on paper how they pictured the face of each apostle from what they learned in the study. It will probably be a good week to ten days before any actual carving begins." William finished with, "I have already begun to sketch my impression of the expression on Jesus' face as he invites people with open arms to come to Him."

On the next morning, after they opened their shop on Bath square James and John walked into the Abbey to meet in the abbot's office. They were warmly greeted and offered a chair to sit on. The clergyman assured the young men about finding it most encouraging to talk with people dedicated in finding a true perspective of the apostles.

Immediately the abbot began a dialogue about the men closest to Jesus and first pointed out the attributes of the brothers Peter and Andrew. He spoke of both men being fishermen, which was considered a rough, menial trade, but the men themselves were not necessarily those of a lower culture. Many fishermen were brilliant and admired.

Then the abbot dwelt on the apostle's individual traits. Peter appeared rough and bold. Bold enough to step out of a boat and walk on water. Bold enough to proclaim Jesus as the Messiah. As the clergyman continued talking about Peter dying in Rome because of his faith, John pictured in his mind a broad face with roughened skin from being out in the weather and sun. Peter's face would have a courageous expression. John thought — what courage it must have taken to face the Son of

God after denying Him, and the to humble himself enough to ask forgiveness.

When the abbot concluded the information concerning Peter he went right onto the brother Andrew. The first point he dealt with was about the tender-heartedness of the fisherman toward God. Andrew's devotion to the teaching of John the Baptist led to his natural turning to Jesus.

The next half hour the clergymen spoke of Andrew's concern for others and the part this apostle played in bringing others to Jesus. He was concerned enough to travel to Sythia to give the people there the hope of eternal life. Andrew was stoned in Sythia.

In James' mind the picture of a slender, muscular, weathered person formed with a face full of compassion.

Both John and James spent a few minutes expressing their thoughts concerning Peter and Andrew. They asked several questions, and then the abbot went on, "Now we will deal with the brothers James and John, co-fishermen with Peter and Andrew."

First mentioned was the fact the mother of these two men followed Jesus, even to the crucifixion itself. Then the clergyman told of how James walked in his mother's footsteps. The Pastor mentioned one after another, and elucidated on, the scripture references where James kept close to Jesus. The abbot said, "John the Baptist was a wonderful "voice in the wilderness" pointing people to Jesus. Now we see James and John were led to the Saviour through him, as well as Andrew."

The last thought left concerning the apostle was the fact James was the first of them to be martyred; beheaded by Herod. The clergyman felt James' character was very warm, but he also thought the apostle was both bold and impetuous.

James Le Espek wondered how he could portray this man of God for whom he was named. He thought, — Am I an example of following Christ, as he was? Could I stand up to death by the sword for my belief as he did? Tears began to run down James' face. Love was the only facial expression he could picture on this apostle's face; a compelling love for his Master.

Now the clergyman talked about the gift of writing given to John, plus the insights he received which allowed him to put on parchment the book of John, three epistles and Revelation. Very clearly John saw the love and faithfulness of his Saviour and acted on it himself. This apostle's love was so very evident it caused Jesus, while dying, to entrust the care of His mother into John's hands.

The abbot ended with, "John's God given insight came to the forefront in that he was the first of the apostles to recognize the risen Lord.

John Le Espec said, "Father, over and over you have pointed out John's love. No other picture than that can come to my mind to put on his face." The Reverend responded, "You are so right. Remember the love stayed fast for the Saviour in the tender care of Mary until her death."

At the conclusion of the session the abbot once more commended John and James in their desire to correctly portray the core of the apostles personality in their carving. He told them they would study four more apostles on the next morning.

The following day the abbot once more graciously received the two Speke men. After the usual cordial greetings the Reverend began talking about one of the controversial names among the apostles - James the less.

The Le Espek whose name was James asked, "Why would anyone be called "the less""? To this the abbot responded, "It is speculated either because he was less in age, or less in height. Probably the former, because in the culture at the time of Jesus' day, it was an honor to be the older."

Then the abbot went on explaining the reason for the controversy within the church. He spoke about the passage of Scripture where Jesus refereed to this James as his brother.

The argument began with one faction of the church claiming Mary never conceived again. They claimed Jesus was her only child. They argue over how they could never understand why Jesus would ever make this claim. Some among the group have settled the problem with the concept of all men being the brothers of Jesus, therefore it was right for Jesus to call James his brother.

Others within the church follow the tradition claiming Joseph's brother Alphaeus died without children. As was the custom of the time Joseph redeemed the widow through marrying her. The children born of this union were legally the children of the first husband. James was considered the son of Alphaeus. He was also the half brother of Jesus.

James Le Espek remarked, "What a perfect picture of our standing, our position in Christ, through redemption. We are physically born to our parents. Then through the acceptance of the Son of God as our Saviour we are redeemed and literally become a child of Jehovah, and a sibling of Jesus.

Both the Pastor and John nodded their heads in agreement. John said, "I see James the less as a small quiet man who revered his half-brother."

Following this description the man of God talked about two more apostles. He said, "Philip and Bartholomew's names are almost always linked together in Scripture, although they are not brothers." One topic covered was about how little is known concerning Philip; only what is recounted in the New Testament, plus any tradition

It is supposed he was a friend of Peter and Andrew's. He was probably introduced to Jesus through them and the most impressive account of him is how he brought Bartholomew to the Lord.

Some scholars discuss why, when feeding the 5000, the Lord asked Philip, "How will we buy enough bread to feed all these people?" One group believe Philip's faith was being tested. Another group say, "No," to this thesis and claim Philip was in charge of the provisions for the twelve and it was right for him to be consulted on such a project.

What is known for sure is, he was one of the twelve who was set apart for the office of apostle. He probably knew scripture well. According to tradition Philip went to Phrygia to preach following the ascension. He was crucified in Syria.

John claimed it was hard for him to get a grasp of Philip's personality when the Abbot first talked about the man. But then the idea came - this apostle was a determined man. Because of Philip's knowledge of Scripture he was determined to see if Jesus really was all of what he heard about the Man from Galilee. Then, on being satisfied that Jesus was the Messiah, he became determined to follow the Lord, and to bring others to Him.

The Abbot said, "Now we will go the Philip's friend Bartholomew. Again, we come across a person of whom not much more is known except for where he is mentioned in Scripture. We do know he was flayed alive and beheaded in Armenia." The Godly man pointed out what could be read, and then recounted how the reading produced one more controversy over the apostle.

Three gospels mention Philip and Bartholomew. The fourth gospel refers to Philip and Nathaniel. Anyone can see the problem this would cause. For those who want to discredit Scripture it can easily be used as a fallacy of Scripture. Then there are those who say these were two different men who were both friends of Philip.

In reality, we believe it is the same person whose name was Nathaniel Bartholomew. John said, "That seems odd." James replied, "Not really. Both you and I know Benjamin Walter. Some people call him Benjamin and others Walter." "Your right," responded John, and he went on thinking out loud about his concept of Bartholomew. "The man must be a very curious person. Also one who needed to see a sign in order to believe what he heard. In a way he showed he was a doubter when he asked 'can anything good could come out of Nazareth?' I Think there must have been quite a surprised look on his face when Jesus said, 'Behold, an Israelite indeed, in whom there is no guile.' My carving will express the joyful surprise of one whose curiosity has been satisfied."

One other point brought out by the Pastor dealt with the common use of second names during Christ's day. He talked about Peter's name being Simon Peter. Perhaps, in this case, it was used to distinguish him from the other Simon

The Abbot agreed with John's concept of Bartholomew, and then went on to say, "The last apostle to be considered today is one whom even less is known about than what we know about Bartholomew. He is Simon the Canaanite, also called Simon Zealotes. We do know he is an apostle and at one time he was a member of the Zealots. They were a class of people who adhered to strict Mosaic rule. In their minds any slightest deviation from Levitical law was to be punished. Simon the Zealot met his death by being sawn in two in Rome."

As the clergyman began to bring the session to a close he expressed being sorry there was not more information he could give concerning Simon Zealotes.

James claimed he could picture Simon without any more explanation. "The man must have had a very stern unyielding countenance." Then went on to say, "Now are we to expect to meet with you again tomorrow morning?" In answering the clergyman said, "I too picture Simon as a very solemn person. Now about your question, tomorrow there is a Diasies meeting and then the weekend follows. We must wait until Monday to conclude with the final four apostles.

Both James and John were thoroughly enjoying the time with the Abbot and they thought they were learning much.

The following Sunday morning sermon proved most interesting to them. The pastor spoke on "Twelve men who gave up everything." To both Speke young men it seemed the Holy Spirit was leading the clergy of the church in a way most beneficial to their study.

Around the dinner table all of the Spekes began discussing the morning sermon. Emma stated, "I never thought much about what each apostle put behind them. Just think they left their homes, their families, their work." Gertrude solemnly said, "Even beyond that, they gave up their lives for what they believed."

Then questions and comments flew. What would we need to see or feel to do the same thing? How awful to be beaten! I wonder how the wives coped? How long do you think it took to travel from Jerusalem to Rome? What must it have felt like to see the Holy Spirit heal someone through you?

The family left the table and the topic of conversation went with them into the sitting room. For several weeks the talk about the apostles lives would pop-up when the family gathered together.

On Monday morning James and William hastened to hear about the four remaining followers of Jesus. On the Abbots desk sat tea, soda bread with currents and clotted cream waiting for the men to enjoy during their final session.

The clergyman first discussed the position of Portitors in Roman politics This was a position of high esteem at the customs house, and usually it was held by aristocratic Roman men whose job was to collect taxes. Matthew, a Hebrew holding this position felt very honored.

When Jesus came to the customs house, probably to pay His taxes, he approached Matthew and said, "Follow me." At that point Matthew quit his job and followed Jesus from that time on.

After Jesus visited in Matthew's home He was accused of eating with publicans and sinners. At this point John said, "Who knows, maybe some of those publicans and sinners came to realize who Jesus really was while they were in Matthew's home with the Lord there."

Thinking out loud John murmured, "Now, from the type of position Matthew held these could have been his only friends and the fellow employees he associated with. Maybe this time in Matthew's home was even a farewell banquet."

The clergyman nodded his head and continued his explanation about Matthew's life and about this apostle being one of the people who saw Jesus ascend to heaven. Then Matthew preached in Judea and went on from there to foreign fields. Matthew's gift of writing was pointed out and how much we benefit from the insights we learn of Jesus' life written in the book of Matthew. Matthew's death came about in Alexandria by crucifixion.

As an afterthought the Abbot dealt with the education John, Matthew, James and Jude must have received in order to write their books and epistles. He said, "Many men did not receive this type of education during the days when Jesus lived."

John said, "I'm confused as to how to portray Matthew. Three concepts keep coming to mind. Because of his position he was a haughty man. Also he was a ribald, party person around his friends and associations. Then too, a dedicated, determined person who was ready to give up all (and he had much to give up) to follow Jesus. It will take me a while to make up my mind about how to portray the face of Matthew.

"Now," the Abbot said, "Since I already mentioned Jude as an author, he will be the next person we consider. There is very little to tell! Historians claim he was the brother of James. It is known he was an apostle. The only inkling as to Jude's character is from the epistle he wrote. In it he emphasized the need for Christians to remain faithful to their Saviour by living a God honoring life.

John indicated the picture coming to mind of Jude is one of a caring man. Yet on his face must be a hint of disappointment over the disregard for Godly behavior of some who claim to be a Christian.

A short break was taken while the Abbot's wife served more hot tea. Now the clergyman went on to the last of the apostles. He said, "Much discussion has taken place over the years about the two apostles left. We will study them one at a time. First there was Thomas, who became known as "the doubter"".

As the clergyman delved into the Scripture concerning this apostle it became very evident to James and John that Thomas was a questioning person. One who wondered how something was possible, and if it couldn't be proved he would not accept it. Thomas needed to think and to see in order to understand. He could not just accept by faith.

After the Pastor drew the topic to a close James said, "My picture of Thomas' face is one of a studious, inquisitive individual, with a hint of joy around his mouth. Joy over discovering who Jesus really is!"

"You both know the story of Judas," said the clergyman. Then he began to put forth the many topics theologians discussed concerning "the deceiver." He elucidated on whether Judas was

1. Ever a true believer, or someone who saw financial profit in Jesus' ability as a leader?

2. Did he steal from the group as a keeper of the funds?

3. With Jesus' knowledge of Judas' traits, why was he allowed to remain one of the twelve?

4. Could Judas have acted differently when he was chosen by God to fulfill the plan of the Sacrificial Lamb?

5. How can the difference between the stories in Matthew 27:5 and Acts 16:25 be explained?

The Abbot closed with a discussion concerning the apparent contradiction between the account in the gospel and the one in Acts over what Judas did with the forty pieces of silver he received after betraying Jesus. He said the supposition is Matthew saw Judas throw the money on the Temple floor. Then he walked away in disgust. Later he heard Judas went and hung himself. Other people remained in the Temple area and saw the priests revile Judas for giving the Temple "unlawfully gained money." They made him pick it up. Then Judas went to buy a field as a place for killing himself and when attempting to hang himself the rope broke causing him to plunge to death upon jagged rocks. This is the story Luke told in the Acts account.

The noon hour was past and the three men were hungry. The morning had been long because of all the discussion.

The Pastor asked James how he would picture Judas. There was silence for a few minutes. The James responded, "I can only see horror and remorse on the face of the betrayer at this point; the terrible guilt over what he did and to whom he did it. Maybe later more characteristics will come to mind, but not right now."

The men closed in prayer, and James said, "Don't forget Father, we are expecting you to come for dinner this evening. I know our wives and children have questions concerning the twelve apostles, especially after hearing the good sermon about them.

All the following week James and John went early in the day to the Le Espek foundry located just off of Bath's town square. The business was in a large building where all their tools hung from the walls. All three men possessed a desk along the west wall, and an open kiln sat in the corner. The two huge doors lay on wooden horses along the east side of the shop and in the back of the building lay the two foot thick, four foot high, eight foot long limestone portal.

William was through with his sketching and ready to begin the actual carving. He would start by using a point chisel to incise into the stone in an area close to the base where the hands would appear. Jacob wanted the hand's open, "come unto me" shape to catch a person's eye before they looked up at the face.

Once John's and James' sketching was ended they would begin on the doors. First, using a pencil they would outline six equidistant squares on the wood. Then the sketches on paper would be re-sketched onto the door panels.

Week after week knives, chisels and drills were carefully employed to bring the faces out of the wood and stone. From time to time the pounding of a mallet against the chisel (to dig deeper into the wood or stone) could be heard vibrating in the building by the people who were passing-bye outside.

Often the Abbot, or a priest, or some other clergyman came to just stand and watch the deft hands forming faces coming to look very alive. Parishioners also stopped in just to watch.

The month of April held two big occasions. On the first day of the month there was a dedication and placing of the portal and doors at the Abbey. Many times Jacob, John and James were thanked for the inspiring carving. People's hearts were touched as they looked at the compassionate face of the Saviour inviting them to come. Also hearts were moved in looking into the faces of the twelve determined men who gave up everything to accept their Lord's invitation to follow Him.

The date of Sarah's birthday was the sixteenth of the month. This was when the culmination of all of the preparation and planning was to finally take place. The men finished building the playhouse two weeks before the birthday, but it remained covered up until everyone gathered.

Sarah's aunts, uncles, cousins and friends all gathered for the noon meal. Her presents would be opened after the food was consumed and everyone moved to the back yard where William, James and John tore the shed down.

Sarah just stood with her eyes wide open for a few seconds and saying, "Oh, thank you, oh, thank you!" Then she and the other children ran squealing with delight ran toward the perfect miniature house. Inside they found child size furniture in the larger rooms and doll size furniture in the many alcoves. There were chairs in the parlor with throws (made by the women) on them; a table and chairs in the dining area and a bedroom set in the third room.

Right away most of the dolls from the main house were moved to the playhouse. Then all afternoon the girls played quietly within the new attraction. The men and boys took bows and arrows out into the field for target shooting.

As the men walked back from the field John told his father, "My friend keeps staring at your gold ring and asking questions about it. Why don't you tell him the story about William the Conqueror giving it to our relative."

So the tale was recounted with the boys all gathered around in the parlor. As William ended the story he told them about the ring being faithfully passed from generation to generation and how this reminded him of the faithfulness of God. He said, "Each generation of our family can tell stories of their reliance upon their Heavenly Father and how the Almighty brought them through many experiences." Then John picked up a parchment copy of the book of Corinthians (which a monk recently transcribed) and read 'God is faithful, by whom you were called into the fellowship of His son, Jesus Christ our Lord.' This verse has come true over and over in our family for the last one hundred fifty years," William concluded.

All the next year the Speke men were commissioned to do carvings in the halls and churches of many small towns around bath. Then they were asked to consider doing a large work in Rochester. The order was so big it would take several years to complete. This came about because of the fame of the portal and doors of the Bath Abbey spreading over all of southern England.

William determined one son must remain at home to take care of the family, property and business. The other son would travel with him the approximate one hundred twenty miles east. They would take turns staying in Rochester for several months and then remain home for a month. The actual amount of months away from home, plus which son would go to Rochester would be staggered in order for two men to be in Rochester all the time and one at home.

The huge job consisted of the majority of the interior and exterior walls of the Abbey to be carved into designs of flowers, doves, and fish. Several angels, cherubs, a crucifix, plus a communion table were all to be chiseled out of huge marble stones and then placed at the front of the Cathedral. The work was so immense the men knew it would take years to finish

William, John and James were each very excited about the opportunity before them. While they didn't look forward to the separation from their wives and children, they did look forward to their gift of carving being used so extensively in a house of Worship. Naturally, practically all the conversation in the home centered on where they were going and what they would be doing.

William asked his grandsons to inquire of Mr. Hastings (Bath's educator and historian) for information concerning the town of Rochester. The boys saw the man once a week for instruction and this would be an interesting project for them.

John and Walter attended school in a room of the Abbey. Here they learned to read, write and how to use numbers. One day a week Mr. Hastings came into the class- room and taught history through telling stories of past events.

The three Speke men shared from time to time the little information they knew about the church where they would be working.

1. St. Andrews Cathedral was first founded in the year 604 by King Aethelbert of England'.

2. The new building for the church was completed in 1130.

Outside of these two facts the men knew nothing. They would remain ignorant of the magnificence of the edifice until they arrived there.

At dinner a week later both grandsons excitedly, one after another, related what they learned in their lesson concerning Rochester.

The older John gave the facts — Rochester is located on the Medway River, in the county of Kent. Originally there was a

Roman town on the site called Durobrival. There still remains a Roman wall. Much trade travels through Rochester because the Medway River empties out into the Channel.

At each pause for breath in John's recitation Walter would pipe-up, "There is a keep there. — It's really big. — Like a fortress. — Keep means "to keep an eye on". — Men stand high up on the top wall. — They keep their eyes on the river and the town."

The adults found it difficult to keep from laughing at Walter's one-track mind. When the boys finished they were thanked. Then James said, "Mr. Hastings must have told you an interesting story about the keep." Both boys said, "Yes." Then John told much of the story and Walter ended with, "Mr. Hastings even drew pictures on the chalk board when he talked about how big the keep was."

So began the trek from almost the west coast of England to just a few miles from the English Channel. William and James went together first. In three months James returned home and John left for Rochester. After the John was with his father for three weeks, William left for home. The precision of time was exact in order for one man to arrive in Bath the same day the other man would leave for Rochester.

The cycle continued. It stretched from month to month and on into eventually years.

On one trip from home John traveled with Norman, a priest who was being transferred from Bath to Redding; a town about halfway the distance to Rochester. John helped to load the belongings of the priest's family onto a wagon and then was responsible for driving the horses for the trip. The priest sat beside him, while his wife and seven children rode with the furniture in the back of the wagon.

Only one topic filled the priest's mind. This was about a rumor passed to him concerning a priest's right to marriage. Norman knew many lay people and clergy felt the monks and nuns were a more religious people because they were celibate.

In their minds the married clergy were not near as holy. Now he heard there was coming a Papal decree demanding celibacy from the priests. Norman also heard there was an indecision as to whether this decree would apply to the already married priests, or just the new incoming men into the priesthood.

For three days John heard, "Oh, what will become of me if the decree becomes effective for priests? What will become of my family? I would need to leave the priesthood!"

Then John heard about how much the priest's wife proved to be a blessing to him. She prayed with him and for him. She was a helper in so many ways, and he would list them.

John sympathized and empathized with the man the entire trip. Then he felt a great relief once they unloaded the wagon and he was able to continue on from Redding without Norman and his family.

After his third trip home William brought Rachael back with him to stay for the three months. She was in Rochester for only a few days when she woke to loudly pealing Cathedral bells. Jacob moaned, and said he hoped the bells didn't mean what he heard there ringing could mean. "What's that?" Rachael exclaimed, and Jacob went on to tell how once the town was badly decimated by a plague. In desperation to God the bells were rung constantly for a full twelve hours in a petition of mercy from the Almighty. Many were healed that day.

Everyone in Rochester quickly dressed and scurried to the Cathedral to learn the cause of the ringing. Once they heard the priest say, "I have rung the bells to gather you because King Richard has signed a truce with Saladin in the Holy Land. The Crusaders were not able to recapture Jerusalem, but the truce allows our Pilgrims to visit the Holy places." A large shout of "Hallelujah" reverberated in the building.

On leaving the church Rachael noticed a man sitting in the vestibule dripping with sweat, and whispered to William, "That man looks exhausted." "Yes, he is" her husband responded. "He is the bell ringer, and the bells are very heavy with long ropes to pull them. I've heard — when the bells are rung for any length of time the men do it in shifts, because it is so exhausting."

In time William brought Rachael to Rochester to live. Half a year later James and his family moved there. In deciding to reside in Rochester the two Speke men built a new home on the edge of town.

John and his family remained in Bath; living in the Speke home and operating the foundry formerly run by the three men. After fifteen years Emma bore John a son and they name him William after John's father.

Chapter 7

December 1285

*W*illiam Le Espek sat at the new organ located high overhead in the Bath Abbey. He was about to begin the prelude for the late Christmas Eve service. As the sweet tones resonated through the edifice a thrill went up William's back. His mind began to mull over the previous year's work of planning and overseeing the purchase of the magnificent machine his fingers and feet were now operating.

In the last year this Le Espek man made many trips throughout England and the continent for the purpose of visiting the organ builders. He wanted to test their instruments tones, plus the response of the keys and pipes to a person's touch. Once he found and purchased the sound he wanted, he alone carefully laid the pipes within Bath Abbey. Next William precisely connected the switches within the organ, then the switches to the pipes. The last decision was where best to locate the bellows (which pushed the air into the equipment.) The place must be convenient for a man to stand and manually move the bellows. After everything was finished William made one last inspection of every connection.

Tonight was the night all the work would be brought to fruition. This man felt there was just one reason to play any organ and this was for God's glory. William was sure no other organ could magnify God more than this one.

As the organ prelude drew to a close William could see the pastors, plus the choir members, all assembled at the rear of the Abbey. They were ready to begin the procession through the Sanctuary to their positions in the front of the church.

The first notes of the French Conductus, "Sing Praise with Alleluias" softly was heard. After the piece was played through once the processional began with the choir members joyfully singing in unison

"Sing praises with alleluias
Loudly sing praise with alleluias
With heart fully devoted to God,
Sing praises with alleluias."

The second time through all of the children in the boys choir sang the melody and at the fourth measure the tenor men repeated the melody producing an inspiring round between the boys and tenors. The third time through the bass men began a harmony part to the round. The whole effect became inspiring to everyone.

Each Christmas eve at the Bath Abbey the service consisted of scripture and songs praising the birth of God's Son, followed with a drama of the Bethlehem story, plus a short devotional by the Pastor. Throughout the two hours William concentrated on worshipping his Lord. The new organ, the choral selections and all parts of the evening's order thrilled him. However in his mind the climax came when the Gloria was sung. Tears ran down his face as he played the introduction and realized the words and music were given to him by the inspiration of God specifically for this evening's service.

The Gloria began in the form of a four-part motet. The soprano boys began with the words, "Glory to God". At the second measure the alto boys and high tenors sang "Glory to God". One measure more the baritones sang the words and at the fourth measure the resonant basses joined in with the same phrase. With the excellent Abbey acoustics the ringing words filled the air, reverberating from wall to wall.

Now the intricately weaved melodies followed with the words

> *"A Son is born.*
> *God's Son is born*
> *To bring us Salvation."*

Each line was sung three times and the motet concluded with the words, "Glory to God" sung fortissimo in six-part harmony. Utter silence reigned for a few minutes as the magnificence of the miracle of God's birth sank into the hearts of the congregation.

William left the Abbey around midnight to go to a cold, empty house. He out lived his sister Sara and now at forty-five years of age ached for his deceased parents, his sister and for someone of his own to love.

Music became William's life and he was extremely involved with it. Most of the year the busy days kept him content, but in the early hours of Christmas morning the only emotion he felt was stark loneliness. The fact was — William did not want to live alone. At one point in his life he was engaged to a lovely woman named Isabella. Her eyes were extremely blue. Her creamy skin and black hair made every young man's head turn.

Isabella grew-up in Bath. Her family originally came from France. Because her father managed a lucrative trade between France, Spain, the Orient and England he determined it would be most advantageous to live in England.

From Isabella's early childhood William thought of her as the girl with the beautiful voice. At times she sang a solo at vespers and her contralto voice fascinated him. In their teenage years William and Isabella would attend church meetings and the local fairs together. They would go horseback riding and walk in the woods in their spare time. At nineteen they became engaged and they set the wedding date for early spring.

A few days before Isabella reached her twentieth birthday she was walking around the north edge of Bath when a dog, whose mouth was frothing, ran out of the field. In a maddening rush he went straight for the beautiful girl's ankle and bit her. It was not a deep wound, but everyone knew what would come to pass when a they were bit by a dog with a frothing mouth.

Isabella went home and told her parents about the bite. Soon the news spread through the whole town. Men sorrowfully came to help her father build a sturdy cage. Because Isabella knew how the bite would soon affect her and the danger she would become to others she willingly walked into the cage and it was firmly locked. Tears fell from every townsperson's eyes when her frothing, flailing and crazy noises began. She died a terrible death. William never seemed to get over the loss or the terrible way his sweetheart died.

Now in the early hours of Christmas day he would sleep for a few hours. Then rise before the sun came up to ride down toward Somerset where William would celebrate Christmas with his Uncle Thomas' family.

Thomas James Speke and his wife Esther moved south from Bath in 1267 to manage a horse riding school and a breeding farm. Their six children all grew up in the lovely country atmosphere. All of their children and grandchildren would be with Thomas and Esther for the holiday. William knew the place would be pure bedlam with many little ones opening their gifts at the same time. He looked forward to the happy noise after the days of quiet in his own home.

Forty-seven faces greeted John. All were familiar, except two. One was a young woman and the other her child. John's oldest cousin immediately introduced him to Constance (a widow for five years) and her ten-year-old daughter Elva.

Of course the cousin was filled with the hope he would be smitten with Constance's charms as she was a cheerful person who appeared to be very caring. Her light brown hair with golden streaks glistened in the light and her eyes were blue. William did not object at all to being placed next to Constance for the dinner meal. To him it seemed an excellent idea.

As they chatted William learned Constance played the harp and at the present time taught a few students how to play the instrument. After dinner Constance brought out her harp to entertain her friends with a few selections. William became more interested in this young woman as the evening progressed. He thought she would be a wonderful help in the music department at Bath Abbey. At this time he would not admit to himself the fact his interest could really be more than Constance's musical ability.

The festivities in the Somerset home continued for two days. Before anyone departed for their home William asked Constance if she would consider moving to Bath to help with the church music. He explained to her the need for people with a musical background to come copy manuscripts for the choir's use because many of the manuscripts were on loan to Bath Abbey from other churches and must be returned to them.

Constance said she would consider and pray about the request and let him know her decision. The big Speke man named William seemed charming to Constance, but she did not want this idea to be what influenced her life. She began to pray for God to show her what He wanted her to do.

The more Constance thought about the opportunity of being involved with church music the more appealing the idea of moving became. Since her husband Adam died she lived in the home belonging to his family. Adam's brother was now married and wanted to live in the home. Shortly she would need to make a move. There was one factor though which kept delaying a final yes. This was her daughter Elva's behavior every time she mentioned moving. There was no disguising the fact the little girl would have very great difficulty in moving from the only place she knew as home. Constance hurt for the child who lost a father she so greatly loved, and who would shortly be loosing her home. If they moved to Bath she would no longer even see her close friends.

A short time after Constance began praying about all the concerns in her life a letter came from William. In it he told about several new manuscripts arriving from the Bury St. Edmonds College music department up in Ware and there was a need was to copy the notes immediately on the manuscripts into Bath's choir books in order for the originals to be returned. If she was willing to come help with this work there was an empty wing in the vicarage for Constance and Elva to make their home.

Also William expressed his concern for Constance's comfort and offered furniture from his own home to fill the vicarage wing. He knew his own home would be a much more comfortable place for them to live. He had servants to prepare meals and take care of the housekeeping. Then too, he could provide a nanny for Elva. None of this they would have in the vicarage. However William knew how tongues wagged and how gossip quickly spread. It would be terribly embarrassing for all three of them to hear the gossip, therefore he did not offer the use of his home.

When Constance read the letter she felt the words written in it were directed by God. She believed the Almighty was leading her to move to Bath. In the weeks following Christmas every day was becoming more and more unbearable with her deceased husband's family pressuring her to leave the home.

There was no reason to hold Constance in Somerset. Her father, mother, brother and sisters were no longer living. They all burned to death in a fire that consumed the whole village where she lived when she was small. An elderly aunt raised Constance and she died shortly after Constance married. Constance was the only survivor. In a few days she wrote to William and told him of her decision to move to Bath as soon as she could arrange for their transportation, plus the few things they owned.

As soon as Elva learned from her mother about the decision to move her tears started to flow. They continued all during the packing and the ride north in a wagon. A very bitter, morose little girl came to Bath.

William was waiting and saw the wagon approach. He ushered Constance and Elva to the vicarage and helped them unpack. Even with the pieces Constance brought with them their apartment appeared very sparsely furnished.

Elva would not look at William. She kept her face averted and constantly looked in a far-off direction. If William could have seen the expression on the girl's face when he first met the wagon he would have recognized pure hatred.

Once Constance was settled in her home she reported into the Abby's music room. There William and his two workers were busy transcribing manuscripts into the choir books.

Naomi, one of the workers, took Constance on a tour of the Abbey and the newcomer gushed her appreciation of the beauty of the Abbey while they were walking into the Sanctuary. The two women strolled down the main isle and up past the pulpit for Constance to see where the two choir lofts were located, parallel to the sidewalls. There was room for forty-nine men on one side of the loft and forty-nine boys on the other.

Constance stepped into the loft and noted the location of one music stand between every three seats. All of the seats were small round disks, just high enough on which to place the buttock. The choir's appearance from the congregation looked like all of the members stood throughout the service. But in reality everyone was comfortably seated.

Placed on the music stands in preparation for the evening rehearsal stood books two feet high. Running across each page were six of the five lined staffs holding the square notes for one voice part; soprano or alto for the boys, tenor or bass for the men.

Sometimes the music of a motet or a conductus was divided into three or four part harmony. The boys would sing first and second soprano, plus first and second alto, while the men sang first and second tenor, plus first and second bass.

One of the large pages might only contain one or two phrases of the Latin words because each of the staffs were two inches high and each note took the space of one quarter inch by one half inch. On the staff appeared no time signature and no measure lines. Notes were placed closer together for a quicker time and further apart to be held longer. All notes were black.

After Constance noted all the information she needed to see in the Sanctuary she and Naomi walked to the room where the manuscripts were transcribed. In the workroom Constance was invited to sit between Naomi and her husband Joseph who was her co-worker.

For a while the newcomer just observed the two workers and their careful handwork. In front of Naomi was one page of music and in front of Joseph sat two pages. They were working on a three-part piece and constantly checking back and forth to make sure the harmony and note spacing meshed. The means of taking two poems and weaving them into three understandable parts was a contemporary medium of music much in use and the type Naomi and Joseph were working on.

The three chatted while Constance watched and she mentioned there were times she needed to transcribe her harp music. Constance admitted her copies did not need to be as meticulously written since they were for her use alone. She also confessed she some times employed short cuts, but that was all right because she understood what they meant.

Naomi and Joseph talked about their being married three years before and also about their beginning to help William at about the same time. Naomi explained about her taking organ lessons from William as a child and how she learned to copy music then. She now often played the Bath church organ when William was called to teach in London.

Constance said, "Oh, I didn't know William was often called away!" Then Naomi told how it was William who was chosen to teach music in the king's household. He usually went to London for a few days twice a month during the middle of the week. But every so often he was called to play the Westminster organ on a Sunday.

Joseph talked about his childhood learning experiences and attending school in the Abbey. He began trumpet lessons under William while in the boy's choir. Some church music began with a trumpet fanfare and it was Joseph who usually played the fanfare.

After the lunch hour of delicious beef and Yorkshire pudding (brought in by the vicar's staff) William gave Constance a blank sheet of paper and asked her to write a prelude using a harp solo for the piece of music Naomi and Joseph were working on. William knew the addition of the harp to the morning worship time would be a great blessing to the congregation. He also knew Constance was greatly talented and wanted the implementation of her gift to begin immediately.

The sisters in the Abbey took Elva under their wing and things appeared to be going well with the girl. Much love and kindness was poured on her, but Elva was filled with hatred. It looked like she was responding, but her actions were a farce.

When the sisters were not looking she would destroy some small thing and hide what she destroyed. When she was out playing she would steal something, then in order to not get caught, throw it away before she went home. Her mind kept working on nasty things to do.

As weeks went by the music copying went well. Naomi, Joseph and Constance enjoyed working together and sharing the stories of their lives.

One day Naomi confided her great disappointment in not conceiving after being married for three years. She said, "How embarrassing it is when people ask you over and over, 'when are you going to have a baby'?"

With Joseph and Naomi's love for children they dreamed of becoming parents and having a large family. Month after month the dream was shattered. Constance assured them she would pray for God to allow them to have a child.

Tears came to Constance's eyes as she told her friends about the circumstances around her husband's death. She recounted about Adam's brother becoming violently sick, and his skin turned yellow. The man was so weak from vomiting and diarrhea he could hardly stand. There were days the brother thrashed around with an extremely high fever, and other times he appeared to be out of his head. The whole family prayed; the wife, the children, the brothers, sisters and the parents were constantly on their knees before the Lord, when the Almighty God healed!

Adam felt so overjoyed when his brother was healed he wanted to thank the Lord by going on a pilgrimage to the Holy Land. He wanted to kneel in the land where the Lord lived and performed many miracles. This Pilgrim was killed shortly after his foot stepped onto Holy Land soil.

An army of fanatical men heard the singing of the thirty marching Pilgrims and surrounded them. With no warning the sound of the voices praising God were extinguished and the bodies were left on the ground. Shortly the next group of passing Pilgrims found them and buried them.

Constance concluded with the words, "It took months for the news of my husband's death to reach me. I did not want Adam to go to such a dangerous place, but he was sure this was God's plan for his life. Then I would not accept the fact my husband was in the group of Pilgrims who were slain. My grief seemed inexhaustible once I accepted the fact Adam was gone.

"Elva was five when my husband died. She is now ten and I am just beginning to enter the stage where I feel like a whole person again."

Several times a day William would step into the room where the three were working to see how the copying was progressing and to offer suggestions. He usually ate the noonday meal with Constance, Naomi and Jacob.

Constantly new manuscripts would arrive with a rider coming from another Abbey. Then the four musicians would study the work to determine whether they should copy it and how to best distribute the work. Sometimes Constance was given a specific part to copy while other times she would be asked to write a descant to accompany the piece, or else to write a solo instrumental section as a prelude, or interlude, or postlude.

Some of the music required very close work as in it there were three voices constantly moving with word phrases of equal length, but at times the parts overlapped. From time to time other pieces required extra care due to triplet notes, known as quavers, or many chromatic accidentals (notes one-half step up or one-half step down).

Then selections would come along with their beauty being the complete simplicity of one voice singing a melody with no accompaniment. There were others slightly less plain with a second voice paralleling the melody. The second person would sing either a third, fourth, fifth, or sixth note higher than the melody.

The four musicians kept involved with many activities. Beside the practicing and playing for services, they enjoyed going to musical performances, fairs, plays and dinners together.

It wasn't very long before everyone could see the interest between William and Constance was more than that of two gifted musicians blending harmony together, more than friendship. They were in love.

Once William realized his heart condition and knew the love was reciprocal, he and Constance sat in Naomi and Jacob's sitting room to determine the future. They knew they must be very careful to prevent malicious gossip concerning the courtship. One thing they decided to do was to always be in the presence of others when they were together.

They did not want for one to visit the other alone in either of their homes in case someone would see them entering or leaving the other home and then spread rumors. Mutually they agreed the nuptials would be announced in two weeks and the wedding would take place in three months.

How the news spread once the engagement was announced. Plans began among all of William's students parents as to what would be appropriate gifts. Plans began among the Abbey clergy and teachers in ways to honor two people so devoted to church music. All kinds of gifts and festivities were talked about for the soon to be wedding. Even the royal students up in London made plans to come down to the nuptials.

King Edward I decided to give William and Constance a trip to Whales for their honeymoon.

With William being a bachelor, plus he and Constance having no family in Bath, all the members of the Abbey took it upon themselves to make the Speke wedding a memorable occasion. Originally the couple planned for a small wedding. Within a month the couple knew the plan would not be a sensible one. The word spread from mouth to mouth. It seemed the whole country was looking forward to witnessing the ceremony.

The Abbey's music staff volunteered to take care of all the decorating. The clergy took upon themselves the plans for the reception while friends held parties to shower the couple with gifts.

At last the September wedding date arrived and Constance's in-laws (by her deceased husband) came up from Somerset. However, before coming they sent a message offering to take Elva home with them for six months while William and Constance traveled on their honeymoon. Elva would even be staying in the home where she lived for the first ten years of her life. The girl looked forward to what she considered going home and seeing her old friends.

King Edward I and his twenty-two year old son Edward, plus their entourage came to the wedding. It was only natural for the king and his son to honor John with their presence at the ceremony, because for fifteen years William traveled north to teach young Edward and his siblings various musical instruments. The heir to the throne was now very proficient on the organ.

King Edward himself planned all the aspects of the honeymoon. He arranged for William to have a six-week absence from his duties at the Abbey. He arranged for the coach and horsemen and he arranged for lodging and meals. The bride and groom were to leave the day after the wedding.

William and Constance planned to spend their first night as husband and wife at the Speke home in Bath. With the reception lasting until late in the evening their arrival home was midnight. This night the terrible midnight loneliness William felt the previous Christmas Eve was gone. Instead the wonderment of the special wife God gave him and the exquisiteness of pure love fill him with joy.

Six a.m. was the usual waking time for both William and Constance, but not this morning. The clock reached eight before they opened their eyes.

Fog, which was not unusual, blanketed the area of Bath. The newlyweds felt thankful to see the fog because then there was no reason to get up and rush to travel. By ten a.m. most of the fog lifted and sunny patches began to appear. The household servants began to load the carriage with baggage for the couple's tour through Wales.

At the present time the bickering between England and Wales was calm. For the past twenty-five years the Welsh people kept revolting against king Edward's demands for their allegiance to him. In a 1292 battle Edward subdued the Welsh, and while the people there still remained angry the conflict ceased.

So the trek northwest began. Some evenings a camp was set up. Some evenings a village or town became the place of lodging. Other nights a castle or vicarage housed the party. There was no need to rush to be at any particular spot at any specific time and how restful this seemed. King Edward did notify subjects along the route to be prepared to house or feed the travelers when they passed through. William and Constance would be treated like royalty.

Constance kept a diary in which the delights of travel were recorded. The first place noted was the quaint city of Birmingham. Because the place was not located on a waterway there was no heavy traffic from maritime trade. Instead they found quaint shops with personally made hand-goods and a few small manufacturing companies.

The newly married couple spent two days browsing in the shops, meeting townspeople and relaxing in a scenic park. After the restful time the caravan of servants, with all kinds of equipment, plus the carriage in which William and Constance rode continued westward toward Wolverhampton.

When the party drew closer to the town they noticed cart after cart of potatoes, carrots, turnips, beets and cabbages being hand pushed into Wolverhampton. Once into the center of town no one could miss the huge market with briskly trading stalls.

Along side of the market William told the driver to stop the carriage. He and Constance wanted to spend the afternoon wandering through this area while observing all the activity and listening to the trading. During the time the two lovers moseyed through the many stalls the coachmen went on to contact the manager of the Inn to let him know they were in town. Then they too were free for the rest of the day to enjoy the town's activities.

More travel was planned for the next day and they hoped to reach the English — Welsh border town of Schrewsbury. The beauty of the Abbey in this town was well known. The edifice was built by Roger do Montgamer and displaying all the grandeur of Norman architecture.

King Edward at one time saw to having a castle constructed for his use in Schrewsbury and this is where the party lodged for the weekend. William and Constance looked forward to worshipping in the Abbey on Sunday morning.

They were not disappointed. The beauty of the house of worship appeared very God honoring and the sermon touched William and Constance's hearts. But the music was what impressed them so. Naturally, being musically inclined them selves this area of worship would either bless them, or leave them cold. The obviously trained voices, the harmonic blend and beautiful tones brought tears to the couple's eyes.

For the rest of the day a peace and a joy filled the couple's hearts and because of these emotions there was enhanced pleasure in meeting the townspeople and great enjoyment in the scenery around the castle.

When the party departed from Schrewsbury the next destination was to be the coastal town of Caernarfon. The arrival to this location was what the newlyweds most looked forward to and beautiful Indian summer weather enhanced the travel. The mild sunshine through the hill country of Wales seemed a most romantic setting for the honeymooners.

Frequent stops to explore villages, or to talk to local people added more pleasure. The party camped for a few days where the highest mountains in all of England were located. One day William and Constance made their way up Glyder Fawr. The higher they climbed the more magnificent the view became. From several spots they could see all the way to Caernefon Bay.

A few miles from the city the traveling party came upon another carriage traveling in the same direction and containing a local nobleman. As William's carriage drew alongside of the other vehicle he began to chat with the occupants. First names were exchanged, and then William mentioned he and Constance were on their honeymoon and traveling to spend a few days in the castle at Caernarfon.

The response was, "You mean Llywelyn, Prince of Wales castle?" In unison William and Constance spoke, "No, King Edward's castle."

Chapter 7

Anger came over the other man's face. He snorted, "That snake!" In a sneering voice he shouted, "Back in '92 he killed Llywelyn, then possessed our former Prince's home. To make it worse, nine years later his son Edward was born in our Prince's castle and your king gave the title of Prince of Wales to his son and future heir. Fury blazed in the man's eyes when he ordered his driver to hasten the horses' pace and to pull ahead.

William's party continued on at the regular trot and arrived at the Castle in the middle of the afternoon. The first place the newlyweds wanted to go was up to every balcony and overlook the vista in all directions. The panoramic views of country and coastline were awesome.

The two newlyweds spent a week of relaxing days in the castle. Some days William and Constance rode horseback up and down the coastline, which changed from sand to rocks and back to sand again. Other days they walked hand in hand along the shoreline.

One day a storm raged and the couple rode a horse down to the rocks to view the pounding water crash over them.

Some afternoons the couple walked out of Edward's stronghold and over the moat to meander through the streets outside of the castle. A few of the days the gates of the city wall were left open for the men who were pushing carts of fresh vegetables into the city to fill the market stalls. At this time William and Constance would go through the gates and on out into the country-side.

On Sunday morning the whole Speke party walked to worship in the little Celtic church built in the fifth century. The service was conducted in the familiar Latin, as was the rule for all churches. The common use of one church language made possible the Welsh speaking townspeople and the English-speaking visitors to all understand what was being said in worship.

Even though the church was small, the music was harmonious, as was the custom with the Welsh people.

Only one of the men traveling with William and Constance spoke the language of the Welsh people. He always accompanied anyone who needed to contact the townspeople for any reason.

Many visitors traveled to and from Caernarfon because of it being the capitol of North Wales. Then too, visitors were drawn to the city to sightsee Roman fort built hundreds of year's earlier/ . A few of the afternoons William and Constance would wander through the fort because of their fascination with the history of the old citadel. Usually they heard someone speaking English on the grounds and they would go over to chat with them.

The last day at the castle turned stormy and cold. Because it was not a pleasant day to be outside William sent his interpreter to the Celtic church to ask if it would be possible for the Spekes to browse through the church music material. Permission was granted and the couple spent the afternoon in the church's choir room.

Two pieces of music seemed meaningful and beautiful enough to be worth copying to take home to Bath. William went to find the little church's music director to ask permission to copy the motets. The director was completely surprised at the request. One reason being he was the person who composed both pieces. Then too people were not usually so gracious as to ask permission. They just went ahead and copied them. Being especially pleased the director responded by nodding his head, "Yes, and responding in Welch, "Help yourself."

The return to Bath was delayed for a day and a half for several reasons; one was because of the time it took to copy the six and four page manuscripts. This was just as well as it gave time for the storm to pass. The day of departure dawned with the last of the clouds scuttling across the sky. By ten a.m. the sun came out and the expanse above became exceptionally blue.

But even with the sun's appearance the air was crisp and cold. Constance went looking through the castle to find spare wool shawls to wrap around themselves in the open carriage.

Traveling south the road wound them close to the water from time to time. The travelers saw waves still crashing on the rocks. Also on the beach as the water remained angry from the storm. Other times they traveled over rolling hills.

Before entering the old Roman walled town of Aberdovey the party camped at the Pen Dinas hill overlooking the town. A day was spent inspecting the iron-age earth works located on the hill and another day for inspecting the town itself.

Leisurely the party headed east with their objective being to spend a few days in Gloucester to view the remnants of the old Roman colony called Glevum. Then travel on home to Bath.

At this time a messenger was sent on ahead to let William's home staff know the approximate time of their arrival. What William and Constance did not know was there was a surprise homecoming planned for them by the church people.

When William and Constance opened their front door they saw people everywhere. A fun time followed for two hours. Constance said, "This is what it must be like when a person is welcomed into heaven."

After the last guest departed Constance was handed a message from her brother-in-law down in Somerset. In it he told how happy Elva was living with them. He said the child cried every time anything was mentioned about her returning to Bath and the note ended with how he and his wife enjoyed having Elva with them, plus how good she was with their little ones. They would not mind their niece continuing to live with them.

Constance broke out into tears and William enfolded her in his arms. He whispered in her ear, "We will need to talk this over and pray about it."

After several weeks of heartache William and Constance decided it would be best to leave Elva with her relatives in Somerset, at least until she would willingly come to live with them.

In the next few years there were times when Elva would come to visit, but she always returned back what she considered her home in Somerset.

John Edward Speke (named after his grandfather) was born to William and Constance on the same day when the town-crier declared the death of king Edward I. The baby was a handsome, big fellow; weighing in at 11 pounds, 8 ounces. Shortly after the baby's birth William needed to leave his wife and son to attend the coronation of his royal pupil. He had no fear of leaving them such a short time after the baby's birth, because they would be in the care of the faithful household servants. William was to be away for a week.

As soon as the new father arrived in London he went to Westminster Abbey to begin practicing on their organ to play for the coronation ceremony. At the reception following Edward the second's crowning most of the conversation centered on the circumstances of the former king Edward's death.

Once more England and Wales were at war and again King Edward I led his troops, but this time he was killed during a battle.

William kept thinking how fortunate he, Constance, and all of the party were, in that there were no outbreaks during the time they were in Wales on their honeymoon. Then he remembered the few times some resentment could be felt in the way people acted toward them when they realized the party was from England.

Before the coronation there were a few times William was alone with the soon to be King Edward II. All the young man wanted to talk about was how inadequate he felt stepping into his father's shoes. Edward believed he had no gift in war strategy.

This weighed heavily upon him, especially with the conflict between Wales and England still continuing. The new king knew his gifts were in the arts, and he also knew such qualities were not greatly appreciated in the ruler of a country.

William tried to encourage Edward in the fact he did have good military leaders who could be depended upon for accurate decisions. The mentor advised his pupil there would only occur problems if he insisted upon making military decisions himself.

Upon arriving home William found his wife crying. He exclaimed, "Darling, what is wrong; are you all right; is our baby all right?" And ran to enfold Constance in his arms.

Through tears and sniffing the sordid story tumbled out about Elva being caught stealing down in Somerset. Constance said, "My brother-in-law paid the fine in order for Elva to not be put in prison. Now she is being escorted back here, and should be arriving later today."

William consoled his wife for a while, and then said, "I would like to see our son. They walked hand in hand into the nursery where William greeted the baby's attendant. Constance gently pulled back the cover to show the perfect little sleeping child. Tears came to William's eyes as he silently whispered a thank you to the Lord for the gift of a child this late in his life.

As William and Constance walked back to the sitting room for a cup of tea he said, "After tea I will go out to meet Elva, but first I need to spend a few minutes at the Abbey to see how things are going there."

Once William walked into the music room Jacob and Naomi rushed toward him with smiles on their faces. Naomi said, "Tell your good wife her prayers have been answered. We are going to have a child."

William congratulated them, but the main thought filling his mind was how best to remedy the problem now entering into his life. He decided perhaps it might be helpful to teach Elva how to play the organ and how to be involved in transcribing music, plus to have her mother teach her how to play the harp. The objective was to never let Elva out of their sight.

In the distance Elva noted the familiar figure coming toward her Uncle and her. She determined to greet him with a smile in order for her stepfather to never know how much she hated him. She thought he would be deceived and she could get away with things not possible if he knew her true feelings.

William greeted Elva and her uncle. Then he assisted her over to his vehicle and returned to the uncle to reimburse him for the fine he paid due to Elva's theft.

As William and Elva traveled toward home she sat in silence. He began talking about the opportunities before Elva in learning all the aspects of home management and child-care.

Elva thought, "Yes, all my aunt and uncle wanted me for was to help around their home and take care of babies."

Then William pointed out to her how fortunate she was to have a mother who was able to teach her how to read, to write and to understand numbers; something most girls were not taught.

Next William filled Elva's ears with the plan for her present teenage years. As she listened to the ideas of all the things this hated man wanted her to learn in regards to music she thought "boring."

All the time the stepfather talked Elva watched his hands. He finally asked, "What seems so interesting about my hands?" Her reply was, "The ring" and she also thought, "What big hands."

With the outskirts of Bath in view William told her the story of the ring; beginning with how it had been given to the Speke named Walter. He concluded with, "One day I will pass it on to your baby brother. In Elva's mind came, "If you ever take it off I will get a hold of it and you will never see it again."

Elva was surprised over how much she enjoyed her music lessons, plus working with Jacob and Naomi. In time she wanted to spend most of her free hours at the organ.

Chapter 7

The loving care poured on Elva began to permeate her hard shell of hatred. She began to realize how caring William and her mother were. Elva became less angry and her business with music lessened her desire to destroy things. By sixteen years of age she determined to yield herself to be of service to God and her attitude about life completely changed.

Ever since William became an adult he chose to no longer use the French spelling for his last name. The Le Espek was returned to the original spelling of Speke.

Chapter 8

May 1430

The Vicar, Micah Marshall, stood in front of his St. Andrews Abby congregation to make an announcement. First he cleared his throat and then said, "Please give me your attention. I am standing here to give the official notice of an up-coming wedding. In six weeks time our own Joan Keynes will be marrying John Speke Esq., son of Sir William and Constance Speke of Bath. John, who has been living in London, will be coming to reside in Dowlish Wake.

John is a lawyer and administrator of oaths. He will continue this profession in our community as well as helping Jane to manage the manor she inherited from her parents."

A murmur of approval sounded in the Abbey as many parishioners thought about the young man, who in the past months came courting Jane. They began to look forward to the coming nuptials and to welcome John into their midst.

By London standards the wedding would be considered small. By Dowlish Wake standards the planned wedding would be the event of the century. Members of the Speke family would be coming from many northern locations. Every person in the small community of Dowlish Wake would be present. Even people from the surrounding area of Somerset would travel to the village to attend the ceremony and reception. One thing the Abbey members felt confident about was that whoever came would be blessed seeing the lovely restoration of the of the old church. The old site was completely rebuilt and refurbished under the direction of Joan's father Thomas Keynes.

On June 30th many beautiful garlands of flowers adorned the interior of St. Andrews. The wonderful floral odor and the beauty to everyone's eyes made the wedding occasion memorable for the friends and family of John and Joan.

After the reception the bride and groom entered a carriage to carry them south toward the port of Weybourne. Their intention was to stay in this seaside town for several weeks in John's lovely waterfront home. Following the time at the shore they would return to live in Joan's manor close to Dowlish Wake.

As many newlyweds desire to do so were the days for John and Joan. They took long walks along the shoreline and they often stopped to sit and gaze at the water. The two of them were constantly holding hands, or in each other's arms or looking into each other's eyes. The bride and groom were able to talk and share their likes and dislikes, their longings and their dreams.

When the two of them walked along Weybourne's Warf they would reminisce about how their first meeting came in this area along the side of one of the ships. John memory dwelt about how Joan's lovely quiet gentleness immediately drew him to her. Joan thought about how she was impressed with John's handsome features with the dark hair and eyes, plus his business-like-manor.

Part of Joan's family's livelihood was the raising of sheep and they were involved in the wool industry. When she first started to help in the business there would be times she would need to accompany their manager to Weybourne in order to learn about the process of exporting the wool.

For many generations John's family owned ships and in these days they were being used in the import - export trade.

Weybourne was one of the ports the Speke family used to load or unload their ships.

From time to time John needed to travel to one of the ports to work out a problem. Almost two years before the wedding John was in Weybourne on business to oversee the Keynes family paper work for loading the wool on one of his ships. John met Joan in his office and almost immediately a correspondence courtship began.

Fond memories filled the newlyweds each time they walked along the water. Around the end of one of their walks John loudly said, "It's a dingy." Way out in the water a tiny spot could be seen riding the top of the wave. The spot would disappear from time to time and then reappear on the crest of the next wave.

All along the waterfront people could be seen rushing towards the wharf. John and Joan joined them to wait for the time when the dingy approached close enough to be of help to the people in it, and soon they saw there were twelve occupants.

Everyone knew when a dingy approached with no anchored ship out in the water it probably contained sailors weary from much rowing. They were usually the only men left from a shipwreck, or a ship captured by pirates.

In the distance shouts were heard. Some shouts from the occupants were just those of relief over seeing land while other sailors were shouting, "The French, it was the French." However, to those on the wharf nothing could be understood as the sounds were all garbled together.

Closer and closer the craft approached. John whispered to Joan, "Look they only have one oar." Immediately John knew the ship did not sink. It was seized, because Pirates only allowed one oar to dingy occupants. Without two oars the dingy would be much slower reaching land and the ship would have more time to get away with the cargo.

A dingy was designed to allow two men to sit side by side, except in the bow, where only one could sit. The boats usually held four or six oars with which the men used to paddle. With only one oar the man on the right side of the boat would take a stroke, then pass the oar to the man on his left to take one stroke; a terribly slow, time consuming procedure.

Finally, the dingy pulled up onto the beach and the town's people gathered around the gaunt, exhausted men who were sitting in the boat. With compassion they were helped out while all along the men kept repeating, "It was the French. The French did this to us. Our keel was filled with rugs and blankets and now everything is all gone."

John and Joan asked everyone gathered to please assist them in helping the weary men up to their house. John mentioned, "We will feed them and care for them until they are strong enough to go to their own homes."

Everyone offered their arms for support, and they were heavily leaned upon, while helping the emaciated men walk the short distance to the Speke residence. Two of the men actually needed to be carried because they were so weak.

The newlyweds hurried home ahead of the others in order to give their household staff notice to prepare food and bedding for twelve men.

After the men were fed and rested for a few days they began talking about the ordeal they just experienced. Townspeople, government officials, shipping officials, plus the local sailors all came to listen to the story which began, "Around two in the morning most of our ship's crew were asleep, except for about a half dozen of us who could not sleep and we were up on deck."

And the story went on, "We didn't hear anything until all of a sudden one of our men yelled, 'Help" and then the beating with clubs began. The men sleeping in their bunks throats were slit, and those who were alerted enough to fight were also killed. The twelve of us who were unconscious from the head blow were thrown into the dingy along with only three days worth of food and a couple jugs of water. We have been attempting to get home for almost two weeks.

The pirates who attacked were very quiet, except once or twice one of them spoke. He seemed to be the leader, and his speech revealed they were French."

The story ended with every one sitting in silence. Then one of the officials broke the silence with, "What sense does it make for one ship to attack another ship when both of them are under the rule of the same monarch, our monarch king Henry VI? Don't they realize they are defeating themselves; their monitory system?"

Then everyone started speaking. The topics began with the fact of pirates being only interested in profit for them selves, and not in a country's profit. They ranged on to the impossibility of nine-year-old king Henry VI being able to reign over both England and France. Lastly an argument developed over the council of lords and senior administrators. Some thought the council was wise in the way they governed for the child king, while others objected to the policies the council put in place in both England and over seas.

The discussions, opinions, suggestions and arguing continued for the whole afternoon and the exhausted seamen were glad to see the group finally leave.

John and Joan caringly provided for the sailors until they were ready to go home. One by one, with profuse thankfulness the men left.

Once the newlyweds were settled into their home in Dowlish Wake John's main interest centered in overseeing the building of a comfortable barn to house his many horses. The hobby of breeding and training various types of horses began when John was a teenager. Now, with his being close to thirty years of age the expansion of the various breeds would need a very large building to house them all.

As John began to figure the number of Thoroughbred, Arabian and Draft horses he owned, and with all of the foals born in the spring, he quickly realized one barn would not be practical, nor would it be sufficient. The final plans called for three smaller barns with each housing one of the breeds.

John kept close tabs on the construction of the stalls within the barns to make sure they would be comfortable for the differing measurements of each breed. This purpose was to prevent the horse any stress. He also monitored the placing of the shelf for hay and grain depending upon the height of the breed.

The next big push was to bring his ninety horses and thirty-two foals (all two to three months old) the many miles from outside London to Dowlish Wake and the trip must be kept at a reasonable pace to prevent the young ones from tiring.

The draft horses were brought southwest in two bunches with the stallions coming first, and then the mares following with the fourteen foals. These strong, heavy animals were well suited to carry knights with their weighty armor, or to pull artillery, or coaches.

Next came the Arabian horses. They too were driven in two groups along with the eleven foals. The breed was trained for hunting, for jumping competitions, and to pull light two wheeled carriages

The last group, the thoroughbred horses were John's favorites. He kept the herd to twenty adult animals with this spring's addition of seven foals.

Horse training and the history of the countries known for their horsemanship was a part of John's interests. He tried to sustain the knowledge through the thoroughbreds, even to the naming of the foals after a city, or country, or person within such a country. The seven new foals were named Susa, Caesar, Hittite, Rome, Asseria, Greece and Persia.

All of the building and transporting of animals took two years and an exciting celebration was given at the work's completion.

Two months later an even more exciting event took place when baby John Jr. was born. Joan experienced no complications during the pregnancy, or the birth itself. She quickly regained strength and found great joy in caring for her tiny son. This little one seemed always hungry. He slept well, but as soon as he woke little John thought it was time to eat again and again before he went back to sleep. His sturdy little body grew stronger and stronger. In ten months time he was crawling around and getting into things.

In the meantime John Senior's law practice thrived well in the Somerset area.

Then he was approached by the government officials and asked if he would consider becoming sheriff.

The idea was appealing and John prayed about the matter. He thought being outside and on horseback would be a better life than inside an office or courtroom, but he didn't want feelings to be the sole factor in a decision. He told the officials, "I will consider your proposition and seek God's guidance for a few weeks. Then you will receive my decision."

John felt a perfect peace over becoming a sheriff and his final answer was, "Yes." He never would regret the decision. Enforcing the law, plus working-out peaceful decisions in squabbles and fights took part of each day.

Then there was also the continued management over his shipping trade and from time to time Joan would need her husband's assistance with managing the sheep herds and wool sales.

Despite John's busy life he always found some time each day (when he was home) to be with little John. Often it was in the late afternoon and out with the horses.

Before little John could even toddle John Sr. would have the baby on horseback with him.

Then when the boy reached three years of age his father allowed him to sit by himself in the saddle while the horse stood still, or else while being led around by an adult. John Sr. began to teach the little one all about correct riding procedures.

The first thing taught was how to mount the horse and it was always from the left side of the animal. When little John questioned, "Why this side?" He was told because the horse was trained for the knights to mount the horse on the left side. Again another, "Why?" John's father replied with a question, "On which side does a knight wear his sword?" When the boy answered, "The left side." Then the father asked, "Could a knight swing his left leg, with the sword hanging there, over the horse's back?" "No", said little John. "All right" his father answered. "Now, you pretend you are a knight and you must get on the horse so your right leg can swing over the back." From then on the little boy would go to the left side of the horse to mount.

Next began a prolonged teaching about horses. Each day John Sr. would make sure his son learned one fact about a proper riding method, or a fact about the breed he was sitting on, or a fact about the job of training a horse. Once little John was mounted the first question asked him was, "What is the name of this horse and why is he named that?"

Depending upon the horse the boy was sitting on the answer would be,

"Blaze, because of the large white patch on the face."

"Star, because of the white patch on the forehead."

"Sock, because of the white patch above the foot."

"Baldface, because the face is mostly white."

"Race, because of the narrow white strip down the face."

"Snip, because of the white patch near the nuzzle."

John learned a sire was a father, a mare a mother, a foal a baby, and more and more information.

By the time the boy was six years of age he was an exceptionally good little rider. By eight years, young John could ride in competitions and often won the race.

During these years John Sr. realized more every day that the shipping business was calling him away from home. Soon he knew he must resign from being sheriff in order to more closely monitor the ships. Piracy at sea and what it entailed was becoming an all-consuming problem, and John felt the need to be on board the sailing ships. From time to time he would act as captain on his ship Stallion, while other times he would be on board just to give advice in a problem.

In the back of John's mind lay the tale of the forlorn sailors at Waybourne. In order to prevent the sudden capture at night John posted extra night watchmen from dusk to dawn on every trip.

The officials in government kept pressing King Henry IV for better control of the sea and to declare a war on piracy. Meeting after meeting took place with the outcome being a decision to appoint privateer men who would go searching for pirates in order to capture them.

John was one of the first appointed with this commission because of his previous service in London to the king and also as a sheriff down in Dowlish Wake. The fact he owned and managed a shipping company that allowed him the use of vessels also played a part in the decision.

Before John Esq. went full time to sea as a Privateer he took the Speke ring and gave it to Joan for safekeeping. He did not feel it would be wise to wear on shipboard with the possibility of it being stolen if he was captured or killed by pirates. The ring would be lost to the family if that happened.

The Speke Shipping Company consisted of ten ships constantly plying trade between England, Europe and the Fareast. John took one of the ships and refurbished her for the sole purpose of attacking and capturing pirate ships. With the Stallion ship being one of the first privateers on the seas, any confrontation the pirate ships met came as a complete surprise to them.

Fighting was fierce, men were lost on both sides, ships were sunk and ships managed to get away. However John's vessel was able to capture pirate after pirate. The Speke privateer became well known among the French, Spanish and Scottish pirates who made it a practice to make great profit from English ships.

In June of 1642 a pirate ship was sighted. However the wind was making it impossible for John's ship to approach the vessel because the seas were high.

The Stallion kept tracking the pirate for hour after hour. Finally the storm started to abate and this allowed the waves to not be as fierce. The possibility of boarding another ship without damage to the Speke ship finally presented itself.

Each person on the pirate ship knew who owned the privateer tracking them and they were prepared to fight to their utmost. They all held a weapon in both hands and some even held a third weapon, a knife, between their teeth.

The man-to-man fighting was terrible. John and the pirate captain met eye-to-eye, then sword to sword. Both were good swordsmen and one did not seem more to the advantage than the other. It was a match to the death, when a young pirate crept behind John's back and stabbed him in the heart.

John died on the spot and all the pirates shouted, "It's done."

Such an action was considered against all rules of battle. Even pirates observed the rule of face to face, one swordsman against one swordsman fighting. The evil plot to attack from behind was planned before John ever set foot on the pirate ship. The plan was made with a pact among pirates to rid the seas of John Speke.

Great anger filled the minds of the Stallion men. To kill a man from behind when he was fighting "face to face" broke all rules of fighting. No matter what army, or navy where in a battle took place, (among noblemen, or ruffians), such conduct was permitted. The all-consuming anger drove John's men to quickly overcome the pirates.

The body of John was placed in a blanket and carried back onto the Stallion to be taken home. John Speke Esq. was buried in a crypt in the sanctuary of St. Andrews Abbey in Dowlish Wake. The church he actively attended and the one Jane's parents founded.

Through out young John's growing years he became more and more like his father, even toward an occupation in law. However, John's propensity toward horsemanship exceeded that of his father, especially in the area of entering jumping competitions.

A course filled with stone wall obstacles of varying sizes and shapes was constructed on the Speke property in order for John to spend some time each day perfecting his control and ease of leading the horse toward and over the different jumps.

His skill became so exceptional he was invited to the various horse competitions, and he usually won.

At nineteen years of age, John was attending a jumping competition in Whitelackington where he was introduced to an Alice Beauchamp, daughter of Sir John Beauchamp and niece of Sir Thomas Beauchamp. Alice, at twenty-two years of age still resided with her mother and three of her brothers at the Gloucester castle. From the time of her father's death her oldest brother Thomas managed the castle. The next three brothers were magnates in Warchester and the two youngest, Aaron and Joshua were very involved with horse training. They were attending the jumping competition in order to compete.

During the next year Aaron and Joshua were involved in every competition John was involved with, and Alice usually accompanied her brothers to the tracks. She often sat with the three men at the banquets following the afternoon of jumping.

At some point during the evening the topic of politics almost always entered the conversation of the men. All of them were thankful for the marriage of king Henry VII to Elizabeth, daughter of Edward IV, because the joining of the York and Tudor lines ended the War of the Roses between the houses of York and Lancaster.

Next, opinions began to fly over the giving of grants of money or property by the king to royal dependents, or men he favored. Those who favored the action always talked about how certain people deserved the grant. Others used examples of how the money or property was misused as a reason to stop the giving of grants. Still others pointed out how the king would accuse the grant receiver of treason when they fell out of favor with him. Once again the topic went around with some men pointing out the reason why the treason accusation was true, while others explained why it was unjust.

Several times Alice told the story about her Uncle Thomas who was one of the people honored by the king with a grant of property. A few years later Thomas, the earl of Ros, spoke out against one of the plans the king was trying to put into action. Thomas was accused of treason.

Eight years after Thomas' death the king issued a pardon from treason to Eleanor, the widow of Thomas. Seven years later a papal dispensation was granted to the deceased Thomas.

At the end of the grant discussion someone always spoke up for the king. The gist of the defense centered in the fact of king Henry's diplomatic ability in regards to matters of government. They agreed some of the king's actions (such as the "personal grant" was not wise) but his overall management of diplomatic problems kept the country united and constantly increasing in wealth.

John began to think of Alice as more than the sister of a friend. The attention seemed reciprocal and soon John began riding to Whitelackington quite often. Within two years time John and Alice knew they were meant for each other and married. Their one and only child, John III, was born in 1455.

In 1483 Sir John and his son John III were both competing at the London racetrack and King Henry VII was in attendance. About halfway through one of the races the younger John noticed a group of burly men attempting to get close to the king. The men looked aggravated and ready for trouble.

The two Johns, plus several other riders who were not involved with the present race began to make their way toward the area where trouble would soon be brewing. As the group strode toward the king's booth they advised other knights along the way about what seemed impending. One after another of the knights joined with the Spekes and their men. They reached the king just a few seconds before the angry snarling group did, but chose not to lash out right away just to make sure something evil was planned.

Out of the corner of the older John's eye he saw a man with a knife in his hand rushing toward the king and John yelled. Both of the John's hurled themselves forward; one to grab the man's hand while the other grabbed the man's body to wrestle him to the ground. The knights began to attack the whole gang to gain control of them and in a few minutes succeeded.

Following the incident Sir John Speke called the knights together to discuss the need for protection of the King. They decided to form a committee in order to plan for the creation of a guard. By 1485 the corps of the Yeomen of the Guard was in place. Sir John Speke, John III and young John IV all were in attendance for the dedication service of the Yeomen of the Guard.

The Captain, Lieutenant and Ensign were peers appointed from the military. Also appointed was a clerk of the cheque and four erons who served as messengers, Sergeant majors and guards of the bedchamber. Then one hundred privates became an active part of the corps.

Their dress code, common to the day, consisted of red tunics striped with purple and gold lace. The knee britches were red as well as the stockings. Each Yeoman's neck was encased in a ruff and on his head sat a plumed hat. They carried a guilt halberd and wore an ornamental sword.

From this time on the king's castle contained Yeomen in most of the rooms as well as posted on guard outside of the building. The Guard surrounded the king's coach where it traveled, and when the king was on foot the men encircled him.

Five years later John IV stood at attention before queen Catherine and he wondered why he had been summoned. John bowed his head in honor to the monarch and waited for her to speak.

Catherine said, "Come closer" and she studied John for a while. Finally she said, "I have decided to commission into your care the welfare of my maid-in-waiting Alice.

It is necessary for her to travel back to Toledo, Spain due to the illness of her father. You are to guard her with your life on this trip and keep in control the men who will be traveling with you."

Two weeks later John (with a company of twenty men) and Alice departed London with the plan to travel by ship to Lisbon, Portugal. Then they would ride overland into Spain and on to Toledo.

This was John's first time away from England, and while on the sea the beauty of the ocean with the mild April weather filled him with pleasure. As the ship sailed into Lisbon's lovely harbor all of the passengers were lined up on deck to catch the impressiveness of the majestic walled city with a fortress sitting high above.

John, Alice and the men were invited into the fortress for a few days to meet with Portuguese noblemen and to enjoy their hospitality. Alice especially appreciated the break as most of the days while on shipboard she was slightly nauseated. In the mean time the men spent their hours making arrangements for comfortable transportation through the mountains and on to Spain's capitol city of Toledo.

Eighteen days later the English party stopped high on a bluff to view the city of Alice's heritage. A palace, fortress and rising Cathedral impressively sat across the chasm on another bluff.

John stared for a while, then quietly said," It reminds me of the stories I heard passed through one generation after another concerning an ancestor's visit to Masada in Israel. That city seemed inaccessible, but Toledo appears even more so with the water encircling three sides of the bluff's base."

Then in a louder voice he said, "Tonight we will camp at the base and tomorrow morning begin the steep climb up the path to the Toledo."

Hour after hour passed while the group from England climbed. They did not reach the homes on the lowest edge of the city until late in the afternoon and there was still higher ground to be climbed before the castle itself could be reached.

In a small cabin next to the castle gate Alice pushed-in a door to see her father. The man lay semiconscious on his bed with one of the king's servants sitting next to him.

Alice's eyes filled with tears as she saw the state of her father and listened to his labored breathing. The servant said, "I'm so glad you are here. Your father has been asking for you for months." The young woman thanked the servant for his faithful care and then said, "Please tell the king I am here and I will be staying as long as my father is alive."

Arrangements were made for John and his men to stay in several of the other huts close to the gate and they were all invited into the castle for meal times. Some evenings two of the men would stay with Alice's father while she joined the others in the castle for dinner. Other evenings Alice would make dinner and invite John, with his men, to join her.

Almost every day the men would walk around the town square and often John, or one of his men, would stay with Alice's father for a while in the afternoon in order for her to be able to have time outside. One place they were all interested in viewing was the daily construction going on of the beautiful Toledo Cathedral; every day the massive structure rose higher. The Bishop's residence was also located on the town square along with a government building and shops.

Constantly being in the palace and among the town people John and his men heard about the many problems the Spanish people were having with the Moors. These Muslim people pushed north from Africa and they were in the process of trying to capture the land of Spain for themselves.

The Moors would overrun one of Spain's cities, then the Spanish king would send troops and recapture the town. This continued fighting seemed endless.

With Alice being home her father seemed to gain strength. There were even times he would get out of bed to sit and look out the window. After the few days up the elderly man would once more become bed ridden and even return to the state she found him in when she first arrived home. Once more he would become strong and the cycle continued week after week.

The time in Toledo was now extending into months. Often in the evening John and his men would sit around to talk about Spain's war with the Moors. One after another the men gave suggestions as to how to best remedy the problem. At the end of one evening all 21 men felt they wanted to be any help they could be to the country they were visiting.

A few days later John went before king Ferdinand to offer the assistance of his men. The king responded with thankfulness; especially with a plan now being formed to drive the Moors completely out of Spanish lands and back to Africa.

For a decade the Muslim invaders lived in the southern town of Grenada and even built the Alhambra palace there for their Sultan. During the present conflict many militant Moor fighters were congregated in and around the city.

King Ferdinand sent the notice "Come fight" to many Spanish cities. Day after day more and more troops responded to the notice and the new soldiers continually gathered at the base of Toledo. After hundreds of troops (with their weapons) gathered the trek south was ready to begin.

John very stiffly went to Alice to tell her he would he would be back to help care for her father as soon as her homeland was safe to live in. The stiff front was because John didn't want to give into the desire to take Alice in his arms and tell her he loved her.

Little did he realize Alice would begin crying as soon as he walked out the door. She cared deeply for John and she feared he would be injured or killed.

The next morning a vast army of men marched south across the barren, arid plain. For two weeks soldiers on horses and the walking men spread across the land. Moor scouts caught sight of the army and dashed south to warn the people in Grenada.

Many Muslims chose to flee back to North Africa. Included in the mass exodus was the Sultan, his family and servants. Still a good armored presence remained in Grenada with the hope of repelling the Spanish soldiers.

Little did the military inhabitants of Grenada realize other Christian countries were notified of the coming battle and knights from these countries would be joining with the Spanish army. There was a good 1500 additional men from England, Germany and France tramping south by the time Grenada could be sighted in the distance.

Several days of fierce fighting ensued and there were many casualties on both sides. However the multitude of Spanish soldiers with their allies insured victory for them.

The Muslim men who survived were allowed time to give proper burial for the dead. Then they were escorted down to North Africa.

The Spanish army remained in Grenada to protect the city from any further attack. There were many lovely vacant homes and in time the families of the soldiers were brought to live in the homes with them.

The Alhambra Palace with the beautiful gardens was kept in its attractive condition in order for it to be used as a place of residence for any visiting Spanish royalty. The city's lovely sub-tropical temperature with spectacular snow-capped mountains in the distance would be a drawing card for their holidays.

The knights from other countries began to return home. John and his men traveled north toward Toledo while other of their countrymen went west to board ships from Lisbon, Portugal to reach England.

Two nights before John and his men began their ascent up the cliff side to Toledo Alice's father died in his sleep. He was lying-in-state in the Cathedral when John knocked on Alice's door. A teary-eyed woman met him and John took her in his arms. He could see her father was not in the house.

Sir John Speke, the fourth, of White Lackington and Alice were married in England the following spring.

John Speke (the fifth) of White Lackington was born the following year. He married Joan, the heir of John Winnisard Esq. of Devonshire. The next generation also produced a Sir John Speke (the sixth) who married Alice, daughter of Sir John Arundel of Cornwal.

Chapter 9

Year 1609

Thomas Speke (son of John the sixth) sat in his library deep in thought concerning his interest in the lives of the survivors of James Towne. Two years before three ships left England for the new land across the ocean. Two of the ships were owned by Thomas and carried 80 of the 120 people over the water. Now there were only 38 of those people living. Of the 62 now deceased, 40 of them grew-up in the area where Thomas lived and attended the same Abbey. They were people loved and appreciated. Thomas heart ached when he thought of the diseases, the extremely difficult living conditions, the hard work and the Indian attacks causing the decimation of the new town built on the James River.

As Thomas began praying for the lives of those remaining in James Towne a knock came on the library door. Thomas quietly said, "Come in," and in charged his fifteen-year old son Thomas II with excitement on his face. He said, "Father, the news has just come that a Virginia Company Armada is being formed and my squad has been assigned to accompany the ships. I must go."

Sheriff Thomas Sr. was shocked and it showed on his face. All he could think about was the terribleness of the dangers his son would face. However, with young Thomas having joined the military just a few months before there could be no question as to his being loyal to the command. The father knew his son would be of service any place he would be assigned and the new land definitely needed help.

The elder Speke put his arm around young Thomas and said, " I know the land across the sea beckons to you, but I am fearful for you and I'll constantly be praying for God's blessing upon you. Have you told Anne yet?"

Thomas assured his father about already speaking to Anne. "I have asked her to please wait for my return and in a few years when that takes place we will probably begin planning our wedding date. Then he asked, "Father, will any of your ships be a part of this second fleet of Virginia ships?" Thomas Sr. said he would probably offer the use of some ships depending upon the size of the fleet being sent. His plan immediately became to look into the need.

On the day of departure Thomas' brothers George and Christopher, his sister Alice, his father and Anne all came to the waters edge to bid him good-bye. As Thomas stepped into the dingy to take him out to the Sea Venture (his father's ship) tears began to flow from all of the eyes as they thought of the possibility of never seeing each other again.

The armada of nine ships looked grand as they set sail down the channel toward the Atlantic Ocean. There was a slight chop to the water, but from all indications the weather looked favorable.

Good weather did hold for two weeks. Then storm after storm hit with mountainous waves and high winds constantly shaking the sailing vessels. Men, women and children became violently sick. Some people only laid in their bunks and moaned day and night.

The first storm carried on for three days. Then two days of milder weather came, to be followed with another storm. So the weather pattern began and continued week after week.

The nine ships attempted to stay together, but it was difficult with visibility being very poor from fog, mist and sleeting rain. The immense waves with high winds didn't help them in seeing any other ships either. Sometimes fear arose over a ship sinking, but it was just in a gully between waves. Then an audible sigh went up when the vessel was sighted again on the top of a wave.

Following one terrible storm only eight ships were visible. The crews and passengers all hoped the missing ship was blown off course and eventually they would all meet again in James Towne.

This was not to be. The ship with all 60 of its passengers was swamped by one of the waves and sank. Everyone perished.

Almost 600 miles from the N. American continent another gale hit. It was the worst blow of them all making it practically impossible to control a sailing vessel. Nor could they be aware of the location of other ships.

Late in the afternoon the people on the Sea Venture began to hear an eerie screeching noise. With this noise Captain Somers knew they were close to an island called Ghost Island.

For a hundred years when ships plied across the Atlantic the people on board would often hear screeching as they passed this island. Quickly the rumor spread about the place being filled with ghosts. No one wanted to go ashore and they determined the place was inhabitable.

The storm's violence blew the Sea Venture closer and closer to the fearful island. Passengers put their hands over their ears in hopes of blocking out the sound.

Suddenly the ship shuddered and the realization came to the Captain the vessel was impaled upon a reef. He rushed out of the bridge and yelled, " We have hit a reef and are in desperate danger. Everyone must be gotten off of the ship. Call for everyone to come on deck and instruct them we are going to the island in the distance where the eerie sound is coming from."

The ship's bell was rung and the clanging noise drew everyone to the deck. Quickly people from every nook and cranny appeared to immediately grab hold of and hang onto the railing because of the high jolting waves.

All ten military men on board, including Thomas, began to load the women and children into a waiting dingy. Since there were only four of these small boats there were many passengers without a conveyance to shore. People were advised to wait for a dingy to return and many did, but in time one after another person would grab some floatable object and jump into the sea. The waves carried them bobbing to shore. Every once in a while, someone would jump overboard and start swimming toward the beach. Miraculously everyone made it to shore.

Of course all through this ordeal people kept praying for the Lord to protect them. Many who waited on deck would softly begin singing a hymn of praise and others would join in. Knowledge filled many people of the awesome fact that no one lost their life and this could be only a miracle.

The first concern of everyone on the beach was to find shelter from the storm. In order to smoothly fill this need, each military man was assigned twelve or fourteen passengers. Thomas was to oversee six men, two women and four children. He and the men quickly gathered driftwood to assemble a roof for the twelve passengers plus Thomas to gather under. All thirteen people huddled closely together against the nights chill and they were thankful to no longer have raindrops pelting them.

Before attempting sleep the group sang the Doxology in praise to God for sparing their lives and for the night's shelter.

At dawn everyone came out onto the beach to see blue sky and a much calmer sea. A shout of joy came from mouths as they looked out over the water and saw the Sea Venture not under water, but sitting high on a reef. It looked like there could one day be a possibility of getting off the island.

With sighting the Sea Venture Captain Somers appointed eight men to use the four dinghies to bring the kitchen supplies from the ship to the island in order for the breakfast and other meals to be prepared. In the meantime several men began to retrieve the driftwood from the beach and began a fire in order to cook a large pot of gruel (as soon as the first dingy arrived back from the ship with the oatmeal).

Much of the wood was soaking wet. However there were enough fairly dry pieces wedged underneath huge piles of the driftwood to begin the burning process.

After the satisfying hot meal in their stomachs Thomas and his six men met with all of the other men to do some planning. The first concern was food. It was apparent there would be abundant seafood, but to supplement that several men were selected to scout the island for edible plants and animals.

For the entire afternoon some men continued the dingy shuttle and brought supplies, possessions and most of the cartable items from the Sea Venture. Some men continued gathering wood with two purposes in mind; to construct more shelters and to have wood for fire.

The Johnson family of five and the Burman family of three, who were a part of Thomas' group began building themselves shelters next to the one they spent the previous night in. All agreed everyone would be more comfortable not so crowded.

Late in the afternoon men began to trickle back into camp; some were carrying the fish they caught and others were holding dandelion greens. With the potatoes brought from the Sea Venture everyone enjoyed a tasty dinner.

As everyone sat around the evening campfire the men who spent the afternoon scouting the island began to share what they discovered. Some talked about the abundant greenery and the possibility of edible plants. Other talked about the large number of a variety of edible birds. Some men remarked about seeing other islands a short distance from the one they were stranded on and expressed the desire to scout these islands as soon as a dingy was free to be used.

One man talked about being appointed to find the source of the terrible screeching noise (which actually sounded like a woman screaming). As he walked there were times the frightening sound seemed very close and other times it seemed high above. Toward the south end of the island the noise became louder and louder. Finally he came to a place where the cacophony of weird excruciating, almost deafening loud calls surrounded him. He was below a rookery of birds where the man's presence was frightening to the birds. Everyone felt relief when they heard the noise source was coming from nothing but birds.

Several of the men reported the fact they did not find any potable water. Every stream and pond they tasted they found the water was either salty, or brackish. Immediately the sense of fear could be felt transformed from the noise of the birds to what will we do with out water?

Captain Somers stood and said, "Of course the containers of water were brought from the ship during the afternoon and we have enough for a few days." Then the question was raised, "Well, what will we do when the water runs out?" The captain replied, "It depends on how much rain falls on this island." Thomas mentioned, "Maybe if we start praying we won't need to worry."

This second evening on the island one more topic discussed dealt with, was there any way possible for them to get off of the island With the ship in view many ideas were offered about how to get it off of the reef without sinking it, plus how to repair the damage.

For the men days became filled with hunting, fishing and gathering provisions for food. Fortunately men of all trades were among the group, so it seemed whatever needed to be done was taken care of.

Women took care the cooking, washing clothes, looking after the children, mending and other normal family tasks. Life became fairly comfortable causing most people to be content with what was necessary to survive.

The weather seemed pleasant with no extreme heat or coldness. Every day a shower came and the rainwater was collected for drinking. Occasionally a storm would come like the one that caused the Sea Venture to hit the reef. There would be extreme wind and torrential rain.

Even though life on the island became comfortable the thought of how to get off of it remained utmost in all the minds. Discouragement came when the men decided there was no way they could get the Sea Venture off the reef. The only way to possibly leave was to dismantle the ship and bring it piece by piece to shore with the plan to use the wood to build another boat.

Day after day men carefully removed one piece of wood after another and day after day the new shipbuilding proceeded. Almost a year passed before the ship "Deliverance" neared final construction.

By now the report from James Towne reached England with the news the Sea Venture was lost in a terrible storm at sea. The town criers broadcast from corner, "There were no survivors."

The Thomas Speke family and Anna went into deep mourning over the loss of sixteen year old Thomas Jr. whom they all deeply loved.

The day finally arrived when the Deliverance was ready to sail. Families hurriedly were gathering their belongings in anticipation of finally reaching the new world; a home long waited for.

Three men stayed on the island, because there was a unanimous consensus of opinion to claim the island for England. The temperature and beauty of the land made for ideal colonizing

The weather conditions for the voyage of the Deliverance stayed calm and clear during this last leg of the journey for the passengers and a shout of joy went up when land was sighted. Children began jumping up and down while the adults raised their arms and shouted Hallelujah.

For the sail between the two points of land and on into the mouth of the James River passengers stood along the deck gazing at the abundant plant life along the banks. Every once in a while a deer, or bear, or wolf, or strange looking person was sighted. In a few hours James Towne could be seen ahead sitting on the end of a peninsula jutting into the river.

Right before sailing into the docking area the ship weighed anchor with Captain Somers announcing from the bridge, "Let us take five minutes in a silent prayer of Thanksgiving to our God for bringing us safely to our destination."

In the meantime, people gathered on the James Towne wharf with curiosity as to whom the ship carried. The British flag was flying, so they were fairly positive as to the country it came from. But there was also the possibility it was a rogue piracy ship flying a fraudulent flag.

The Naval attachment was not aware of the possible arrival of a ship from home. Nor did they know of any English ship with the name of Deliverance.

Once the ship unloaded the passengers there was much rejoicing among the townspeople. It was like loved ones returning from the dead. For a whole year everyone in the Virginia Company assumed the ship Sea Venture sank with everyone on board. Now they learned the ship was wrecked and no one died in the accident.

Every home became open for the newcomers until a place of their own could be built and a huge welcoming feast was planned. On the same evening of the feast another ship arrived. There was no question as to the ownership of this ship as both the English flag and the colors of Lord De La Warr were flying.

Everyone knew the lord was commissioned to govern and help develop James Towne. He would live in a home built close to the military quarters where Thomas and the other service men recently settled into.

Thomas found his life in James Towne most agreeable. The people were friendly and his job assignments challenging. Some days he was involved with construction of homes and shops. Some days he was on guard duty about the perimeter of the Towne. Then came the assignment he most enjoyed. He was part of a squad sent by Lord De La Warr to scout the land for the purpose of getting the lay of the land, to locate Indian villages, and to find other suitable locations for settlements of English people.

In the "Towne" itself there was the constant challenge of keeping the peace with the fierce Indian Chief Powhatan. Thomas heard the story over and over about how the Chief captured Captain John Smith. What was amazing was the fact Powhatan released John with the honor of being a lesser chief.

Now Pocahontas, the chief's daughter, was in the care of the Towne. She was being taught the English language and also about Jesus being the Son of God. One hope of the teacher was to bring about a good relationship between Pocahontas' father and the Towne's people.

The ship carrying the news back to England concerning the safe arrival of the passengers of the Sea Venture to James Towne returned a year later to the New World with interesting news from the homeland. The Towne crier proclaimed, "King James is becoming active in church reforms." Actually the king was attempting to modify the penal laws against Catholicism, plus bring about unity between Anglican Puritans and Hampton Court.

The news became discussed everywhere in Towne. There were people with affirmations and those with condemnation. There were polite discussions and angry arguing. However the topics of conversation were nothing in comparison to what went on after the last news was given. This was about King James ordering a translation of the Bible into the English language. The Towne's people were flabbergasted. Such a thing as the Bible in the language of the people was unheard of.

Ten years after Thomas was called to serve in the new world he was reassigned back to England along with all the other men in his squad. A few months after returning home Thomas and Ann were married.

King James' son Charles experienced much sickness as a child. He grew up to be an extremely thin young man, who was very timid, and one who endured the anguish of stuttering. In preparation for the future of Prince Charles and his ascension to the throne King James attempted to arrange for him a marriage to Maria, the daughter of King Philip III of Spain. All of the English government officials thought this would make a good alliance.

Before any marriage alliance would be accepted, Charles, along with the Duke of Buckingham, plus a military bodyguard of eight men traveled to Madrid, Spain to meet with the perspective bride.

Spain's princess rejected the betrothal. The entire English party returned home with a very angry prince and duke. The embarrassing refusal brought about a war with Spain.

Actually England became embroiled with two conflicts; one in Europe, plus another one in the homeland between the Catholic and Protestant faiths. The king and his government leaders were mostly Protestant and their desire was to put to a close any Catholic influence with- in the country, plus bring the Scottish Presbyterians and the Church of England into a united form of Worship. Nothing but turmoil followed for years in England, with upheaval in the churches and a war overseas.

Thomas Speke was involved with the fighting in Spain when King James died and his son Charles ascended the throne. However Ann was able to attend the festive crowning of the new king.

Charles began his reign with an alliance with France; sealed by a proxy marriage to the French King's sister, Henrietta Maria.

Ann's home was with her father-in -law and a good part of her day was spent in caring for the elderly and in poor health gentleman. Her biggest pleasure was for a short time each afternoon when gathering the street children into her home to read to them and tell them stories about Jesus. Ann's biggest disappointment was not having a child of her own to read to. Her hope and prayers were for God to some day allow her to bear a child.

Once again Thomas returned to his homeland. Now as a full colonel with twenty years of service, he was assigned to maintain peace within the different religious disagreements taking place within his homeland.

The elder Thomas (now bedridden) was cognizant of the fact his son was home and a smile constantly played on his face. Two months after Thomas' return, his father while sleeping, passed on to his heavenly reward.

More and more friction developed between the Catholics and the Protestants. For a while king Charles kept some Catholic men he valued working with him, but now it became necessary to cull the few who were left from their government posts. One particular man the king especially thought greatly of was lord Baltimore, but being Catholic he was asked to leave his position. In appreciation for the years of valuable service king Charles offered lord Baltimore land in the new world.

In 1639 Thomas Speke and his wife Ann were chosen to be a part of the party lord Baltimore would send across the ocean to develop land north of James Towne. At this time little did the Speke's know that lord Baltimore's plan was to make the area a Catholic state.

For Thomas and Anne the days spent aboard the ship Dove were like a second honeymoon. There were calm days with smooth sailing and light breezes where Thomas and Ann would sit on deck while chatting and relaxing. Then when a storm came along and raged for a few days the two Spekes would stay in their cabin and read.

A few Catholic laymen and two Jesuit priests were sent on the ship to establish a Catholic Church in the first town settled. Several days a week and on Sundays a Catholic Mass was offered on shipboard. This had not taken place before on any English ship traveling to the new world.

During the Mass time Thomas and Ann would go to their cabin and open their new copy of the King James translation of the Bible. How encouraging and enlightening for them to be able to read the Word of God in English. Following their Bible study they would hold hands and pray. Their future was uncertain and just talking to the Lord about the unknown new life before them gave Thomas and Ann a peace and an assurance concerning their future.

Month after month passed while afloat on the Dove. Then one morning a sailor called out "Land ho" and by late afternoon the Virginia cape was rounded for the ship to sail into sheltered water. By evening the anchor was released in the bay along side of St. Clements Island. Here they would wait two days for the Ark, their sister ship to arrive.

For most of the passengers on both ships the ocean crossing seemed to take forever. True it took months to sail from England to the horn of Africa and on across the Atlantic Ocean to the West Indies. There was a layover in the islands and now they could say the New World was right before them.

Everyone met on the island to discuss the most suitable area in which to settle. Many questions were asked of Thomas because of his experience scouting the area as a younger man. One place he suggested was north east of the island and up a bay where there appeared to be fertile soil and a good water supply. The men suggested it would be best for a few of them to take a dingy to see this area and two other areas Thomas mentioned.

Three days later the men returned to let everyone know they believed the best place to settle was the first one Thomas mentioned. Before the Dove and Ark ever left England, Lord Baltimore determined the first city in Maryland would be named St. Mary's after Henrietta Maria, the wife of the king of England. The new settlers decided to name the inlet to their city St. Mary's Bay.

Gentry and nobility passengers on the Dove and Ark were given land grants by the crown. However the majority of passengers were men who were coming to the new land as indentured servants. They would work for seven years for the owners of the land and then gain their freedom.

Before any land was parceled out Leonard Calvert (Lord Baltimore's brother) plus all the nobles and gentry on board, and twenty more men went to shore to visit with the Indians living there. They found the natives a peaceful, agricultural people whose main crop was tobacco, but they also grew corn, beans, peas, squash and other vegetables.

Leonard was to be the governor of the new colony and while he knew King Charles assumed the new land rightfully belonged to the crown, he also knew a more peaceful situation would exist if he attempted to give gifts as purchase for land from the Indians.

The Natives looked on the friendly arrivals as people who would be their allies against warring tribes. Gladly they accepted cloth, hatchets and hoes in exchange for land. Once the exchange was made the party returned to their ship for Leonard to announce, "You gentlemen may now claim your land grants."

Thomas and his indentured men returned to shore the next day to see his particular piece of property. It was located on the north end of the Bay and Thomas thought it looked very promising for the growing of crops. Later in the day the rest of the land owners and their servants returned to see the location of their grants.

Ann and the seven other wives stayed on board. They chatted with excitement over what the future would hold for them. Being in her late forties Ann felt almost like a mother to the other woman and in her mind she pictured the blossoming families who would be raised in St. Mary's. As these thoughts came to her the ache for a child returned. To her it was understandable not being able to conceive while in England when Thomas was away from home so much. However she and Thomas had been together month after month while crossing the ocean and still there was no sign of pregnancy. Tears filled her eyes as she looked on the younger women.

As soon as Thomas set foot on his soil he drove a stake with the Speke crest into the ground. Then he and the men went into the woods to look over the timber he would use for the buildings. They found the woods plenteous with many of the types of trees good for construction. The plan was to build a three-room cottage for Thomas and Ann, plus next to the cottage a long one-room building to house the ten men. Immediately the men became anxious to get back to the ship in order to get their bags full of tools and start building.

Early the next morning Thomas and his men left the ship with their axes and other tools start work on the property. The trek from ship to property and back continued daily until the buildings were far enough along to have a roof over them.

In the heat of the summer flash thunderstorms could occur at any time and the men did not want to spend a night without some protection from the pouring rain. Once the roof was in place, Thomas, Ann, the men, and all of their possessions moved into their new home.

Ann wanted a lean-to built next to the side of the house where a fire could be made for cooking. She knew while she was preparing food she would enjoy looking at the lovely bay in front of the house and also at the lush woods along the side and back of her home. Then too, in the hot, muggy summer time the outside heat of a fire would not make the house stifling hot. Ann hoped by the time cooler weather arrived a fireplace for cooking in the kitchen would be completed.

Days became extremely busy for everyone. For the men the top priority was the clearing of land in order to prepare the ground for spring planting. However, two of the men were assigned to help in the preparation of food. Their main jobs were hunting and fishing, plus the cutting of the meat and the cleaning of the fish.

A plenteous supply of potatoes filled the holds of the ships in the bay and men on each property saw to the digging of root cellars in order for the potatoes to be safely stored once they were brought from the ship.

Soon there became a constant interaction between the Natives and the townspeople. Out of curiosity the Natives would stand around watching what the white people were doing and the white people visited their tribal neighbors for the same purpose. Friendships were built.

The tribal philosophy of "sharing everything" meant the townspeople really never lacked food. For generations the Natives grew plenteous crops and they now began sharing the produce with their new neighbors.

Each family was kept very busy clearing their land and establishing a home, yet everyone realized it was also very important to set up a governing body for the community.

Leonard Calvert and all of the men who received land grants met three evenings a week to plan how best to govern St. Mary's. Of course Leonard was chosen as the governor and three advisors to him were elected. Then Thomas and the other landowner's sat in the upper and lower house of the Legislature Assembly. They were also expected to take care of a smooth running court system.

By the time October arrived everyone know the gentry would spend the following year building manors with lovely bay views. The free men would oversee the indentured servants duties of clearing the land, planting, harvesting, plus all the maintenance care of the properties. This left the main function of the gentry as the roll of community leaders in government.

One thing Leonard wanted constructed before Christmas was a Catholic church. Therefore half of the indentured people were assigned to this project.

Chapter 10

Year 1646

Things were not going well in the town of St. Mary's. What was now taking place in the new colony was the exact opposite of what took place and continued to take place in England.

Lord Baltimore's determination to make all of Maryland a Catholic region was bringing about the oppression of non-Catholics. The Quaker people and the Church of England people were being condemned and ordered to desist services. The use of the King James Bible was banned and the people were ordered to only use a Latin Bible. One freedom after another was being removed for non-Catholics; including the right of Protestant gentry to take part in any governing body.

Thomas began considering moving north. In his mind came a picture of a perfect spot along the Potomac River. A place he once previously visited as a young military scout and the picture became the land Thomas wanted to own. A plan to make it possible came into action.

It didn't matter the Speke's manor along St. Mary's Bay was complete and lovely. It didn't matter the crops on his land were producing well. The only thing of importance to Thomas was to get away from the oppression.

In Ann's thinking all of this turmoil was affecting her health. She was constantly irritated and felt nauseous almost every day. Ann hated the thought of leaving her home and the friendly Indians, plus the dear people who met in her home for Bible study and Sunday worship. Yet, she felt the present oppression would become worse and worse. Ann pictured in her mind the terrible treatment of the Catholic people while she lived in England. This woman knew the same action could become just as bad against Thomas and her, especially since they were holding Bible studies in their home.. She understood they needed to get away.

Ann tried to drive away thoughts concerning the move. She tried to eat easily digested foods. She thought menopause might possible be starting. But nothing Ann did changed the symptoms of her health problems. Finally Ann confided about how she was feeling, plus all of her other problems to the ladies who came to have Bible study with her. In one voice they said, "You are pregnant." Ann responded, "Impossible, I am almost fifty." The ladies quietly giggled and after a few more weeks Ann realized the ladies were right. Her sour attitude turned to one of joy.

A beautiful tiny baby boy was born on May 12th 1647 and named Thomas after his father and grandfather. As soon as Thomas felt sure Ann and the baby were coming along well he left them in the care of the ladies in the Bible study group, and then went north with a newly arrived free man, and ten indentured men to go claim the land on the Potomac River. Once the area named Speke's point was stepped on Thomas drove the stake, with the family emblem on it, into the second land he now possessed in the new world. The new men were given the plans for all of the buildings to be constructed and the land to be cleared for planting. Thomas spent a few days to make sure everything was going well and then traveled back to St. Mary's.

Three years later Thomas, Ann and little pudgy Thomas moved north. They left the land grant at St. Mary's in the care of the now free men who were originally their indentured servants; men who appreciated all the years of love the Speke family showed toward them. In gratitude the men promised to faithfully grow productive crops for Thomas and his family. Most of the men were now married. They either brought sweethearts over from England or else married the native women in the area and each one now owned a small piece of land they would care for along with the Speke land.

Over and over during the past two years Ann kept hearing questions from Thomas about how she would like certain rooms to look in their manor being built up north. She would give a few suggestions and then try to picture in her mind what she would see once she arrived there.

Thomas kept his small boat in excellent shape and used it now mostly to travel down St. Mary's Bay, then up the Potomac to where his new house was located. The trip would take a couple of days.

The day the key to the house in St. Mary's was handed to their faithful freeman Thomas, Ann and their baby said goodbye then boarded their boat which towed a raft behind to carry a few things north. Two indentured men came along to row the boat. The party carried some food on the raft for the evening meal and some food with them in the boat to eat while on the water.

Thomas kept a fishing line in the water the whole distance. Each day he would catch enough fish for the evening meal. Once on shore Thomas would gather small dry wood then start a fire with it for cooking. The other men would cut branches to assemble a lean-to for the night's sleeping.

Ann's hands were kept busy with little Thomas. For the entire day while they were in the boat she attempted to keep him busy in order to prevent him from leaning over the side of the boat and falling into the river. If she became distracted for one minute he would immediately put his little arm over the side of the boat and try to touch the water.

On land, her fear was the little one would slip into the woods and disappear from sight. The only time Ann allowed herself to be free from watching the boy was while she prepared dinner and the following morning's breakfast. Even then, before releasing the little one to his father's care she made sure her husband understood his responsibility.

The weather remained clear and warm for the whole trip. Every once in a while an Indian family could be seen on shore; often the native man was fishing. Ann and little Thomas would wave with the Native family usually responding with a wave. From time to time the home of a settler family would come into view. Once in a great while they would catch sight of a stately manor house.

Around noon on the third day a most lovely manor on the left bank of the river caught Ann's eye. She wondered who lived in the stately home with a large verandah across the front. The next thing she realized was the fact her boat was gliding toward the point of land the manor sat upon. Ann thought they were stopping to visit some friend of Thomas'.

Thomas said, "Welcome home." He took Ann's hand to help her out of the boat and then picked up the little one for their walk up the beach. The look on Ann's face was one of astonishment over the beauty of her new home. First she stopped to look at the verandah pillars. Then walked onto the verandah and on through the front door.

Ann kept saying to little Thomas, "Our new home, our new home" as her husband began to take them on a tour through the manor. The entryway was spacious with archways into a room on the right, plus into the room on the left. At the back there was a spiral staircase going to the second floor. Thomas walked into the large living room on the right of the entry with Ann and the boy right behind him. This room would mainly be used when guests were in the house. Ann told her husband she appreciated the fine looking furniture and their location in regards to the fireplace. She felt the guests could sit comfortable in chilly weather.

In the back wall of the living room there was an archway going into to a large dining room where Ann looked at the rich dark wood of the table, chairs, buffet and china closet. For comfort, a fireplace was centered in the dining room's back wall.

Now the little family went back through the living room and into the room on the other side of the entryway. Thomas murmured, "Our families sitting room." The room was a few feet smaller than the living room and appeared cozy with the stuffed furniture close to a fireplace. The portal at the back of this room went into a vestibule containing three exits; a door on the left to the house's side entrance, and archway into the dining room on the right and straight ahead a door to the back porch. Ann wanted to look more carefully at the three rooms, so she let go of little Thomas' hand.

Immediately the boy saw he could run from room to room, through doors and arches. Round and round in a circle he ran until he finally just plopped down in the middle of the sitting room floor to get his breath.

Daddy took the little one's hand to walk up the staircase to show his wife the four large bedrooms with each containing a private area for bathing.

When they returned down the stairs they were met by Charles, one of the house servants, to inform the Speke three there was tea and scones ready for them. Little Thomas' eyes kept closing between the bites of the scone with jam. Even before his last bite was consumed he was sound asleep sitting up in a little chair.

Ann picked him up and carried him upstairs. Then she asked the servant to please let her know as soon as Thomas woke. Charles assured her he would watch over her son. Then hand in hand Thomas and Ann walked out onto the back porch for him to show her the rest of the estate.

To the right sat a cottage containing a sitting room and bedrooms for the house servants. To the left there was a roomy building for the preparation and cooking of food. Both building's walkways to the porch were covered to prevent the servants from getting wet in inclement weather.

Still there were many buildings to the right and to the left for Ann to inspect and the couple started walking in the right-hand direction. The first building they went into past the residence of the servants was the washhouse; tubs and scrub boards were lined along the wall. In back of this building stretched a good size laundry yard; one big enough to handle the largest of washes. Ann could picture sheets, towels, tablecloths and clothes going from line to line.

The third building was the coach house where both an open-air coach and an enclosed coach sat side by side. There was also room in the building for a few guest coaches. Naturally, the stable was located next to the coach house. Ann stood in the stable doorway to count ten stalls and noticed six of them were occupied with horses.

By now Ann and Thomas strolled along the circled path to the front of their home. As they started across the veranda Ann's eyes were glued to all of the beautiful flowers between the house and the Potomac River. She thought, my, when we docked I concentrated so at looking at the house I didn't even realize what a feast for the eyes lay all around me.

Ann led her husband down into the midst of the lovely garden. Then they went up one path and down another while stopping often to sniff blossom after blossom.

On the other side of the house, past the garden, stretched a wide green for the game of lawn bowling. Along side of the Bowling Green, and toward the back of the house stood a large greenhouse where many unusual plants and an abundance of vegetables grew.

By now Ann was walking ahead of Thomas in her anxiousness to see the remaining buildings. Into the Spinning house Ann went and there she saw two women at spindles as well as a few women making blankets and one was knitting a shawl. Thomas introduced his wife to them and they chatted for a while.

Next to the Spinning house sat a Storehouse. This building contained two rooms; one for storing household items and the other containing groceries. At the far end of one room there was a door, situated in the floor, for entry to the root cellar where potatoes and other fresh vegetables could be kept for better preservation.

Now Thomas and Ann were back to the kitchen and he knew they were going to spend more time in this building than any of the others. Ann would want to talk with the cooks. Then give a good inspection of the fireplaces with the cooking apparatus, plus look at the supply of pots, pans and utensils.

Thomas sat down by the door after he introduced Ann. He could hear the women's chatter about food preparation; even going into the recipe details. When Ann was ready to leave she found her husband leaning back in his chair and sound asleep.

Before going through the back door of their home Thomas pointed down the back path to the buildings about a half-mile away. Ann knew the buildings she saw in the distance would be the homes of those servants who worked in the fields. On another day she would go there to meet and chat with these workers.

Life settled into an enjoyable pace for the Speke family. Ann continued to be mainly occupied with the care of little Thomas. Her biggest concern was the boy's fascination with the river. She felt she needed to be constantly by his side all of the hours he was awake. Little Thomas' favorite sport was throwing stones into the water and then running into the river to see if he could find them.

Ann built a good relationship with the household servants. Even though this woman was very precise and meticulous in the way she wanted the place cared for she requested the service in a pleasant, kind manner and the servants grew to love their mistress.

Little Thomas enjoyed following his mother into the laundry and spinning houses, plus the kitchen, He would chatter away with the servants and always wanted to help them in what ever they would be doing. During this time his mother would look over the finished tasks and make suggestions for the future work projects.

Thomas Sr. oversaw all of the other property care. He dealt with the gardener, the stable boys and the field hands.

During the years while the manor was being built, the land prepared for crops and the servants brought from England Thomas would spend as much time at Speke's point as he did in St. Mary's. While he was at Speke's point he made sure to spend some time locating neighbors and learning about their life. Now that his family was with him at the point the three of them went together to visit the neighbors.

Some of the days Thomas, Ann and little Thomas would travel either north or south on the Potomac river in their boat. They would pull into shore at cabins or wigwams and spend time just chatting.

Other days the three would take their coach inland to visit at individual homes as well as at places where there was a cluster of houses. Once in a while their travel would take them to the Indian village of Accotink.

The Speke's grew to love their neighbors and cared enough to help them in any and every way possible. In return the caring became reciprocal. However, Thomas and Ann were interested in their neighbors being introduced to Spiritual help as well as meeting their physical needs. With this in mind Thomas usually carried his copy of the King James Bible with him.

Often when discussing some matter with a neighbor he would say let's see what God has to say about the subject and take out his Bible to read a verse pertaining to what they were talking about. Thomas hoped in the future to build a small Chapel and bring a Pastor from England to minister to his family and his neighbors.

In time Maryland's government recognized Thomas' ability in the military, as well as his helpfulness in political situations. By 1651 Thomas Speke was invited to represent the county in the

House of Burgesses. In four more years the Governor appointed Thomas to be county commissioner, as well as colonel of the militia for the county. Through this he became the presiding judge of the King's Commission of Peace in the county.

On a sunny October afternoon in 1655 the Speke three were riding west to attend a birthday party for the son of their neighbors, the Alexanders. The boy was the same age as young Thomas.

About half way to their destination Ann complained about a terrible pain in her head. She no sooner finished speaking when she fainted. Thomas thought this was brought on by the unseasonably warm October sunshine and he believed his wife would soon revive.

Usually eight year old Thomas chatted a great deal while the family traveled. But after his mother fainted he became quieter and quieter. He thought his mother was napping and he didn't want to wake her.

A half hour later Ann stopped breathing. At first Thomas didn't recognize the fact his wife was no longer with him. When the horrific realization came he turned the carriage around to go home.

Immediately young Thomas wanted to know why they weren't going to the party. Thomas Sr. didn't want to frighten the boy with the truth and told him his mother wasn't well and they need to return to the manor.

As soon as the stable boy saw the coach returning he knew something was wrong and went to get his father Charles. Thomas quietly whispered to Charles, "My wife is dead" while the two men were carrying Ann's body into the house. Young Thomas' sharp ears heard what was said and he exclaimed, "Oh, no, my mama can't be dead, she is just asleep."

Immediately the servants took horses and rode to the neighbors to inform them of the calamity. They told everyone they met there would be a viewing on the next evening and the funeral would take place the following morning.

Young Thomas walked down to the river with his fishing pole to wait for his mother to waken. It seemed strange to him to not have her by his side, or know she was sitting on the veranda watching him. As far as Thomas was concerned his mother was his best friend.

An hour later Thomas Sr. came down to the river to sit with the boy. When young Thomas glanced his father's way, the boy thought he looked terrible with red swollen eyes. Thomas asked his father, "When do you think mother will wake up." Thomas Sr. swallowed hard and said, "Your mother has gone to be with Jesus." The boy responded, "But Jesus lives in heaven. How did my mother get there?" The Senior Thomas replied, "Jesus came and took her there. She will not return to us, but some day we will go to be with her in heaven."

Because the father didn't want his son to see his mother laying in a coffin, or being put into the ground he arranged for young Thomas to visit in their neighbor Dr. Thomas and Susanna Gerrard's home. The doctor's grandson (also named Thomas) was Thomas Speke's godson and he was about the same age as young Thomas Speke. The two boys often played together and Thomas Sr. knew his son would be loved and cared for at the Gerrards.

Frances, the Gerrard's daughter taught fifteen children in the little school house on the Speke property Young Thomas held a special love for his gentle teacher.

For two days the Speke boy enjoyed playing with his classmate and time went quickly. Then after he rode home all he could sense was a great loneliness because the loss of the presence of his mother was deeply felt. With each passing day he became quieter and quieter. Soon everyone sensed the child's deep sad spirit, especially with the lack of joy usually seen on his face.

No one was more sympathetic with Thomas' loss than his teacher. The boy felt this and usually he would be in no hurry to leave the classroom after school was over. He would ask, his teacher, "Is there anything I can do to help you?"

Miss Gerrard would often suggest to Thomas to erase the blackboard, and when he was finished she would walk to the manor with him. Often she would stay fifteen or twenty minutes to chat with Charles, or Thomas Sr. and then she would be taken home in a carriage.

As the days passed Frances would be encouraged to stay longer and longer. Some days she would stay through dinner. Meanwhile Thomas Sr. began to realize more and more there was a deep bond building between the teacher and his son.

After a few months Thomas Sr. knew he too was developing a deep affection for the teacher. When six more months passed both the father and the teacher became aware of the fact they were falling in love. Thomas asked Frances to marry him one year and three months after the death of Ann.

Young Thomas and his father were returning from a hunting trip when they glanced north and saw smoke rising in the distance. Thomas Sr. stared a few minutes and then said, "I wonder if last night's storm caused a fire by one of the lightening strikes. Young Thomas replied, "That's a possibility. Then too, an Indian family could have set up camp and the smoke is from their fire." Both of them thought it would be a good idea to row up stream to find the cause of the smoke.

A few hours later the two Spekes pulled the boat to shore by a spot where trees were piled around a cleared area. One of the piles of wood burned brightly and several men stood by watching.

Thomas Sr. and his son walked over and introduced themselves to the new landowners. The oldest of the men put out his hand and said, "Hello, my name is John Washington and these two fellows are my sons Lawrence and Augustine. The other men introduced themselves as friends of John's who were there to help John in erecting a new home on the property.

A short distance away another fire was burning where four women appeared to be preparing food for the hungry men. John invited his guests to stay for dinner and the men walked over to be introduced to the women who were Ann, the wife of John and their daughter Mildred. The two women servants who were helping were also introduced.

After a tasty dinner of fresh fish and biscuits Thomas told his new neighbors, "it is time for my son and I to leave. John said, "It will be dark in an hour, you better stay for the night." However, Thomas assured John about the current flowing south and the fact they would get home in half the time it took for them to row north against the current. He thanked his host for the kind hospitality and told him, "My son, my servants and I will be most happy to help you in the building of your home. Please send someone down to my place to let us know when and how we can help.

As the boat carried the father and son south young Thomas remarked, he thought Augustine Washington would make a good friend.

For all of this day the sun shone brilliantly. The Speke's were about two thirds of the way home before the sun went down and darkness surrounded them. Deep darkness is something people traveling in a small boat on water do not greatly appreciate. However, in a few minutes the two Thomas' were delighted with the moonlight beaming down on them.

Thomas suspected the night would be filled with the light of the moon even before leaving the Washington homestead. He prayed this would be so when they stepped into the boat, and thanked the Lord when his prayer was answered.

While rowing home Thomas and his son talked about how good it was to see more families moving to the new world. Into their conversation the thought of the many people coming from England to escape religious persecution was covered. They were not only coming to Maryland, but north and east as well. While the two men did not know any individuals among these people the Puritan group was mentioned.

One nineteen-year-old young man, Abraham Temple, son of Robert Temple of Leicester, England was among the first group of Pilgrims arriving. Abraham chose to settle in Salem, Massachusetts.

Shortly after Abraham arrived his marriage bands (allowing him to court a young lady) was announced in church. Abraham knew the young lady Ann when he lived in England, and her family traveled on the same ship with him while crossing the ocean in 1636.

Abraham was granted five acres of land the year he arrived and a year later he was given five more acres of land. On the third year Abraham was granted an acre of marshland. This pleased him greatly, because salt was extracted from the marshes. This gave him one more commodity to sell beside the potatoes, turnips and carrots he grew.

The courtship was rocky with many arguments and disagreements. After a year and a half of this, Abraham declared he did not want to marry Ann. Then, as usually happened, Ann brought a lawsuit against Abraham for breaking the marriage band.

Within another year Abraham began to be very discontent in Salem. People were shunning him because of the lawsuit. Then too, there was a sense of trouble coming with the large focus on certain behavior being caused through witchcraft.

Abraham waited another year and then put his property up for sale. He moved to the northern end of Long Island, New York but he only stayed there for five years. Abraham moved back to Massachusetts to the area of Cambridge.

The first group of people who arrived in Delaware came to establish the town of Lewis in 1635. One person in this group was William Burton who was from Shorpshire, England. His father was Thomas of Longer Hall, and he descended from Sir Edward Burton, a man who was knighted by King Edward IV after the battle of St. Albens.

William met and married a young woman by the name of Ann Stratton. Then came ten children; one girl and nine boys. First there was Agnes. Then came William (1680), John (1681), Thomas (1682), Benjamin (1684), Joseph (1685), Stratton (1687), Woolsey (1688), Jacob (1690) and Samuel (1672).

In 1677 William received a patent for land from the Governor General Edmond Andros. The home William and Ann built on this land was named the White House Farm.

During the year of 1682 the Burton family became involved in helping to establish the Lewis Presbyterian Church.

Life changed for Frances Speke due to the rule about a female being no longer allowed to teach after she married. Frances was not an exception to the rule and an indentured tutor was brought from England to fill the role Frances once held. The new teacher moved into the apartment over the schoolroom.

Thomas Gerrard stayed with the Speke's Monday through Friday and then returned to his own home for the weekends.

On the next trip north to the Washington's land Thomas Sr. took six of his servants to stay and help in the construction of John and Ann's home. He also invited John to allow his sons Lawrence and Augustine to stay at Speke's point for schooling until the Washington's could bring over a teacher from England.

After thinking about the invitation for a few days John and Ann agreed their boys would benefit by staying with the Speke's. A week later Lawrence and Augustine were headed south. The boys found themselves in one of the extra bedrooms and followed the same schedule as Thomas Gerrard with five nights at Speke's point and two nights at home.

The four young men grew to greatly appreciate the company of each other. They would hunt together, fish together, play table games and also croquet, plus kick a ball, or throw a ball to each other.

One year later John Washington brought to the new world a tutor who would live over their newly constructed schoolroom. Lawrence and Augustine returned home to continue their education. However, the four young men continued to get together on the weekends. The adult Spekes and the Washington family also spent much time together because their personalities meshed well.

From time to time fall storms would be a topic of conversation. The residents of Maryland and Virginia were amazed at the terrible wind, rain and storm surges often occurring between late August and October. The phenomenon was labeled "a nor'easter". The monster storm would approach from the Atlantic Ocean and scream up the Chesapeake Bay, then on up the Patomic and Patapsco Rivers.

In 1659 one of these terrible storms approached the new world. Within a few days there was great destruction from trees being blown down and treacherous flooding.

Many lives were lost. One of those was Thomas Speke Sr. who was returning to his home from the stable when a large branch was wrenched from one of the old huge trees. The branch knocked Thomas down and broke his neck. He died swiftly.

Ann Washington was also killed in the storm. She was caught in a swift current flowing over the road she was traveling on.

There were many tears flowing from residents along the Potomac River. Some families held joint funerals; one being the Speke-Washington funeral. Frances and John cried together while attempting to console each other over the terrible losses they were experiencing.

Young Thomas was a big help to Frances in managing the plantation. With each year of his growth Thomas became wiser in the production of the crops, and wiser in his relationship with the servants, and the workers came to greatly love their teenage master. Speke Hall never looked better and many products went to market to bring in a good income.

As the years passed the friendship between the Spekes and the Washington family continued. John and his boys were also flourishing financially. The two families constantly encouraged and helped each other

When Thomas entered his twentieth year his stepmother and John Washington decided to marry. This brought Thomas to an even closer relationship with John, Lawrence and Augustine. While he continued to manage Speke's point it seemed he spent as much time on the Washington's property as on his own.

As time progressed all three young men matured more and each became very involved with the care of their own property.

Thomas loved his land and the people who worked for him, but he began to feel something was missing in his life. It didn't take him long to realize the something he needed was a special young woman and he began to seriously seek out the young women of the neighboring people.

More and more new families began to settle in the area. A few settled between Occoquam and Manassas. However there were more settlers moving toward Manassas than any other place. The small village was starting to become a town. Doctors, lawyers and merchants were all making their way to Manassas. The business of the town and the opportunity for trade began to bring people from the plantations into the town.

Even though it took almost a day for Thomas to travel to Manassas he began to feel there were good opportunities for his business in going there. Then too, he felt it was now time to begin contact with a good lawyer for advice in all of the plantation's financial dealings.

Thomas visited the town's four lawyers and he decided James Bowling was trustworthy. James was about six years older than Thomas and seemed to be a man who lived his faith.

James and his younger sister Elizabeth came to the new world shortly after their parents died. Several years before coming to the new world James thought he would gain better business opportunities in America. There was also the excitement of going to live in a new land and he was ready to come three years earlier when James realized the health of his parents was failing rapidly, and he knew if he left, his sister would be alone to deal with funeral arrangements and grief. This was not something James could do, so he stayed until both his father and then his mother died. Then Elizabeth was free to travel with her brother.

The more Thomas worked with James the better he liked him, and a social friendship progressed. Thomas would invite James to come to Speke's point on a fishing trip, and James would invite Thomas inland to go hunting. On some occasions the Washington young men and Thomas Gerrard would join in on the trips.

In the meantime Elizabeth would stay at home. She was having a difficult time dealing with the grief over the death of her parents. It was not easy for her to adjust to the different way of life in the new world and she preferred not to socialize. James felt it would be best to let her progress through the mourning before encouraging her to go out to meet others.

For two years James watched his sister retreat into herself. He became more and more concerned and began to share his feelings with Thomas. Together they decided Elizabeth needed some Pastoral counseling. So Thomas suggested to James to bring his sister out to Speke's point to meet with the Pastor there.

James began bringing Elizabeth out to Thomas' home on Saturday for a dinner with Pastor Miller and his wife. After the meal the Millers would sit around to chat until bedtime. Following the Sunday morning service the two Bowlngs would return to Manassas.

Pastor Miller kept encouraging Elizabeth in two ways. One was by constantly reminding Elizabeth of the fact her parents knew the Lord, and there would come a day when she would be with them again. He advised her to daily rejoice in this fact. Then the Pastor gave Elizabeth pointers on how to work through grief, one of which was to become active in helping others.

Month after month passed before any change in Elizabeth became noticeable. Finally she began helping and teaching the children of indentured plantation servants and found much joy in doing this. A sparkle came into Elizabeth's eyes and a smile appeared on her lips.

Both James and Thomas were thrilled with the new young woman. However Thomas' appreciation was more intense because he now realized he was in love with his friend's sister. Because the Speke gentleman did not want to rush things he waited six months before telling James of his feelings, and then Thomas asked his friend for permission to court Elizabeth. James was not surprised, as for quite a while he suspected Thomas loved Elizabeth. Because the Speke gentleman did not want to rush things he waited six more months before beginning to court Elizabeth.

The wedding of Thomas and Elizabeth took place at Speke's Chapel on June 10, 1664. For the next year the newlyweds traveled to England and Wales to visit with aunts, uncles and cousins. Thomas knew his plantation would be well looked after by James and the Washington men

Once the land of England was reached the Speke's traveled by coach to Somerset and Dowlish Wake. They spent ten days there and worshipped in the ancestral St. Stevens Cathedral at Dowlish Wake. Later they traveled north to Bath to visit more of the Speke relatives, and then north to London and Wales to visit with Elizabeth's family.

Chapter 11

Year 1666

*E*lizabeth was six months pregnant when she and her husband returned to Speke's point. Their memories were filled with wonderful family times in England and Wales. This gave them a determination to keep up a correspondence with those they loved back in the old world.

Here in the new world Elizabeth decided to redecorate their home. The walls of each room were to be re-wallpapered with pastel designs and some new furniture would be purchased for the parlor. Most of the old parlor furniture was placed in the sitting room and the slightly worn sitting room furniture was put in the indentured servant's quarters.

Then Elizabeth wanted one of the upstairs bedrooms to be made into a studio for her to use when she painted. Her already finished pictures of the sea and of gardens would be hung on the walls. She turned the bureau into a brush and paint supply container and the removed bed was replaced with a chair and easel.

The evening the last bit of redecorating took place, Elizabeth's labor pains began.

The labor was long. Thirty-six hours later baby John Speke was born. He weighed nine pounds, four ounces, and his hair was a dark brown. Baby John wrinkled up his little red face and let out a loud cry. Thomas thought his baby was beautiful.

A large Christening was planned for the church at Speke's point. Close to 100 friends came from around their home and as far away as small towns within a thirty mile radius. At the ceremony James became the Godfather of little John.

The Washington family brought much food for the celebration feast after the ceremony.

John proved to be a contented, happy baby and after the first six weeks Elizabeth found some free time to devote to her painting.

Servant Lucy would stay in the room with the baby in order to notify Elizabeth in case he woke and cried. But until that happened Elizabeth shut the door of her studio and relaxed with a paintbrush in her hand. For a few hours several days a week she drew various pictures of the river. Then pictures of the servants working in the fields and also portraits of various family members appeared on the easel. Elizabeth's plan was for the pictures to be given as gifts for special occasions of family members and friends.

This woman was gifted in music as well as in art. When Thomas and Elizabeth were in England (on their honeymoon) there were many evenings when musical ensembles provided entertainment. Often Elizabeth would accompany the ensemble on the harpsichord. At this time, because Thomas so enjoyed hearing his wife play he determined they would bring a harpsichord back to the new world when they returned.

On many evenings after little John was asleep Elizabeth would light the candles on top of the harpsichord and sit down to play. While her fingers roamed the two keyboards and beautiful music filled the room a sense of complete peace came over her.

Often Thomas just sat in his rocking chair with his eyes closed while his ears drank in the beautiful clear tones. Much of the music Elizabeth played was church music with many of the pieces recently composed by J.S. Bach

An idea began to come alive in Thomas' mind — why not introduce the community to the lovely ensemble music heard in England? He began to formulate plans about how to make this possible.

First Thomas went to the neighbors to inquire as to whether any of them ever played an instrument. Then he went door to door among his indentured servants. Two violin players and three trombone players made themselves known. At this point Thomas determined he would begin to bring over from England teachers for each instrument found in an ensemble. This consisted of strings — violin, cello, viola and double bass, plus the wind instruments — flute, French horn, oboe and bassoon.

Locating these teachers took several trips to England for Thomas and his family. Elizabeth and baby John would stay with her family while Thomas visited one conservatory after another to hire talented people.

In one of the schools Thomas heard new sounds coming from a trumpet player. For all of the years before this time a trumpet was only used for military calls with the same note progressions arranged in different orders for different military actions.

Now new notes could be heard coming from the trumpet and when Thomas asked about the reason he was told J.S. Back taught different lip pressures to produce the new notes. This now made possible the use of a trumpet in an ensemble.

Thomas decided he would learn to play the trumpet using the new technique. For three months he took lessons from a Conservatory using the new Bach method. Then he would practice a half hour each evening. When the Spekes returned to their Maryland home Thomas continued practicing and in a years time became quite proficient.

Soon people around Speke's point wanted to take lessons and even more people wanted to learn after they heard their neighbor's playing beautiful music.

Before long, eight first violinists, six violists, four cellists, four double bass players, two French horns, two flutes, two oboes, two bassoons and one trumpet player were all practicing. In three years time the musicians were proficient enough to start practicing together and the local ensemble was born.

Not too long a time later, the players sounded good enough to be in a concert hall and Thomas began the construction of one located next to the church on his property. The seating capacity was made for 150 people with the plans for two concerts a month to be held there.

Every Saturday, for four hours, the musicians gathered in the new building to practice. They practiced for six more months before the first concert was announced.

Thomas made sure programs were prepared for the event with every musician's name and instrument listed.

For the first concert about fifty people showed up. In the audience sat Elizabeth with two month old James in her lap and sitting next to her was seven years old John.

Like electricity, the news traveled from household to household about the enjoyment the audience felt at the first concert. Thomas' vision of a small musical group for family enjoyment became a concert series with the auditorium almost filled to capacity for every performance.

Speke's point became known for harmonious pleasures and the Chapel itself for the beautiful organ music. The organ was purchased the same time as the harpsichord and Elizabeth would go over to the church some afternoons to play it. Thomas brought an organist from England to play for the church services.

So a pattern began to develop for Elizabeth. Tuesday and Thursday afternoons she would play the organ for an hour and then come home while on the other afternoons she would go to her studio and paint. In the evenings after the boys fell asleep Elizabeth would sit at the harpsichord and play for a while. From time to time this musical lady would accompany one or two of the ensemble selections.

The simple, realistic beautiful paintings produced by Elizabeth began to catch the attention of neighbors and town folk. People started to come to ask Elizabeth if she would paint a picture of a family member, or else some lovely rural scene, and very happily she obliged them.

Chapter 11

Both John and James were lively, laughing, healthy boys. They loved fishing and hunting as their father did. Thomas would usually take both boys with him when he was engaged in either of these activities.

The teacher now at Speke's schoolhouse was named Luke. The two Speke boys, plus neighbor children, now brought the school's enrollment up to 23. John and James both loved their teacher and attempted to work hard in their studies to please him.

Mr. Luke, as the students called him, wanted music to be emphasized as a part of the studies mainly because of the influence the concert series held in the community.

Even before John began his schooling Thomas started to teach his son how to play the trumpet. By third grade John was quite proficient on the instrument and in the middle of the semester Mr. Luke gave John the assignment of playing a piece on his trumpet each Friday at the school's closing exercise.

As soon as James reached the age of three Elizabeth started teaching him how to play the harpsichord. Oh, even before then, he often sat on the bench beside his mother when she played. Other times he would climb up on the bench when his mother wasn't playing just to touch the keys and listen to the sound they made.

Other students in the classroom developed a desire to play an instrument. In time all of the ensemble players were giving lessons to the children. Speke's point now added one or two numbers by the youth ensemble to their concert series.

Thomas and his two sons often went out into the woods to hunt for rabbits. To the male Spekes a rabbit stew, or some fried rabbit, were tasty dishes. To satisfy this hunger often sent the men rabbit hunting.

Of course, if a deer came into their sights they would feel fortunate to be able to put venison on their table. With the wild game, plus the plantation-raised beef, lamb, pork and chicken, and all the seafood from the river the table at Speke's Point was always well laden.

On May 13th, 1681 Thomas and his sons were out in the woods west of their home on a rabbit hunt. It was a lovely morning with the sun filtering through the branches overhead.

Suddenly Thomas fell to the ground. Both John and James were walking in front of their father and it took them several seconds to sense he was not behind them. They looked at each other and then both young men turned at the same time to see their father lying on the ground. Immediately they ran to him and found an arrow protruding from their father's back. He was dead. The arrow went right through Thomas' heart.

Two emotions filled the young men. One was anger and the other was the fear of being shot themselves.

John and James ran back to the plantation for help. Within twenty minutes there were men searching the woods to find the person who shot Thomas. No one could be found and once it was determined the woods were safe to enter the two young Speke men, plus six servants went to bring the body home.

Weeping Elizabeth stood in the doorway as they brought the body of Thomas into the house. Once he was placed on the bed she cradled his whole upper body in her arms. Sobs racked her body and she murmured over and over, "Oh no, Oh no! How can my thirty four year old husband be dead?

Hundreds of people came to the funeral of Thomas Speke who was laid to rest along side of his father and mother in the cemetery ground by the Chapel.

Elizabeth, with her two sons and her brother James hosted the dinner for the many guests. The Washington family came and sat at the same table as the Spekes. It was a solemn time, but also a time when much love was expressed, plus honor given to Thomas.

Each day after the funeral Elizabeth sank deeper into depression. She felt there was no reason to live and wanted to do nothing but sit in the room where she previously enjoyed painting and to stare at a picture she drew of Thomas hanging on the wall. Elizabeth's demeanor regressed to the same state she was in following the death of her parents.

Fifteen-year-old John and his younger brother didn't know what to do. Foremost in their minds was the condition they saw their mother in, and they were completely frustrated in knowing how to help her. Then too, the boys tried to fulfill all of the responsibilities their father once shouldered and felt they fell far short.

John determined he should go to see his Uncle James for advice about his mother's problems. However, James now lived across the river and to visit him would take two days.

Ever since Speke's Point was established, small towns began springing up on the eastern side of the Potomac River. This was due to the tobacco trade being funneled through that area of Maryland. The trade became larger and larger every year. One reason for this was because many doctors were advising their patients, "Smoking, or using snuff is beneficial to the lungs". People began thinking any lung problem could be cured by inhaling tobacco smoke

Two years before Thomas' death James thought he should set up his lawyer's office where high trade took place. Then when he realized much trade was centering across the river in an area named Port Tobacco he moved to that part of Maryland.

Before leaving Speke's Point John asked his younger brother to look after the plantation while he was gone. Three of the servants accompanied John on his trip.

Fortunately the point where the Spekes lived jutted out into the Potomac, and the shore across the water held a strip of land jutting west into the water; this place was one of the narrowest on the river.

There were two ways possible for John to reach his uncle's home. One way was to row straight across the river and then ride the horses east for sixteen miles to Port Tobacco. The other way was to row south on the river, then north up the inlet leading to Port Tobacco and to ride their horses a few miles from the town to James house. Either way the horses would need to swim the river alongside of the boat. Going straight across seemed the most sensible thing to do to prevent the exhaustion of the horses.

John and the three men set out early in the morning. The day ahead would be a long one with the two-mile row across the river and the sixteen-mile horseback ride.

The sun was barely over the horizon and the morning air was filled with haze. As the day progressed the weather improved. By the time the men stopped to eat the prepared lunch they were carrying the sun was shining and the air was clear.

Late in the afternoon James sat on his veranda reading and resting before going in to eat dinner. With the sound of approaching voices James looked up and found four men riding up the lane to his house. As they drew closer James recognized his nephew John and a surprised look came over his face. This was the first time John had traveled to visit him at Port Tobacco. After the surprise emotion there followed one of fear. James knew the only probable cause for his nephew's coming to visit would be due to some problem at home.

The uncle quickly rose from his chair to stride across the veranda and down the steps to meet the approaching party. In the meantime John slid off his mount in preparation of running to his uncle. The two relatives grabbed each other and hugged. James shook hands with the three other familiar looking men and then he led them into his house. As John gazed around he did not think the home looked as spacious as his own.

The young man's uncle determined it would be best to feed the company before showing them around. He knew it would be wisest to wait until everyone was fed before finding what was troubling John.

James went to notify his housekeeper Alice about the fact there were four more people for dinner. Alice went to stir a big pot of stew and assured James there was plenty of food for extra people. She said, "I'll mix up another batch of biscuits and dinner will be ready in about half an hour."

James now decided since there was a half hour before dinner he would show the men his home. Being a bachelor he felt he did not need to have a home as large as the one his sister lived in.

The tour began in the four downstairs rooms consisting of a small parlor, a sitting room, a large dining room and James' law office. From the dining room a door opened onto a ten-foot breezeway leading to the kitchen, laundry and root cellar. All were contained in one building. Next door to this was the two-room cottage where Alice lived.

A long flight of stairs went from the sitting room to the three bedrooms upstairs. Then there was a hallway over the breezeway leading to two guest bedrooms. John would sleep in one of the main bedrooms and the men traveling with him would go into the guest rooms. James would use one of the upstairs bedrooms from time to time, but often he would just sleep on a sofa in his office.

Dinner was served at exactly six p.m. Once the delicious smelling chicken stew and biscuits were placed on the table James, John, the three men and Alice bowed their heads to say grace. Immediately plates were filled with chicken, potatoes, carrots, celery and onions. Then smothered all the food in the stew's gravy. The biscuits were buttered and dipped in the gravy. A silence descended for a short while as the hungry people enjoyed their food.

Then casual conversation began about the beautiful weather, the trip from Speke's Point and the cases James was working on.

Following the main course Alice brought in a berry cobbler covered with vanilla pudding and whipped cream. A round of compliments were placed on Alice and thank-you, thank-you, thank-you followed.

Now it was time for James and John to go to the sitting room and for John to tell his uncle the reason for the visit. John continually choked-up as he described his mother's behavior and the effect this held on his younger brother.

James shared with John how he went through similar emotions when his sister withdrew and went into a depressed state after their parent's death.

John was completely surprised to learn about this area of his mother's life; a topic never once mentioned in all of his growing years. He was also encouraged to realize his mother once overcame this state and there might be a possibility she could do it again. James and John went to prayer over the matter.

The uncle and the nephew decided the best thing to do would be to bring the Speke family across the river to live with James. The older and younger man both knew the overseer at Speke's Point was a very capable person and there need be no fear in leaving the plantation's care in his hands.

James, John and the men who accompanied John all traveled west to Speke's Point. When James knocked on his sister's painting-room door there was no answer. He knocked three times and finally called out, "Elizabeth it's your brother James." Finally and very quietly, a "come in" was heard.

Before James sat a very disheveled woman with stringy unkempt hair and a sallow sad face. He strode over and enveloped Elizabeth in his arms; holding her and telling her, "Your son's and I love you." Tears streamed down Elizabeth's face.

A little later after Elizabeth calmed down she joined James, John and the younger James in the sitting room. Elizabeth heard her brother gently tell her how her sons and he thought it would be best if the Spekes would move to Port Tobacco to live with him.

The men were surprised when they saw a smile come over Elizabeth's face and she said, "That is a good idea. Here in this house everything I see, everywhere I turn I think of my dear husband and feel terribly his absence. Maybe with living away from the familiar surroundings the feeling of loss will be less."

Now began the tedious job of moving some furniture, plus all the personal possessions of three people across the river and overland to Port Tobacco. Three months passed before everything was accomplished.

The most difficult piece of furniture to move was the piano. There was fear on the river it would shift in the boat and cause it to tip, and then dump the piano, plus everyone into the water. Following the boat trip came the possibility of completely destroying the instrument as it swayed and bounced in the wagon while traveling overland on the rutted, bumpy road.

As soon as the piano was placed in James' sitting room Elizabeth sat down to play it and found the tones coming from the instrument sounded terrible. James promised to locate a piano tuner. He even promised to buy a new piano if this one could not be fixed.

A few weeks after everything was moved into place and the three Spekes were settled into their new home James began hiring workmen to construct an addition off of the sitting room. Once the hammering stopped and the dust settled the new room became Elizabeth's painting-studio.

Elizabeth's grief condition began to improve. She became friends with Alice and together they oversaw the care of the home.

After the piano was tuned Elizabeth would spend at least an hour each day playing classical music and hymn tunes. Then for a few hours she painted. These two things brought a peace to Elizabeth and as time passed she again became involved with the small church located nearby.

Once the three Speke's began attending the church where James was a member Elizabeth became concerned over the music. There was no instrument to accompany the singing and she wanted to donate her piano to the church.

Up until this time no one in the church played a piano or an organ, therefore there was no use to have such an instrument in the building.

James told his sister he would purchase either a piano, or an organ for the church, but it was up to her to decide which instrument would be best, and she must be the one to purchase the instrument for him.

The more Elizabeth became involved the more her grief eased. She found great joy in locating a small organ and playing it at the Protestant church. Soon the beauty of the music became a topic of conversation in the community. The church began to set aside one evening a month for just music with John and James playing their instruments along with their mother at the organ. People began comparing the music of the newer Protestant church with that of the well-established Catholic Church built in 1641.

Upon hearing Elizabeth's playing a few parents began to ask her if she would teach their children. In time she was teaching four piano students and two organ students.

Five years after Elizabeth and her sons settled into James' home the church determined it was time to build a larger edifice. She felt the building should contain the grand form of organ. So Elizabeth traveled to England to locate an organ with two keyboards, the proper stops and 61 pipes. To Elizabeth's surprise she found in one of the shops not a two-keyboard organ, but a three-keyboard one.

Immediately she sat down to test the tone and found the instrument's range was five octaves. The pitch of every stop (flute, string, reed and organ) sounded perfect. Elizabeth knew right then she would bring this organ back to the Port Tobacco church.

Six months later the organ was placed in it's new home. However 200 of the 1600 bellows were missing. Another six months passed before the needed bellows arrived. Finally Elizabeth could sit down at the keyboard of the magnificent instrument to play for the morning service.

Chapter 11

Both young Speke men became involved with the planting of crops on James' property. The lawyer was too busy with all of the legal aspects of the town to be involved with planting and harvesting. Therefore he was very happy to have his nephews take over the management of the land for crop production.

All kinds of vegetables (those grown underground and those to grow above ground) were planted. Peas, beans, tomatoes, lettuce, cucumbers, peppers, potatoes, beets, turnips and carrots all thrived. In two years time they were making a profit for their uncle. Then the boys planted a tobacco crop and it also did well.

The soil and weather of the area seemed perfect for growing, and with Port Tobacco's export trade the location seemed ideal for trade.

The road from the town down to the river was especially designed to easily roll the bales of tobacco to the ships. James' home was just two miles from the beginning of the road. Men brought from Africa would roll the bales out of James' driveway and along the road to the descent to the water

Both John and James felt joy over the move from Speke's point. They now understood the satisfaction their grandfather experienced when he first broke ground in the new world.

Shipload after shipload of people continued to stream to the new world and some began to settle north of Port Tobacco in a place they named Annapolis. The streets of the town were laid out as those constructed in London following the city's great fire of 1666.

In 1696 the Maryland capital of St. Mary's was moved to Annapolis. James Bowling traveled north to take part in the celebration of the new capital. And while he was there he saw the opportunity for another outlet for the produce grown at Port Tobacco.

Once James returned home he discussed with his nephews the possibility of opening a produce store in the new capital and all three men decided the idea was a good one. Young James traveled north to oversee the building of the store.

The young man was constantly traveling back and forth from his home in Port Tobacco to Annapolis. Once all the aspects of moving the produce and keeping it fresh until it arrived in the new city was worked out James Speke made plans to permanently moved to Annapolis.

However, before the actual move James was the best man at his brother John wedding.

John Speke with his wife Winifred, stood teary-eyed at the graveside of their five-year old son James. Beside them little three-year old Thomas could not quite understand why he could not see his older brother any more. When he looked up and saw his parent's tears he began wailing.

John picked up his little son and carried him into the quiet, well-established courthouse of Port Tobacco. On they walked to the second floor where their uncle James' law office was located. Once inside both Thomas and his wife tried to console their boy.

As Thomas' sobbing quieted John carried him to the north wall of the office where hung a picture painted by his grand-mother Elizabeth. Thomas particularly liked the regal Indian head at the top of the painting and he clapped his hands every time he saw it.

Then Thomas would point his chubby little finger at the letters P O T O B A C and say the words several times. John always told his son to remember the letters were the name of the Indian Village before the white man arrived.

After the boy completely quieted, John, carrying Thomas, and Winifred left the courthouse to walk around the town square. A new structure in the square was partially completed and the young family stood in front of it. John whispered in his son's ear, "This is going to be our new home." The boy's eyes grew wide and he whispered back, "Big". Yes, the building was big because it was going to be the Inn of Port Tobacco.

For several years the job of finding accommodations for visiting merchants became more and more difficult. John and his wife decided the only answer was for the town to have an Inn. The completed structure would contain an apartment for the three Spekes.

When the land claims clerk filled out the paper work he listed the last name as Speake, not Speke. John didn't notice the mistake for several months and when he did see the mistake he decided not to change the name on the paper, but to change his name. To him the new spelling seemed to fit the pronunciation better.

The people and business of Port Tobacco thrived more each year. It became the second largest export terminal in the new world. Many of the inhabitants began to stress the need of a good education for their children.

By the time Thomas was six-years of age a one room schoolhouse was completed and a teacher was brought from England. John finished eight grades of schooling in this building. Then he became bookkeeper for his father at the Inn.

In 1729, when Baltimore was declared a city Thomas moved there with his bride to open the Baltimore Inn.

Chapter 12

Year 1754

Ten-year-old John Bowling Speake rushed to help his father move new furniture into one of the bedrooms of the Baltimore Inn. The steamy summer heat seemed to slow down most people's movements. However, John moved quickly because he knew when the job was finished he would go to spend a month with his grandfather in Port Tobacco.

John loved his grandfather as well as the place he lived. Port Tobacco held John's interest with all of the town's people coming and going. He enjoyed playing games with his friends in the town square. Sometimes they would just sit on the grass of the square and watch the people, the horses and the coaches passing by. Some times the boys would sit by the road descending to the water and watch the men roll the bales of tobacco down it.

These things were fun to do, but there was one thing more fun for John and that was to walk down to the river and watch the boats being loaded. Every time he went to the river he thought about becoming a boat captain when he grew up.

A short distance from the dock was a sandy beach where the townspeople often swam. Of course John would go swimming every chance he could.

Days seemed ideal to the boy because he not only enjoyed the playtime; he thoroughly enjoyed helping his grandfather with duties at the Inn. John's special jobs were showing guests to their rooms and clearing the tables in the dining room.

All the time John worked he would listen to snatches of conversation by the guests. One topic coming more and more to his ears was the dissatisfaction of the people in the new world over the rule of the English monarch.

The boy determined he would do something about the problem when he was a grown man. He didn't have any idea what he would do, but he knew he would be ready when the time came.

Almost twenty years later John still heard all the arguments about British rule. Now he was involved with the conversation himself in condemning the main issue of taxation without representation.

As a grown man he still held duties at the Baltimore Inn. This would soon be his sole responsibility as his father Thomas's health was failing. Despite this work, John's childhood interest in cargo ships became his main occupation. He owned two ships and was the captain of one of them.

In 1774 John was sailing toward his homeport of Annapolis and was surprised to see a ship burning in the harbor He weighed anchor in the center of the harbor and waited until the blaze was contained before sailing on to the dock. Immediately John's first interest was to find the cause of the blaze, where upon he learned the captain of the demolished ship was forced to set fire to his vessel because he paid tax on a shipment of tea.

John could foresee great trouble coming in the future over the area of taxation.

With the tax on tea becoming such a big issue some of the merchants began to smuggle tea from Holland. Almost everyone in the new world drank tea and they loudly made known abroad that any tax on it would not be tolerated.

Still another problem with the ruling country kept coming to the forefront. England was now releasing prisoners from jail to be sent to the new world as servants.

The Burton family in Lewis, Delaware, felt this pinch. Every time they brought over new workers to work in the fields some would work for a day and then disappear. Often they would take something of value when they left.

The Burton family was not the only landowners facing the problem; many other families did also. The problem didn't apply to only the field workers, but some of the house servants were released criminals as well.

Many of these new comers were thankful for the new work opportunity and they were reliable people. However, about one in five of the new arrivals continued their illegal activities in the new land where (without choice) they were shipped.

Before the American Revolution began John Temple, son of Return Temple and grandson of Abraham Temple of Massachusetts, established a home in Ewing, New Jersey. He married Rachael Vanhorne and four sons were born to them, William, Andrew, Levi and Azariah. Giving three sons Biblical names no doubt was a result of the families strong ties to the Ewing Presbyterian Church.

The main road from the north to the south passed between Ewing and the larger town of Trenton. Because of the Temple family's home location and the fact John was involved with local politics many dignitaries stayed in the Temple home when traveling from Massachusetts down to Pennsylvania, Maryland or Delaware, or visa versa.

Following the Boston Tea Party men from Delaware, Maryland, Virginia and other southern areas joined their northern neighbors to oust English rule from their country.

In the late seventeen hundreds and early eighteen hundreds immigration to America increased yearly. The leading numbers of people came from England and France. Quite a few of the immigrants from France were still fleeing from persecution of their Huguenot faith.

The Charshee family fled from France to England and lived close to London. Then when the opportunity came they moved on to America. Their son Edward was the first child to be born at the Charshee farm close to Perryville, Maryland. The year was 1818.

Henry Barnett, his wife Didemiah and their baby Merns arrived in America in 1838. Their second son John was born in the town of Chestnut Hill, Pennsylvania.

John's mother died in childbirth. Henry was devastated over his loss, plus he was filled with the anguish of needing someone to look out for his little son and the baby boy. A wet nurse was found for the baby and she agreed to look out for both children.

Two years later, while attending a business meeting, John met a widow from Delaware. Her name was Mary and she was the mother of two children. Mary's parents cared for her children while she worked.

After several meetings Henry suggested to Mary it would be advantageous for both of them if they married. Her children would have a father and his children would have a mother. Henry could farm the land Mary inherited from her husband and she would no longer need to work. They both agreed the idea was a good one.

In time Henry and Mary fell in love with each other and four children were born to them at the Magnolia, Delaware farm.

The large family of James McCracken Sr., his wife Jenny and ten children crossed the ocean in the 1860's. The crossing was very difficult with five boys and five girls, plus their parents often being seasick.

Storm after storm hit. The ship would plunge, steeply rise and plunge again. One major problem was the fact the boat's passengers could not go up on deck because it was often covered with the water sprayed by waves and they would have been swept off.

Each family in the ship's hold used a bucket for their sickness. The problem was no one could go on deck to empty the bucket and people who were not seasick would retch from the odor.

Great relief filled everyone when the ship sailed into the quiet New York harbor.

Every family on board felt joy when they went on deck and gazed upon the Statue of Liberty.

New York was not the McCracken family's destination because James was promised a job in a gun maker's shop in Baltimore, Maryland.

As soon as the family was well settled-into their new home James' boss took the McCracken family on a tour of the Baltimore waterfront; a place many visitors went to see. The drawing card was not the enjoyable view of the river, but the significance of the writing of the Star Spangles Banner during the war of 1812 while Fort McHenry was being bombarded.

Ezekiel M. Wilson, his wife Elizabeth and their two sons also arrived in the United States just before the Civil War. Because there was a famine in Ireland the family believed they would be better off in America. Their ship sailed up the Delaware River and into the port of Philadelphia.

Because Ezekiel was qualified as an engineer he fit right into his job at the shipyard and the family settled into one of the row homes in the center of the city.

They sought a church home and found it at the Episcopal Church in their neighborhood.

When the Civil war broke out every family in America was affected.

Ezekiel Wilson was immediately conscripted into the Union Army and because of his engineering training he was made an officer in the army engineering corps.

Because Maryland was just below the Mason-Dixon line some of the residents favored the freedom of slaves, while many of those involved in agriculture felt slavery was necessary. James McCracken Jr. believed all men should be free. He rode his horse north and joined the Union Army.

James Speake believed in the southern cause. His main war effort was for all of his ships to escape the naval blockade of Confederate ports. He knew the only way the south could financially support their life style was by selling the cotton and tobacco products overseas.

James would study the Union Navy's maneuvers and slip his ships through the blockade at night. He would sail to Bermuda, Jamaica and even England without the enemy's knowledge.

Peter Waples Burton who lived on the Lewis, Delaware farm put much effort into providing food for the northern troops. His army contract was to supply produce to the Pennsylvania and Delaware army corps.

Edward Charshee's farm home was one of the under-ground railroad stops to enable African American people to flee their slave owners. Because the farm was south of the Mason-Dixon line there was always the danger of people with Confederate leanings learning about the secret dealing of the farm. It could have meant death if it was found out. One good aspect of the location was the fact it was only a day's journey to the free soil of Pennsylvania.

Edward felt his family fled Europe because of religious persecution and slavery was a form of persecution based on color. He was very opposed to any persecution and willing to risk his life to prevent it.

Enoch Armitage Temple now lived in New Jersey and was involved in the clothing business. He was given a contract with the Union Army to supple uniforms for the men. Enoch, along with his wife Martha, spent hours of every day at the factory sewing machine.

In 1861, at 23 years of age John Barnett, son of Henry enlisted in the Union Army from his local Kent Country address. John became a private in the third brigade, second division, second corps of the army of the Potomac. For military training the young man was sent to Lewis, Delaware. During his time there he met Sara Ann Burton whose father constantly invited soldiers in training into his home for dinner. On Sunday's John began attending the Lewis Presbyterian Church with the Burton family.

John and Sara were married six months after they met. For three months Sara lived with John and his father at their Magnolia, Delaware farm during the time John attempted to recruit more Kent County men into the army. Then he was called to be involved with the corps military engagements.

The division rode down to Norfolk, Virginia to join the other members of the brigade in the capture of the city, and this was accomplished on May 10, 1862. Four months later John was involved with the fighting at Antietam, Maryland,

and in December he fought at Fredericksburg, Virginia. At the latter battle John was wounded by a shell piece piercing his shoulder.

Five months passed before the shoulder healed and for some of this time John was at home while recuperating. He was so thankful to once again be able to hold his petite wife. How he missed her! Once healed John's desire was to again help free the slaves and he returned to the military. John fought at Chancellorville and on to the July battle at Gettysburg, Pennsylvania.

The Auburn battle took place next and at the following battle, the Bristol Station battle, John was injured again. A piece of enemy artillery ran over Private Barnett and he was badly bruised. However, this soldier was again ready to fight a month later at Mine Run.

John's two-year term of service ended in November of 1862, but he re-enlisted before the end of the year to serve in the same regiment as before. During the next year the corps fought one battle after another; Mortins Fjord, VA, Wilderness, Pa River, Spottsylvania and North Anna.

In June of 1864 a skirmish took place at a place called Gold Harbor where for a third time John was wounded. This time his leg took a minnie ball. Private Barnett spent three weeks in a hospital, but the doctors were not able to remove the minnie ball.

He was released from the hospital and sent home on furlough.

When Sara saw John riding up the lane she ran to hug him. He held up his hand and said, "Don't come near me. Please bring a tub outside and fill it with warm water so I can bathe. I'm covered with lice." John took of his clothes and while naked burned them, then he stepped into the tub of water. When he was finished bathing Sara handed him a towel and they hugged.

Sara believed her husband's absence was over. A relief came over her because she thought there would be no more days when his location was unknown to her. No more waiting to receive notes from him and no more fretting over the hours he would be traveling from battle to battle.

For almost two years Sara had helped John's father in every way possible. She cooked for him, washed his clothes, whenever possible she helped with farm chores and then kept him company in the evenings.

Henry Barnett took good care of his farm. He plowed, sewed and harvested the fields, plus cared for the chickens, pigs and cows. He kept Sara supplied with wood for cooking and heating, plus carried the water for washing. On Sundays Henry would hitch-up the horse and wagon to drive Sara and himself to the Methodist Church in Magnolia.

All of these duties would continue for Henry and his daughter-in-law, but now John would be able to help them.

Around the dinner table at night John told many a story of comradeship (some were hilarious),but there were also ones of hardship and heartache. There was laughter and tears.

John's leg healed, but his leg remained stiff because of the minnie ball lodged close to a bone.

News reports of Indian fighting in the west reached Delaware and this began to weigh on John's mind. After six months at home he re-enlisted. This time for one year in Captain Jesse Custers' Company, to serve in the eleventh Regiment Indian Volunteer's infantry under the command of Col. Dan McCanley.

The ship of James Henry Speake was captured by the Union Navy at the close of the civil war. James was killed in the final battle. His wife Harriet Jane was left with their only child, George Washington Speake.

George was 14 years of age when his father was killed and for all of his young life his father kept telling him, "You have been given this distinguished named because of the past history of the Speake family with the Washington family. Washington children were always considered cousins of the Speake family and they kept close contact with each other.

Year 1866

Finally all of the fighting was finished allowing both the north and south's military men to return home to stay. The post war years were very difficult with much poverty. Farm families struggled to make ends meet. However they were better off than many of the people living in the cities because they could raise their own food. The farmers grew fresh fruit and vegetables to eat in the summer and the surplus of these they canned for winter consumption. Most farmers also grew chickens, pigs and cows for meat and milk.

Jobs in the city were scarce with the pay very low. People were hungry and church organizations tried to help as much as possible. There was no government aid.

Most African Americans remained in the cotton fields. They never received any other job training and there was no other place for them to go to live.

Almost every family swelled in size when the soldiers returned home. This greatly added to the worries of the time.

Before the war Edward and Harriet Charshee were the proud parents of three sons and a daughter, Grover, Elizabeth, Robert and Edward. Following the war three more sons were added; Lorenzo, George and John.

All six of the boys left home between twelve and fourteen years of age to work on the Baltimore and Ohio railroad. First they went into an instruction class and then they were apprenticed to well-qualified workers. Young John was helping to couple boxcars when he slipped and fell under the wheel of a rolling car. His leg was severed, but he lived and went on with life.

George became a Railroad Conductor by the time he was eighteen. The other four boys eventually became engineers.

James McCracken Sr. immigrated to America with ten children but only three were living following the Civil War.

When James McCracken Jr. returned from the war his younger sister Elizabeth Jane was preparing to marry another returned soldier named John Walker.

James reopened the gun shop where his father once worked and eventually owned. Guns were still in demand, but not as greatly as they were during the war.

Elizabeth and John Walker were married three months after James Jr. came home. He escorted his sister down the isle and gave her away. The wedding was lovely and the bride's face glowed.

In early 1864 Ezekiel Wilson was welcomed home by his wife and their two children, James and Ezekiel. Nine months later baby Sara arrived. Four more children arrived in the next twelve years, one boy and three girls, John, Mary, Lillie and Elizabeth.

Ezekiel returned to his engineering position and he did not feel the financial breakdown so many of the post civil war veterans experienced.

From 1866 to 1886 John and Sara Barnett became the parents of six children and two foster children. The oldest boy, John Gilbert (called Gillie) left home at sixteen years-of-age to go to the Baltimore and Ohio railroad to begin working as an apprentice break man.

Gillie found a room in the same boarding house in Wilmington as the one where George Charshee lived. The two of them went to the same railroad station at the same time and they soon became good friends. From time to time George would invite Gillie to his home in Perryville, Maryland and

Gillie would invite George down to his home south of Wilmington, close to Magnolia.

Gillie's younger sister Lillie began to think she should also go to Wilmington to find work because the family was experiencing much difficulty in purchasing any supplies with the lack of cash. While Gillie sent money home it was not near enough to meet their needs.

One afternoon before Lillie left for Wilmington Sara was hanging clothes on the line and noticed a wagon coming up the lane to the farm. It was George Charshee and he was the bearer of tragic news. Gillie was killed the evening before in an accident while at work. The wagon George was driving held John Gilbert's body and George had driven all night to bring the body home.

Great anguish overcame the Barnett family while they made preparations to hold the funeral at the Magnolia Methodist church with internment following at the Barrett's Chapel graveyard. Friends of Gillie from church and school attended the service to share in the grief and give condolences.

George himself was extremely sad over the loss of his good friend. Then his heart became wrenched as he watched the tears flow down Lillie's cheeks.

Every other weekend for several months George would drive south to see how the Barnett family, and especially Lillie was doing. When George was transferred to the Dover, Delaware terminus the relationship between George and Lillie became a courtship. George and Lillie were nineteen years of age when they were married at Magnolia's Methodist Church.

One year later on July 17th, 1891 tiny Lulu Blanche Charshee was born. For the year of awaiting the baby's arrival George and Lillie lived with Lillie's parents. Then they bought a home at Bowers Beach by the Delaware Bay. This was an ideal location as long as George's terminus was Dover.

However, Dover was not to remain a permanent terminus. Some years it would be Wilmington, some years Philadelphia and some years Baltimore. The little family would rent an apartment in Philadelphia or Baltimore for the winter months and then Lillie and Blanche would go to Bowers Beach when summer came. George would come down to Dover by train on Friday nights after work, and return the same way to his terminus location on Sunday evenings. Of course every one was glad when the terminus would be Dover for a while.

So Blanche was constantly changing schools when she became of age to attend one. Before she started school, Lillie noticed a little swelling on Blanche's cheek. It kept growing and growing. There was nothing Lillie could think of to make the swelling go down. Finally she was taken to a Doctor and he said, "Blanche has a tumor. It must be removed." The dangerous surgery was performed and everyone was thankful no infection followed, but there remained a great hallow at the side of Blanche's left cheek.

In 1907 George was again sent to Baltimore for his terminus. The family decided to rent a little house in the city at this time, because it looked like George would be there for several years.

The health of Blanche was not good once she reached her early teens. Fatigue and lack of energy plagued her. The doctor said her system was low in iron and she should eat raisins and liver. Liver and raisins were two foods she detested and she resisted all attempts of getting her to eat them. Finally, at the end of tenth grade the doctor and her parents thought it best for her to quit school. Blanche was content to stay home and help her mother with the cooking. Then too, she thoroughly enjoyed making clothes on the sewing machine, or doing embroidery work. This work along with church activities and those of her friends Blanche pleasantly busy.

Enoch Armitage Temple, his wife Martha and their two children Charity and Sarah moved from New Jersey to Elkton, Maryland because they longed for the more rural life. Then too, the clothing business was not doing well and they thought farming would do better.

Two more children were born to them, Lorenzo and Jonathon Evans. The two boys grew up helping their father with planting, harvesting and caring for the animals. As John grew older he was the one who took the excess produce to a near-by market. The older John became the more he enjoyed the constant driving of a wagon and decided this would be his life employment. He moved to Philadelphia and went to work at an ice distributing company. Every day he moved blocks of ice to homes to be stored in iceboxes.

At a company picnic Jonathon met the daughter, of another employee. Her name was Sara Ann Brown and Jon thought she was very pretty. He began to date her. In time they were married at St. James Episcopal Church. In the following ten years Jon and Sara became the parents of four children, Jonathon Evans, Charles, Sarah and Ethel.

At work Jon Sr. was transferred from the homes to the Saloons and Bars delivery route. Things went well for a while until the bar tenders at the drinking establishments started to offer Jon a drink for delivering the ice. Soon at the end of every day it was only the fact the horse knew the way home that allowed him to safely arrived there.

When Jon Jr. reached his teenage years he decided his preference for work would also be to work at delivering products. First he applied at a packaging handling company and was hired by them to make deliveries from Philadelphia to Atlantic City, N. J.

In the office of the company worked a woman by the name of Elizabeth Hecker Johnson, nee Wilson (daughter of Ezekiel). Elizabeth was a widow with a nine-year-old son named Raymond. William, her husband, was killed before Raymond was born in an accident at work.

William worked at a ship building company in Philadelphia and he was loaned to a Boston, Massachusetts company to work on the construction of a large ship in their harbor. William was killed in the launching of the ship. The news was printed in a Philadelphia paper even before Elizabeth received the notice of the accident. Reading the article brought on the premature birth of Raymond and Elizabeth began the long grieving process.

Elizabeth was now the accountant for the company Jon worked for and her parents took care of Raymond during the day. She usually arrived for work the same time as the truck drivers and they would all chat together before beginning work..

Jon and Elizabeth started to take their half hour lunch together. In a few months John became almost a permanent guest for dinner in the home in Ezekiel's home where Elizabeth and Raymond lived.

Elizabeth was fifteen years older than John, but that didn't matter to either of them. They were in love and were married on November twenty-first in 1911. During the following ten years there were five children born, Dorothy, Mildred, Jonathon, Eleanor and Charles.

The widow of James Speake and her son George packed their belongings and moved to her parents home in another section of Baltimore. George continued his schooling until he was sixteen and then he became apprenticed to a stonemason. He worked hard and was happy in what he was doing. One other aspect of the stonemason's guild thoroughly enjoyed by George was the parties put on by them. While attending one of these parties he met a young widow by the name of Janette Olivia McKennie. Her maiden name was Walker, and she was the granddaughter of James McCracken.

Janette spent three years of a happily married life before her young husband was killed in an accident. It now seemed to her that every joy in life was gone, and there was no purpose in life. To fill time she went to work in the office of a construction company. A company with stone mason employees, and George Speake was one of them.

Party after party went bye with George and Janette meeting, chatting together and dancing together. Then they decided they were in love, and there was not a long courtship. They were married in the fall of 1881 at Olive Branch Evangelical United Brethren Church.

Janette was raised in this church, but left it after marrying her first husband who was Catholic. Following his death she returned to the church and found out she wanted to attend there for the rest of her life.

George spent his young life attending the Sunday school at an Episcopal Church where his mother's family attended. After he met Janette he accompanied her to Olive Branch Church and agreed with her about the good quality of worship there. However, with the alcohol problem he developed while attending the many guild parties he did not choose to attend church regularly.

Over a period of twenty-two years George and Janette became the proud parents of twelve children, eight of whom lived to adulthood, Grace, Pearl, Ella, George Washington Jr., James Edward, Harriet, Raymond and Elva. While these children were growing up they felt much family love.

Janette was determined her children would be raised in a church where they would hear the truth about God and have the opportunity to claim his Son, Jesus Christ as their Saviour.

George and Ed were very close in age and close in companionship. They played together, got into trouble together and were punished together.

Both boys always wanted a dog, but their parents would not allow it. Often George and Ed would roundup a stray dog and sneak it into the basement of their home. They believed their mother would not find out. However, every time they returned to the basement the dog would be gone.

Some times their mother would be hanging wash in the basement when the boys put the dog through a front basement window. Janette would grab the dog and put him out through the back basement window.

Financial stress constantly plagued the Speake family. Not because the occupation of stonemason was a low salary job, but because George Sr. was an alcoholic.

On payday the head of the house would often be brought home from a local saloon with little money left in his pockets. Then there were times he would not come home at all, but disappear for several days until he sobered up.

All of the children watched the behavior of their father with sorrow, or shame, or anger, or disgust. They vowed they would never touch any alcohol, nor ever have it in their home when they grew up.

While attending one of the church's Sunday school picnics Janette and the children were all baptized in the water of the lake where the picnic was held.

Most of the Speake children only finished six grades of school, and then went out to work in order to help feed, clothe, and house the large family. George went into a glass blowing factory and Ed started work in a shoe store.

On hot steamy afternoons when George and Ed were off from work they would often go down to the harbor of Baltimore and walk aboard one of the ships. Then climb up to the highest deck and march up to the bow of the ship. The two young men would take off their shirt and trousers (underneath were bathing suits) and dive down off of the boat into the Patapsco River. Sometimes they would dive in unison and other times one after another until they tired of doing it. Of course their mother knew nothing about this activity because they waited until they dried off before going home.

One Friday evening Janette asked her son George to go check the local saloon to see if his father was there. It was payday and she knew if her husband stayed late there would be no money for food.

George saw his father as soon as he stepped into the establishment. Up to the bar George walked, sat down next to his father and said, "Dad, it's time to come home." George Sr. was already partially drunk and did not want to leave. He said, "No".

Young George replied, "If you won't come home then I'll join you with a drink. The elder George looked horrified at his son and said, "Don't ever start. I'll go home with you."

As the Speake young men reached their late teens they began to realize the type of work they were doing was not what they wanted to do the rest of their lives. George determined he wanted to be a Pastor and began saving money toward the training he would need.

Ed applied for work at the post office and learned he needed to take a physical before the post office would consider hiring him. At the physical the doctor told him he did not weigh enough to be hired. Then the doctor looked him in the eye and said, "Drink a quarter cup of olive oil each night and when you reach the required weight come back. Jim drank the horrible stuff, gained weight and was hired.

Church was important to all of the Speake young people. They attended all activities, taught Sunday school, and helped in Daily Vacation Bible School. Hattie Speake (George and Ed's younger sister) introduced her teenager friend Lulu Blanche Charshee to the church. Blanche became as involved with Olive Branch as the Speake young people were.

When the Charshee family arrived in Baltimore they chose to attend a Methodist Church, but after George and Lillie saw how much Blanche felt at home at Olive Branch they too started to attend there. On Sunday morning's Blanche and Hattie would sit with George and Lillie while the whole Speake clan sat in the row in front.

Beside the girls being together in church, Blanche and Hattie were constantly in each other's homes. They became involved in many evening activities together and then they found themselves busy helping with the weddings of Hattie's two older sisters Grace and Pearl.

Following the weddings a void was felt in the Speake family because both Grace and Pearl married men who lived and worked in Virginia. To visit either Cape Charles or Newport News, Virginia seemed practically impossible for the any of the Speake's. They did not own a vehicle and the cost of a boat or train trip seemed beyond their means. They started saving pennies with the hope that maybe once a year they would get to see each other.

In a short time another marriage took place at Olive Branch Evangelical United Brethren Church. This time it was between James Edward Speake and Lulu Blanche Charshee. The quiet family wedding took place in April of 1911.

Epilogue

*E*d's work with the postal system was in the mail delivery section and he was assigned to train duty. When trains passed through small towns without stopping the towns' mail was hung in a bag on a pole close to the track. Ed's job was to lean from the train's mail car and grab the bag. Then sort the mail in the car and oversee the delivery of it to the post office once a major city was reached.

For a year Ed's terminus was Baltimore and during the year Blanche Ruth Speake was born. Then his terminus became Troy, New York where Ed and Blanche's baby boy George Edward was born in 1915.

The Post Office promoted Ed to the position of Postal Inspector and assigned him to the Philadelphia, Pennsylvania office in 1921. Five years later little June Mosena came into the world.

To read more about the Speake family and in particular June's childhood, her marriage to Charles Wilson Temple and their life on the mission field you will find the continuing story in the following books

1. Growing in His Light

2. Through Pastures and Valleys

3. Bush Teacher in B.C.

4. Bush Teacher in B.C. II

5. Opened Doors

6. Come Traveling with June

June has also written two Devotionals and one study of seven women in the Bible.

1. O Come Let Us Adore Him

2. Adoration, A Prelude to Worship

3. Stars on Earth

Bibliography

Battle of the Standard — The First Stewart Battle, Stewart Society

Catholic University of America, The, Washington, D.C. c.1967

Cistercians in the British Isles, Catholic Encyclopedia

Dictionary of National Biography, Volume VI, Library of Congress

Domesday Book English Heritage Book of Abbeys and Priories, Coppack, Glyn, B.T.

Batsford, London

Feudal Kingdom of England 1042-1216, Barlow, Longman, London & New York, c.1998

Leisure Hunt Search, Kirkham Priory, Kirkham Hall, Kirkham Abbey

Leisure Hunt Search, Rievaulx Abbey, York, Y06 5LB, UK H

Maryland — A History of Its People, Johns Hopkins University Press, c.1996

New Catholic Encyclopedia

New Encyclopedia Britannica, The15th edition, 1995

Norman Heritage, The, 1066-1200, Trevor Rowley, Routledge & Kegan Paul, London, Boston, Melbourne & Henley, 1983

Oxford English Dictionary, Second Edition, Volume XV, Clarendon Press, Oxford, c.1989

Oxford Popular History of Britain, Morgan, Parragon, United Kingdom, c.1996

Union Soldiers and Sailor's recoreds, Washington, D.C.

Walter Espec d.1153, Oxford University Press 1995

Warfare in England, 1066-1189, John Beeler, Cornell University Press, Ithaca, NY 1966f

World Book Encyclopedia

Dr. June M. Temple

FOREVER FAITHFUL

Художник *М. Литвинова*
Компьютерная верстка *М. Литвиновой*

TO ORDER BOOKS

in Canada

Centre for World Mission
Box 2436
Abbotsford, B.C. V2T 4X3

in the United States

Julie Wood
ACW Press Distributor
1200 Hwy 231, S. # 273
Ozark, AL 360

or

Faith Works / NBN
15200 Faith Works / NBN Way
Blue Ridge Summit, PA 19214

ЛР № 01234 от 17.03.2000
Подписано в печать 27.01.2005. Формат 84x108 $^1/_{16}$.
Бумага офсетная. Гарнитура Minion
Печать офсетная. Усл. печ. л. 25,2
Тираж 1000 экз. Заказ 791

Местная религиозная организация
«Христианская миссия евангельских христиан "Шандал"»

197198, Россия, Санкт-Петербург, а/я 614
E-mail: mission@shandal.ru; manager-sale@shandal.ru
www.shandal.ru